PRAISE FOR
LOVE ON TOUR

"Lee Adams' experience in the country music industry, from supporting artists' lifelong dreams and artistic visions to sharing her love and passion of music with the fans makes her the perfect person to write a book like *Love On Tour*. She knows the music industry down to her core. It's a part of who she is."

—**DUSTIN LYNCH**, #1 hit maker, singer, and songwriter

"Lee Adams is one of the best and most talented people in the country music industry. She has many years of inside knowledge and behind-the-scenes experiences to write a book like *Love On Tour*."

—**CRAIG MORGAN**, #1 hit singer, songwriter, and author of *God, Family, Country: A Memoir*

"Lee Adams knows the country music world and she knows how to write a romance that will make your heart beat fast. Put the two together, and you have a recipe for this smart, swoony, love song of a book."

—**JEFF ZENTNER**, author of *Colton Gentry's Third Act*

"A heartwarming, country music romance from a fresh voice in women's fiction. Get ready to fall in love!"

—**JENNIFER MOORHEAD**, author of *Broken Bayou*

A Novel

LEE ADAMS

SHE WRITES PRESS

Published 2025
Printed in the United States of America
Print ISBN: 978-1-64742-918-8
E-ISBN: 978-1-64742-919-5
Library of Congress Control Number: 2025903948

For information, address:
She Writes Press
1569 Solano Ave #546
Berkeley, CA 94707

Interior Design by Tabitha Lahr
Illustration, page 2 © Shutterstock.com

She Writes Press is a division of SparkPoint Studio, LLC.

CHAPTER ONE

Christine stood on the corner of Broadway and Third Street in downtown Nashville, group-texting her friends. New York wasn't the only place where neon lights were bright on Broadway. Music City had grown into a mega tourist attraction with flashing signs advertising various bars and grills owned by country music's finest artists, along with trinket shops and boot stores. She stood outside Miranda Lambert's Casa Rosa bar, smelling the tacos and wishing she had time for a quick bite. But she was running behind and needed to focus. The CMT Awards would be starting soon and her friends were holding her ticket. Finding them trumped getting tacos.

She wrote, *Driver was twenty minutes late, but I'm here at our meeting place. Where are you?*

Her friends, Julianna and Phoebe, didn't reply. She called. No answer.

She texted again: *Doors are closing in ten. I don't want to miss the awards! Are you getting my texts?*

This was an important awards show for Christine. The year before, she had pitched a song to a rising artist, and now the song was up for a video award. This was the first time Christine had placed a song that reached number one on the charts *and* was nominated for an award.

She looked down the street at the arena where the ceremony was about to take place. Amidst the throng of lookie-loos was a hint of the red carpet where A-list artists made their way inside. A blonde head poked out of a limo and was followed by the most amazing set of legs in country music. The blonde reached for a man's hand, and he helped her gracefully exit the car. Carrie Underwood had arrived. The tall man, who had dark hair and a megawatt smile, laughed as he leaned in to the woman beside him. It was Luke Bryan himself. The host of the show. Who else had that smile?

Christine looked down at her phone. Still nothing. *I'm walking toward the front door. Please meet me outside with my ticket,* she texted.

Her eyes darted left and right, searching the crowd for a familiar face. The streets were closed off near the venue, forcing ticket holders to walk the last few blocks. Women balanced on six-inch heels, hanging on to their dates, while men reached for their necks to loosen their ties ever so slightly. This blue-collar town had put on its glamour face for one of the biggest awards shows in country music.

Her friends were not amongst the crowd.

Her text alert chimed with a message from Julianna, her best friend. *Hurry, Christine. We're at the front door convincing the guard not to lock it. Run! You can make it.*

Christine knew it would be close. The doors closed thirty minutes before showtime, and she was pushing it. She was always prompt and had ordered her Uber the night before. She should have had plenty of time to spare. But the best-laid plans didn't always work when you factored in the nightmare of Nashville traffic.

A group of young women cruised by on a pedal tavern. Their T-shirts screamed of a bachelorette party. They waved and raised their glasses, hooting and hollering. Christine guessed it wasn't their first drink of the evening.

Christine's heel broke as she ran toward the venue, causing her ankle to twist and her leg to buckle. Her body did an ungraceful, slow-motion twist downward, leaving her sprawled half on the sidewalk and half on the street, asphalt burns on the palms of her hands. She grabbed her ankle and winced with pain.

Her phone chimed with an incoming text from Julianna. *I'm so sorry, my friend. The guard locked the doors and made us go back to our seats.*

"No." It came out as a pained cry. Tears flowed, causing mascara to run down her face as she lay half in the street.

A gleaming black tour bus with a large AG logo in metallic blue roared to a halt at the red light, right beside her.

"No, no, no," Christine said. "Please don't be who I think you are."

The door opened and Christine looked up into the gorgeous green eyes of Austin Garrett, new male artist extraordinaire.

"Are you okay?" Austin asked. "You took quite a spill."

"I'm definitely not okay. Doors just closed. I didn't make it. And even if I could beg my way in, my friends have my ticket."

"Shit, girl. Bless your heart. Come on—get up here." Austin leaned out of the bus and offered his hand.

Christine hesitated. She was humiliated enough without having to face the newest hunk in country music.

"Light turned green so we have to hurry." He wasn't backing down, so she reached for his hand and let him pull her into the bus. Christine limped to the plush sofa in the seating area.

The driver continued down the road, passing a group of tourists flocking to Nashville's famous honky-tonks. The bus passed the main arena doors, and Christine grimaced knowing her friends were safely inside and she had missed her opportunity to be with them.

The bus pulled around to the back of the arena.

"Don't I know you?" Austin said. "You work at Hit Songs Publishing."

Christine's head shot up. "You know where I work?"

"You were in my song meeting a year ago," Austin said.

"You remember that? No offense, but you looked like you were stoned."

"It's a good cover. Most people think I'm a dumb singer. I'm actually pretty smart." He smiled at her.

"Then why the dumb act?"

"You'd be amazed at what people say in front of you when they think you don't understand them," he said.

"I bet. The executives often have bigger egos than the artists."

"You speak the truth. You're the plugger who found my last song, right? 'Promises to Me.'"

Christine had always disliked the term "song plugger." There had to be a better way to define a job where a person liaised between songwriters and artists, matching the perfect penned tune to someone who could sing it.

"Yes. That was one of the best meetings I've ever been in," Christine said.

"Why's that?"

"'Cause I knew I had the right song for you. I could feel it. And I knew I could sell you on it if given the chance to try. My job rides on me finding the perfect song for an artist. That's a lot of pressure. But when you know, you just know."

"You had the only song I liked. I remember listening to it and envisioning myself singing it onstage. I had to have it."

"When you said, 'I love it. I want it. Put it on hold for me,' it was the best day of my career. Then you decided to make it your next single to radio. And as we know, getting a radio hit is still the biggest thing you can do as an artist and songwriter," Christine said.

"For sure. Radio taking it to number one makes everybody more money. And if it becomes a streaming hit, even better. You have a good ear."

"I've always had a knack for it. I'm glad you think so," Christine said.

"I told my producer, 'That chick Kristen was the only person in the room who really got me.'"

"Christine."

"Huh?"

"It's Christine. Not Kristen."

"Right. I'll tell you what. If I win Breakthrough Video of the Year, I'll thank you from the stage," Austin said, giving her a thumbs-up.

"Unfortunately, I won't see it. I'll be in an Uber on my way home." She frowned.

"I forgot. You don't have a ticket." He reached into his pocket and produced two tickets. "And I don't have a date." He wiggled his brows and grinned.

Christine choked. "Right. *You* don't have a date."

"I don't. My sister was going to come with me, but her flight out of San Jose was delayed. I have a ticket, you need a ticket, and we have fifteen minutes until showtime. Let's go."

"You've got to be kidding. Look at me." Austin's gaze traveled over her broken shoe, runny makeup, and disheveled appearance.

"Yeah, you look a bit rough. How fast can you clean up?"

"I can be ready in about ten minutes," Christine said, standing up. Then she pointed to her foot. "Other than a broken shoe."

Austin chuckled and looked toward the rear of the bus. "Relax. Look in my back room, second closet to the left. You'll find some women's shoes."

Christine raised her eyebrows before he continued.

"I entertain some ladies and sometimes clothing gets left behind." He shrugged.

"Oh my God. Gross."

"One woman's gross is another woman's awards shoes. Go find a pair that fits, go into the bathroom, straighten up your makeup, and let's roll. Ten minutes," Austin said.

"Are you serious?"

"Never been more. Now go." Austin pointed to the back room.

Christine thought, *What the hell. Why not?* She rummaged through the closet, moving aside his numerous T-shirts, trying not to notice the lace camisole, fishnet stockings, and miniskirt. Christine had never worn anything resembling this kind of clothing. And how does a woman leave without her skirt?

She never wore higher than a three-inch heel, but all Christine could find in her size was a pair of black five-inch strappy heels. Luckily, Austin was tall. She guessed at least six foot three. At five feet, seven inches, she wouldn't tower over him. She'd never been overly graceful and was sure she wouldn't be able to walk ten feet in these stilts, especially with a sore ankle. But it was the best she could do, and she wasn't going to let a little pain stop her. She quickly wiped off the mascara that had streamed down her cheeks and reapplied. Then she ran a brush through her hair, glad she'd had a blowout earlier that day. The weather had zero humidity. Maybe, for once, her hair would stay straight. A quick reapplication of her lipstick and she was ready to go in seven minutes.

Austin nodded with a smile. "I love a lady who can get ready fast."

They stepped off the bus and headed in through the arena's back door.

"Didn't you want to walk the red carpet tonight?" Christine asked.

"I did. But I was waiting on my sister. My time slot came and went before I could get here. Family first. I'll catch it next time."

A man came running up to them, grabbed Austin, and steered him toward the front of the arena.

"You're late," the guy said.

"Sorry, unavoidable. Chrissy, this is Matt Miller, my tour manager. Matt, this is Chrissy."

Christine shuddered at the name Chrissy.

"It's Christine," she said, looking at Austin. "Please don't call me Chrissy."

The name Chrissy brought back the taunts from her high school bullies. *Chrissy is a sissy; Chrissy is a sissy.* How much time would it take to erase such a horrible memory? So far, it hadn't been enough.

"Hello, Christine." Matt stopped walking and shook her hand. He looked her straight in the eyes. She froze. His hand was warm and his gaze made her feel at ease. Time stood still. Everyone disappeared from the room. Matt seemed familiar, yet she knew she'd never met him. He was like coming home to a warm fire on a snowy night. This night was shaping up to be a very good one. She held on to his hand a little too long.

"Ahem." Austin cleared his throat.

Christine released Matt.

Matt smiled and the warm feeling spread through Christine's body.

"Let's go," Matt said, ushering them to their seats before returning backstage. The Bridgestone Arena had twenty thousand seats and was home to concerts and Nashville Predators games. It also hosted events like Disney on Ice and wrestling. But tonight, it held the country music video awards. The floor seats held country music's top artists and their dates. Farther back on the floor were industry executives. The middle tier was a mix of fans and industry people, and the upper tier was almost all fans. They screamed loudly each time they recognized a favorite artist.

The countdown to the show had started. The emcee was at T minus forty-five seconds. Christine looked around. She'd never been this close to so many artists at once. From A-list artists in cowboy hats and bell-bottom pants, to newcomers, every artist was on display. Christine watched them casually chat with each other, just like normal people, and wondered what millionaire singers talked about.

"Look at me and smile," Austin said when they were seated.

"Why?"

"Just do it," he said in a firm voice.

She did.

"Okay. Just checking that you don't have anything in your teeth."

"Why does that matter?"

"Because you're probably going to have a close-up on TV, and it would help if you didn't have broccoli in your teeth."

"I don't want to be on TV. I'm a behind-the-scenes kind of person," she said, looking around at all the cameras. Some hung from the rafters, others were attached to camera operators, and still more were on cables moving around the arena.

"Too late. Smile."

She looked up. Her face was magnified a gazillion times on the giant screens gracing both sides of the stage. She and Austin gave big camera-ready smiles.

He leaned into her and said, "Don't look up. We forgot to check your nose for boogies."

She broke up laughing, and the cameras cut to someone else.

"You made me laugh on national television. Nobody looks good with their mouth wide open."

"It looked cute. Chicks dig cute. It's all about the press, baby."

The hosts kicked off the show with witty banter, and then it was time for a commercial break. Christine's phone vibrated in her purse, so she pulled it out. Her friends were texting simultaneously. She visualized them, decked out in their formal wear, sitting high up in the bleachers somewhere. Julianna with her straight blonde hair and legs up to her neck. And Phoebe, who was stunning to look at with her jet-black hair and blue eyes but had a very difficult personality.

Julianna: *OMG! Is that you sitting next to Austin Garrett?*

Phoebe: *How in the hell did you end up sitting next to the country stud?*

"What are you doing?" Austin asked.

"Texting. My friends saw me on TV."

"You don't text in the second row. You text in row one twenty, not row two."

"I usually sit in row three-zero-two," she said, pointing to the back of the arena.

"Not tonight. Gotta shut it off."

She texted, *Long story. Will explain later. Gotta go. Not allowed to text down here.*

She shut her phone off and glanced at the people around her—singers and actors sitting within feet of her. This was her Cinderella moment.

"Next commercial break, I have to go backstage. Everyone up for Breakthrough Video gets to sing a minute of their song."

"A whole minute? Wow, you've hit the big time," Christine said, giving an awkward chuckle before realizing he might not appreciate her sarcasm.

"I like you. You're funny." Just then, the commercial break started and a guy with a headpiece gestured for Austin to join him. "I've gotta go. Wish me luck."

"Good luck." He found her funny. She liked that. Christine had a reputation for being too serious and was often told to lighten up. Tonight, she was funny.

Austin took off, and a college-age kid promptly nabbed his seat.

"Excuse me, that's Austin Garrett's seat," she said.

"I know."

"Ah, you're a seat filler. Empty seats do make for bad television." The kid grunted a response.

Christine wanted to give herself the proverbial pinch. She was actually sitting next to someone designed to keep floor-level seats from being empty. She usually sat so high up that nobody cared when seats went empty.

"Do you get paid for this? Sweet gig."

His brow furrowed. He shook his head and turned away.

The commercial break ended and the cameras came back up on Austin. Onstage, he looked even more striking with his long legs, muscular torso, and strong arms. He had some seriously toned arms. He sang an excerpt from "Promises to Me," stripped down with only an acoustic guitar for accompaniment. It was a song about heartbreak, someone making promises they didn't keep. The subject wasn't anything new. But the lyrics had spoken to her: "You promised me, only to lie. What happened to, until we die? Even apart, I'm still not free. I can't let go of your promises to me." You'd expect the song to be from a woman to a man, which is why she'd thought of Austin when she first heard it. With his raw-sounding voice and manly exterior, it would be unexpected and heartfelt. Now he was onstage singing it. Her heart skipped and her hands flew to her chest. She'd found this song for him. Without her, he wouldn't be singing it, right now, for millions of people all over the country. Pride surged through her for both of them.

For only having one minute, he nailed it. He pointed to her from the stage and gave a thumbs-up. The camera panned back to her face and there she was on the giant screens, beaming at him.

Austin stayed backstage while they announced the winner.

Christine held her breath.

He lost. The camera panned to him as he gave a high five to the winner, followed by a hug. *He's a gracious loser*, she thought.

"Maybe he *is* smarter than everyone thinks," she said.

"Who?" the seat filler asked.

"Never mind."

During the next commercial break, Austin returned to his seat.

"You okay?" she asked.

"Oh, yeah. I didn't expect to win. That guy's been out way longer than me. But next year, the award is mine." He nudged her with his shoulder and she nudged back.

The rest of the show went by in a blur of awards. Christine was so awestruck after George Strait walked past her to get his Performance of the Year Award that her thought process shut down. She couldn't repeat the name of one other winner. She focused on not fidgeting, making sure she sat correctly, and not doing anything embarrassing when the camera panned past her. Her face hurt from smiling. The last thing she wanted was to be caught on camera with resting bitch face.

When it was over, she stood with Austin as he back-patted his fellow artists. Amidst the biggest stars in the country scene, Christine felt awkward and wanted to bolt. But Austin kept reaching back for her like she was an appendage he couldn't forget. They made their way backstage where Matt was waiting.

"Limo's out back. Ready for the after-party?" Matt asked.

"Sure. Is the band coming?" Austin asked.

"They're waiting outside," Matt said.

Christine wanted to gracefully make her exit. These parties often had a preapproved guest list, and her name would not be on it. She didn't want Austin to have to politely explain that she couldn't go with them.

"I'm going to call an Uber. Thanks so much for this amazing night." She turned to shake Austin's hand. His smile faded and he squinted his eyes.

"You don't want to go to the party?" he asked.

"Oh, well, I can. I mean, sure. Why not?" She wondered if that was even a coherent sentence.

"Is that a yes? It was hard to tell."

"Yes. Of course, yes."

"Then let's go," Matt said, leading them out the back door to a waiting limo. She saw a group of people near one of the limos, and Austin told her it was his band.

"Hey, everyone. Meet Chrissy, my song plugger. Chrissy, this is the most awesome band and crew in all of Nashville," Austin said.

Christine smiled. "It's Christine. Nice to meet you."

"This is Cat, my guitar player; Kennedy, on bass; and Red, my drummer." Christine shook hands with each of them. "And this is Alicia," Austin said, putting his arm around a young woman. "Best merch person ever." Alicia blushed.

The band members were dressed in a similar style. Black jeans, black T-shirts, and sneakers. Christine knew a lot of money went into building a band's brand. The last thing anyone wanted was a band of misfits taking attention away from the lead singer. Looking stylish while also appearing uniform didn't happen by accident. Even Alicia was dressed the same, only she was wearing combat-style boots. She was pretty with big brown doe eyes and small features, but she had a toughness about her. She fit in well with the guys.

"Hi, Alicia," Christine said. "Nice to meet you."

"Yeah, you, too." Alicia reached out her hand and Christine shook it, giving Alicia a warm smile. Christine knew women in this business could be territorial and the band was Alicia's territory. Christine respected other people's positions.

Christine turned away and saw Matt speaking with security guards about the best way to get the limos out of the parking lot and away from the waiting fans. He ushered Austin into a seat and gave the limo driver directions. Christine had always been attracted to a "take charge" kind of guy. For her, it was a total turn-on. Her mom used to say, "Find a man who can assess a chaotic situation and get it under control and you'll always feel safe." That's what had attracted her mom to her dad. He was decisive and never panicked. Her mom had been raised by a man who would hyperventilate at the mere sign of a problem. It had left her feeling unsettled as a child. She'd done her best to warn Christine about what she considered to be wishy-washy men. Christine was from a generation that didn't need a man to take control, but she secretly craved that feeling of safety.

THE PARTY WAS HELD ON THE GROUNDS of Austin's record label. A big tent and huge port-a-potties stood on the lawn. Inside the tent, most people were dressed in tuxes and gowns. A few guys wore jeans and T-shirts, and numerous young women were in what looked like dressed-up T-shirts. Christine's dress was somewhere between tea length and panty-showing short. It stopped mid-thigh, allowing a modicum of modesty.

"I can't decide if I'm overdressed or underdressed," Christine said to Matt, who was standing to her left.

"Yep. That's an industry party for you. Everything from holey jeans and T-shirts to suits and dresses. The good news is, you can never be dressed wrong."

Christine turned and took a good look at Matt. He was handsome. She guessed he was in his mid-thirties. He had spiky blond hair and blue eyes, and he was dressed in a modest yet tailored suit. Nothing stood out and said, "Look at me." But she couldn't stop looking at him. She had that same easy feeling she'd had when first meeting him. When his eyes met hers, she quickly glanced away. But not before seeing him smile.

"Anyone else need the bathroom?" Austin asked, coming up beside them.

"I'll walk out with you," Matt said.

"Uh, sure," Christine said, following behind. She spotted Cat and Kennedy talking with a group of men. She'd lost sight of Alicia and Red.

The port-a-potties were the biggest she'd ever seen. Three normal-sized stalls could fit inside one. She wondered if they each held more than one toilet. As they got closer, one of the doors flung open, and out walked a blonde-haired woman. She was dressed in a white blouse with a flowing floral skirt. She was pretty. Very pretty. Not in a Barbie doll way, but definitely eye-catching. When she talked, she had the strongest southern accent Christine had ever heard.

"Holy crap, that's a big shitter. I mean, it's like a *condo* shitter. I could live in that thing."

Christine howled. She looked at Matt, who was shaking his head. "I love her," Christine said.

"That's our Andy," Matt said.

Andy walked over, said hello to Matt, kissed Austin on the cheek, and introduced herself to Christine.

"I'm the record rep, Andy. Short for Andrea, but nobody calls me that. Unless I'm doing the naked dance with some dude. They hate yelling out 'Andy' in the throes of an O. Like I enjoy yelling out 'Bubba.' Who the hell names a guy Bubba? That just ain't sexy, you know what I mean?"

Christine was shocked into silence.

Matt let "uh-huh" slip from his lips.

"Okay, gotta roll. Later, peeps." And with that, Andy was gone.

"I love her," Christine said.

"You already said that," Matt told her.

"It was worth repeating."

Christine used the condo shitter, more out of curiosity than need, and when all three were finished, they returned to the party.

Austin ordered three Fireball shots, which they sucked down. One was usually her limit, but when he ordered another round, she knocked it back. When her next sentence came out slurred, Austin appeared oblivious to the fact she was buzzed, but Matt stayed close by, plying her with water, while Austin worked the room. Christine could feel the fuzziness creeping into her brain. She usually didn't drink because she didn't like feeling out of control. She fell mute, sticking with the old adage: it's better to keep quiet and be thought stupid than open your mouth and prove it. She tried not to think about all the times she'd embarrassed herself, trying to be cooler than she was. She'd found a niche she was comfortable with. A talented song plugger known for her hard work and professionalism. She was pretty sure getting drunk at an industry party and slurring her way through conversations would not enhance that reputation.

A number of people came up to chat with Matt. Christine nodded and smiled, but aside from a few basic introductions, she stayed quiet. She recognized some people in the room but didn't know them well enough to strike up a conversation.

"I never say the right thing when I drink," she said to Matt. She had leaned in to whisper in his ear but misjudged and her lips touched him.

"Who does?" He grinned and lightly touched her arm. It gave her chills. "Are you bored yet?"

"Parties aren't really my thing," she said.

"Mine either. I'm the tour manager, the right-hand man, the wingman. So I have to be here, ready to jump and ask how high. But right about now, my sofa sounds pretty damn good."

A visual of Matt lying on his couch, shirtless and in sweatpants, breezed through her mind. She wished she could screenshot it.

"You two look awful cozy," Austin said.

Christine looked up. She hadn't noticed Austin walking their way.

"Just killing time," Matt said.

"I'm ready to hit the road if you are," Austin said. "I told the others to hang as long as they want. They can Uber home."

"It's only one o'clock. I expected you to party all night," Christine said, most of the Fireball having worn off.

"If it was my party, I'd go all night. But at this kind of party, it's best to leave early."

"Why?"

"Three reasons, Chrissy, and these are important."

"It's Christine," she said. "Lay these reasons on me."

"One, you never want to show your ass in front of the record execs. Two, most of the chicks you're considering doing the bunk bump with are either a record exec's trophy wife, their daughter, or their niece. And last, stars leave the party early and alone. It adds to the intrigue."

"I have so much to learn," Christine said.

"If you're going to hang with me, you do."

"If I'm going to hang with you?"

"I was just talking to my producer about it. I want you to go on the road with me. I think you'll get a better feel for my musical style if you do. Think about it." He pulled out his phone. "Bring it in for a quick selfie." He turned on the camera, reached out to Matt and Christine, and snapped the photo.

"Let's go." He grabbed her hand, and they ran to the limo.

Come on the road with me? Was he kidding? She could think of nothing worse than being on a bus with a bunch of guys for a weekend. The thought of the smells alone made her want to say no. But opportunities like tonight didn't happen to Christine ever, much less repeatedly. She would think about it.

She desperately wanted a copy of the photo but didn't want to ask. She was steeling her nerves when Matt spoke up.

"Hey, send that pic to Christine and me, please."

"You got it. Chrissy, what's your number?" Austin asked, ready to tap it in.

Christine gave Austin her number. "Please put it under Christine."

"Got it. Now you'll have mine. See if you can find me another big song. Maybe hit me up next week." He sent the picture.

Not wanting to appear too eager, she decided she would look at it later.

"Where do you live?" Austin asked.

"Brentwood. You?"

"Franklin. We can drop you off on the way home or you can spend the night at my place."

What?!

Christine's head nearly exploded. Had Austin Garrett just invited her to his house? That's leading lady stuff. Christine saw herself as more of a supporting actress in life. She didn't play a bit part, but she wasn't top-of-the-line either. A million thoughts crammed into her brain in a matter of seconds. She imagined herself talking to her friends the next day. "Did I mention that I went back to his house and we had sex all night long?" A smile crossed her face. But Christine prided herself on being pragmatic and leading with her brain, not her hormones. The next vision she had was of herself doing the walk of shame. She'd never hear from Austin again if she slept with him. And it would get around the industry.

"Hello? Are you there?" Austin brought her out of her head and back to the moment.

"You can take me home. Thanks for the offer, though."

Christine saw a smile cross Matt's face. Austin shrugged like he could take it or leave it. She gave the limo driver directions to the Brentwood Apartments. When they arrived, the driver came around to open her door.

Christine turned to thank Austin and found herself in his arms with his lips on hers. It happened so fast that she didn't know how to react. Her door opened and Austin pulled away.

"Um, uh, thank you, um . . ." Christine said.

"Austin," he said.

"Huh? Right, yes. Austin. Thank you. Sorry, I must be really, um, tired. And thank you, Matt," she said, reaching to shake his hand.

"You remembered Matt's name and not mine?"

"Matt didn't just kiss me."

"Was that an option?" Matt asked.

Christine blushed.

"I didn't kiss you either. At least not properly."

Christine suddenly forgot her own name.

"Next time," Austin said, his eyes lingering on her lips.

Christine couldn't think of one thing to say.

She got out of the limo, and before the door closed, she heard Austin say, "That chick is cool as shit."

She giggled. There were a lot of words people used to describe Christine. Loyal, smart, hardworking, talented—but never, ever, cool as shit. She stood a little taller, liking this new description.

The limo didn't pull away until she was safely inside.

Once in, Christine turned her phone back on, and the first thing she did was save Austin's number. The second thing she did was look at the selfie. She thanked the selfie fairy for making her look thinner than she was and for keeping her eyes open— and for her hair staying flat for once. She'd half expected to see Medusa's snakes making their usual appearance. She saved the photo and then emailed it to herself to make sure it didn't get lost. She also thought about the kiss. For just a brief second, she had a flash of a memory. Another kiss. A bad one. She shook it off. She would not let that moment ruin this one.

CHAPTER TWO

C hristine's alarm went off at seven. She grabbed her phone, shut off the offensive noise, and saw she had missed some messages. Julianna and Phoebe had both texted asking if she wanted to have lunch. She texted back yes and got ready for work.

Even after a late night, she was still the first one in the parking lot. She parked her red Toyota in the lot outside the brick building on Music Square. She gathered her purse and computer bag, unlocked the front door of the office building, locked it again for security's sake, and sat at her desk. Her office was sparse with a desk and office chair, and two additional chairs in front of the desk for when she met with songwriters. She wasn't a trinket person, so other than a cup of pens and a coffee mug, nothing but her computer took up space on her desk. The walls were solid white, broken up by a few framed photos with inspirational messages like "You're capable of so much more than you think." These were her self-reminders to recognize her talents instead of beat herself up.

She opened her email and started reading. Most of the emails had to do with her being on TV. Song pluggers weren't usually seen on television. They worked behind the scenes, headphones on, listening to song after song after song. Nobody wanted to see that on any screen. She weeded through the pleasantries but then got down to work, aiming for the emails that contained songs from writers she had expressed an interest in. She'd specifically requested that a few new writers send her songs after she saw them at the Bluebird Cafe. Discovering a talented songwriter before anyone else found them was one of her favorite parts of the job. She was into her third song when her boss stumbled into her office.

"Rick? Are you hungover?" she asked.

"Define hungover." He had dark circles under his eyes and his complexion was pale.

"Feeling like crap after having too much to drink. Same definition as it's always been."

"I'd say that sums it up. Give me about ten minutes and then come to my office. I need to talk to you."

"Um, yeah, sure. I'll be right there."

Ten minutes later, she knocked on Rick's door, and he yelled for her to come in. Christine sat across from him. It was never good to be called into the boss's office. Her eyes darted back and forth. What had she done?

"So, you and Austin Garrett, huh?" Rick said it as a statement and not as a question.

"It's not what it looked like," Christine said, having no idea what it did look like. Her voice rose an octave as her vocal cords tightened. Would Rick frown on her fraternizing with a client? What was it about bosses that instantly put people on high alert?

"Whatever it is, it's good for this company. He's a rising star and everything he touches climbs the charts. I want you to focus your efforts on finding songs for him. If you have an inside track, we need to use it."

Christine bristled at the idea of using Austin but then remembered that he wanted her to find him songs, so it would benefit everyone.

"He's asked me to bring him some next week. I hadn't had him scheduled in, so I'll take a bunch home this weekend and listen. There's an old box of cassettes that I've been wanting to dig into. There can be some real diamonds in the rough in those old songs."

"So true. Songs that were ahead of their time can be relevant to today's sound. Good call on that. Do you have something to play them on?"

"Actually, I do. An old cassette player that has followed me from home to home. I could never bring myself to toss it," Christine said.

"Good girl," Rick said.

Christine cringed at being called a "girl." Rick was sixty years old. To him, she probably looked like a girl. He went silent but continued staring at her.

"Anything else?" she asked.

"You know the music business has suffered monetarily for the last decade or so. Proceeds have dropped twenty percent annually for more years than I can count."

"I know."

"Hit songs used to bring in a lot more money for the songwriters and publishing companies than they do now."

"Yes, sir." Christine had no idea where Rick was going with this.

"And let's not even talk about the pandemic. No live music. Bars, clubs, and restaurants closed down. The public doesn't realize that all that music being played is licensed and goes toward our bottom line," Rick said, running his hands through his hair.

"I know. And we're all still trying to dig out. Even with the government compensation," Christine said, nodding in agreement.

"I've been running the numbers and contemplating making some hard decisions with regards to songwriters and employees. Scaling back. But this, Christine? Austin Garrett? It could turn everything around."

Christine's eyes widened. Had Rick just laid the company's future on her?

She squeaked out, "Understood." And with a nod of his head, she was dismissed.

Christine went back to her desk. She stared at the wall, her thoughts incoherent. She shook off the fear and thought about what Rick had said. She was the one who could turn business around and save jobs, including her own. She'd always been a non-cutthroat person in a cutthroat business. She prided herself on not using people to get to the top. She wasn't one who left carnage in her wake. But being tough and being cutthroat were two different things. Maybe it was time to be a little more assertive. And if Austin could help her rise through the ranks of song pluggers and keep the publishing company profitable, it would benefit everyone. Including Austin.

CHRISTINE ARRIVED AT HER FAVORITE chicken restaurant. As far as diners went, it wasn't much to look at, but the food was great and the service was quick. Julianna was already there, but Phoebe was running late. Phoebe liked to make an entrance. And with her long black hair, striking blue eyes, and off-the-charts self-confidence, she always did.

Christine took a moment to look at Julianna. She was gorgeous—what every young girl dreamed of looking like. Long, thick blonde hair, shapely legs that went on forever, and a waist the size of most women's thighs. Christine caught a glimpse of herself in the window. She'd gotten used to her body and had learned to appreciate it. Her thighs weren't thin, but they were strong. Her breasts were a bit too big for her liking, but after watching women spend thousands of dollars to get what she had naturally, she'd learned to be thankful. She had a love-hate relationship with her hair but was trying harder to appreciate her curls. She'd flat-ironed it to perfection that morning, but it had only lasted until she stepped out into the humid air. Now, it was so big it needed its own zip code. She'd have rocked the big '80s hairstyles. She used to slouch so she'd fit in with petite women. But not anymore. She stood up straight, smoothed her shirt, put on a big smile, and walked to the table.

Christine's relationship with Julianna was the only reason Phoebe even knew she existed. Two years earlier, when Hit Songs Publishing hired Julianna as an executive assistant, she and Christine found they had an easy rapport. Julianna's friend came as a package deal. Phoebe was not a warm and fuzzy personality. She was reserved and could be somewhat curt. Christine had tried to disarm her with charm, but so far, it hadn't broken through Phoebe's walls. She remembered the first time they'd all had lunch together and Julianna introduced her to Phoebe.

"Phoebe? As in the character on *Friends*?" Christine had asked.

"Nope, as in Cates. Mom loved *Fast Times at Ridgemont High*. Long live Spicoli," Phoebe said, her upper lip lifting into a sneer. Christine had given her a knowing grin, remembering her own mother making her watch that movie. Phoebe was a Belmont alumnus. She had interned for a record label, and then they'd hired her for a full-time social networking role. She was brilliant at it.

That first meeting had solidified Christine's place as Julianna's friend, but Phoebe was Julianna's sorority sister and those bonds ran deep. So Christine had learned to deal with her.

"Hey. It's the lady of the hour," Julianna said, looking up and motioning Christine over as she walked to the table. "And damn does your hair look good."

"It's a curly mess," Christine said, fluffing it.

"Not even. Your long locks look amazing."

"Damn. Can you come give me a pep talk every morning?"

"I can." Julianna's face was bright, her smile huge. "Tell me everything."

Christine shrugged out of her black leather jacket and hung it on the back of her chair with her purse. She'd discovered in college that she looked good in black leather jackets when some hot random guy on campus told her she did. It wasn't much of a fashion statement, but ever since that day, she'd felt a sense of confidence when she wore them. And having confidence went a long way in the music business.

"I was standing on the street corner, looking amazing in my dress, and he said he couldn't help but stop and ask me to be his date."

"Seriously?" Julianna asked.

"I may have paraphrased a little. I clearly needed a ticket, so it worked out perfectly."

"I'm so sorry we couldn't hold the doors any longer. We begged the security guy," Julianna said.

"I was late. That's on me. And it turned out well for me. I mean, how many times do I get to ride in a limo to an after-party?" Christine picked up her menu and perused it. She was being coy—not her usual style—but so often, she was the one who *heard* this kind of story. She enjoyed getting to be the one telling it.

"Limo? After-party? Keep going."

Christine told Julianna about the night, embellishing a large part of it. She ended with Austin's offer to go home with him and exchanging cell phone numbers.

"He invited you to his home and you said no?" Julianna said.

"He didn't ask me to have sex with him. Just to go home with him."

"What do you think he meant?"

"I don't know. It never happens to me," Christine said.

"It did last night, and you said no," Julianna said.

"I don't need a one-night stand or courtesy sex. I'm fine," Christine said, thinking she might have lost her one chance to have sex this year. *Damn it*, she thought. *I'm such a dork.*

"When was the last time you got laid?" Julianna asked.

"What year is it?" Christine said with a smirk. "He did kiss me. And did I mention his tour manager is super cute?"

"He kissed you?" Julianna's eyes went wide.

"He did, and his tour manager, Matt, asked if he could kiss me," Christine said, wiggling in her chair.

"Yeah, yeah. Tour manager, whatever. Tell me about Austin," Julianna said.

"I'd rather talk about Matt. He is so handsome, and kind, and he's—"

"Matt? What about Austin?"

"Oh, Austin. Yeah, he's gorgeous and funny and has really soft lips."

"Then why are you talking about Matt?"

Christine felt a huge grin cover her face. "'Cause Matt could be the one for me. And I haven't said that since . . . never."

"You just met him," Julianna said, giving Christine the are-you-crazy look.

"You know how they say you sometimes just know?" Christine said.

Julianna looked like she was going to say something else, but then the server came by. They ordered lunch, Julianna getting Phoebe a Caesar salad and then a Greek salad for herself. Christine ordered the soup and sandwich.

"Please don't mention Matt to Phoebe. Or anyone else. Or mention the kiss. Oh, this is all so weird for me," Christine said. "I feel like I'm in high school or something."

"I won't say a word."

Phoebe rushed in, panting, but not a hair out of place.

"Christine, I'm so sorry."

"It's not your fault. I knew they'd close the doors if I was late. It says so on the ticket," Christine said.

"What? No, not for that. For what his fans are saying about you on socials. It's just horrible," Phoebe said. She knew the cyber world better than anyone.

"What are you talking about?" Christine asked.

"You haven't seen?" Phoebe asked.

"Seen what?" Christine asked, looking from one friend to the other. Julianna wouldn't look her in the eyes.

"Don't you follow Austin Garrett on Twitter?" Phoebe asked.

"I prefer Instagram."

Christine grabbed her phone, went to Twitter, typed in *Austin Garrett*, and nearly cried. One message read, *OMG! Who was the girl with AG? You can do better, Austin! Call me.* Another one read, *Um, what's with the average looking date AG had? He should be with a model!* Another tried to be kind: *I heard he was taking his sister, so don't be so mean.* This was rebutted by, *That's not his sister. I googled it. His sister is way hotter than his date was.*

And on and on it went. Comment after comment. Every so often, just to break things up, someone would say something nice like, *She looked like she has a great personality. She grinned a lot.* But some were also scary: *Someone needs to remove her from him, NOW.*

"Did you know about this?" Christine looked at Julianna.

"I'd seen a few of the comments but didn't want to make a big deal out of it."

"It's a pretty damn big deal. I'm trending, for God's sake. And not in a good way," Christine said. She kept reading more comments. *I liked her shoes!*

"When did they get a shot of my borrowed hooker shoes?"

Christine shook her head to clear her thoughts, then gave a quick huff. The mean people couldn't win. She would just choose to ignore them.

"Well, that was ... dark. So what if I'm not tall, blonde, and size two? No offense, Julianna," she said, slamming her phone down.

"None taken. You okay? I'd be freaking right now if this was about me," Julianna said.

Christine envisioned the worst day of her life. It was in high school. The circle around her, the taunts, the threat. This was nothing.

"People can just be mean. They are insecure and jealous. That's all."

"What?" Phoebe asked, her brow creasing.

"It's what my mom always told me when people teased me in high school. She said that people who are secure with themselves don't need to tear others down. They must have been jealous of me. So what if I didn't sit at the cool table or hang with the best-looking guys?"

Christine had known that, deep down, she wanted to date the hot guys, sit at the cool table, and go to parties. But she'd hung on to her mother's words, and the older she got, the more she realized that it did take an insecure person to belittle someone else.

"Huh. Well, that's one way of looking at it," Phoebe said.

"And you're hanging with the hot guy now," Julianna said, wiggling her eyebrows.

"And obviously sitting at the cool table. I mean, we're here," Phoebe said, pointing to herself and Julianna. Christine chuckled.

"And I do go to some cool parties. See? They're just jealous," Christine said, nodding. She didn't add that the comments still stung. Words can hurt. Sometimes worse than a punch.

Their food arrived and they dug in. Christine was glad when Julianna broke the silence and changed the topic.

"Are we still hitting the Bluebird next week? It's the weekly songwriters round, and I hear there are two new writers who show a lot of potential," Julianna said.

"It is our monthly outing. I plan on being there. Hopefully none of Austin's cyber friends will be," Christine said.

"I'm in. The talent they get is always promising," Phoebe said.
Christine's phone chimed, but she ignored it.

"You have a text," Phoebe said.

"I heard," Christine said.

"Look at it. It might be Austin," Julianna said with urgency.

"It's not him," Christine said.

"You don't know that." Julianna met her eyes.

"I do know that," Christine said.

"Just look."

"Okay."

It wasn't him. They paid their bill and headed out.

AS IT TURNED OUT, AUSTIN DID call Christine—at 3:00
a.m. She reached for her cell, shocked to see his number on
the screen.

"Hello?"

"Hey, hello. Yo. Is this, um, is this . . ."

"Christine?" she said.

"Yeah, Chrisshy."

Christine sat up in bed and turned on her bedside light.

"Not Chrissy, Christine."

"What?"

"Never mind. What do you want?"

"Don't you live in the Brendwood Aperments?" She could
hear his labored breathing and imagined him swaying. Drunk
people tended to be heavy breathers.

"Brentwood Apartments? Yes, why?" She got out of bed and
walked into the kitchen, getting a glass of water.

"I think I'm in one, and I need to get out, but I can't drive
'cause I've had a couple drinks."

"A couple?" She took a sip of water.

"Maybe more. I didn't count."

"Why can't you stay where you are?"

"'Cause this chick I came home with is frucking crazy!"

"Frucking?"

"I tried to say freaking but it mingled. You don't seem like the type of girl who appreciates the F-bomb at . . . at . . . hold on." He made a rustling noise. "At three in the morning."

"I'm not the type of girl who appreciates anything at three in the morning. Why do you think she's crazy?"

"I tried to leave, and she stole my pants and locked them in a cabinet. I can't find the key. She's passed out, but I have no pants and can't drive." He exploded in a fit of giggles.

"Where are you?"

"In an apartment. Can you come get me?"

"Which apartment?"

"Hold on." More rustling, a door opening, a door closing.

"Apartment 21B. Now I'm stuck outside without pants. I can't get back in. The door is locked."

He laughed, but it was muffled over the phone.

"Stop laughing. Someone will hear you."

"Okay. Got it," he said, continuing to chuckle.

"Do you at least have on underpants?"

"Yepper. You won't see my boy if that's your concern. But if you did, it's pretty damn impressive, if I say so myself."

Christine closed her eyes and tried not to conjure an image of Austin's *boy*, which she assumed would be as perfect as the rest of him.

"I'll be right there." She hung up the phone and tried to visualize 21B. It was at least three streets away. She threw on a pair of sweatpants and a tank top, grabbed her keys, and drove over. When she arrived, there he was, Austin Garrett, the heartthrob, who was now passed out in his tighty-whities on the lawn outside the apartment complex. Christine got out of the car and shook him until he came to.

"Oh, hey, Chrisshy." He grabbed her arm and pulled her down beside him, laying a sloppy kiss on her face.

"Quit that." Christine wiped her mouth and stood, pulling him with her. Along with his underwear, he was wearing a black T-shirt and a leather jacket. "Get in the car, now. Someone might see you."

"Yes, Mom." He stumbled into the passenger side of her car.

Christine bristled. Why did she always have to act like the mom? She was the responsible one, the designated driver, the person you could call at three in the morning.

"Want me to leave you on the lawn outside Crazy Woman's house?"

"Nope."

"You'll behave?"

"Yep."

She closed his door and got into the driver's seat.

"What about your wallet? Car keys?"

"In my jacket." He patted his pocket. "Not my first rodeo with crazy chicks."

"Why would you choose crazy chicks?"

"You know what they say. Crazy in the head, crazy in the . . ."

"In the what?"

"Really? You don't know? Bed, Chrissy girl. Crazy in bed."

"Oh, dear Lord. No comment. And don't call me Chrissy."

He rolled his head to the side, blew her a kiss, and promptly started snoring.

She drove to her building, woke him up, and helped him into her apartment. He sauntered in, went straight to the bathroom, then weaved his way into her bedroom and passed out on her bed.

"Oh no you don't. Uh-uh. You get the spare bedroom. Austin. Austin. Austin Garrett." She reached out and tapped him. Then she shook him with one hand. Then she used both hands to shake the mattress.

Nothing. No response. He was gone.

"Damn it." She gave up trying to wake him and went to the spare bedroom. How had it happened that Austin Garrett was asleep in her bed? Or that he was in her home at all? Her friends would love this story. If she told them. It was hardly romantic to save him from the clutches of a crazy woman. She was irritated that he thought it was okay to call her, a virtual stranger, to come save him. And that he'd taken her bed. She forced herself to calm down so she could fall asleep.

When her alarm went off at 7:00 a.m., she snuck into her room and grabbed some clothes. She paused to look at Austin, peacefully sleeping. He was so handsome, even after a night of debauchery.

She showered and left with a quick note: *Coffee in the machine. Just turn it on. Help yourself to any food you can find. Ciao.*

On the drive to work, she obsessed over her use of the word "ciao." What was she? Italian? Why had she written "ciao"? She felt like an idiot.

When she got to work, she didn't say anything to anyone. It wasn't as if he'd called her while he was sober and asked her out to dinner. She kept her mouth shut and turned her phone off for her morning listening meetings so she could give her full attention to every song. She hoped she'd find a song for Austin that would be so big he couldn't help but agree to record it, release it to radio, and make it a hit. It had to be different, yet authentic to him. He could get rousing party songs from anyone, but she wanted to dig deeper. He had so much potential to go bluesy, do more ballads, and even do classic country. But after eight songs that sounded like the party songs he'd already recorded, there was nothing left. Every time she hit PLAY on a new song, she hoped it would be a career-changing hit for an artist. They were few and far between, but when you found one, the high was better than any street drug. Those moments reminded her why she'd chosen this job. This was not one of those moments. And she needed it to be, more than ever, after what Rick had said.

Frustrated, she removed her headphones and took a break. When she turned her phone back on, her texts blew up.

9:45 a.m.: *Hey, Chrissy. It's Austin. How do you work the coffee machine?*

"Really?" she said aloud.

10:10 a.m.: *Hey, Chrissy. This is great shampoo. Where do you get it?*

She thought, *He was in my shower?*

10:35 a.m.: *Hey, Chrissy. I can't figure out your remotes. Which one turns on the TV?*

11:10 a.m.: *Hey, Chrissy. I figured out the remote. Thanks for your help. Ha-ha.*

11:30 a.m.: *Hey, Chrissy. Can you run out and buy me some pants? I'm a 32 waist, 34 long.*

11:50 a.m.: *Hey, Chrissy. I rummaged through your drawers, not your panty drawer cause that would be creepy. But I found some big sweatpants and they kind of fit me. I'm dressed enough to head home. Thanks for your help. See ya around.*

"I have no words," Christine said to herself.

"No words for what?" Julianna asked from the doorway to Christine's office. She wore a miniskirt, off-the-shoulder shirt, and high heels. Only in the entertainment industry was that standard business attire. She sat on the spare chair and put her long legs up on Christine's desk.

"So how's our rising star?"

"Our rising star?"

"Yours, mine, ours. We're friends. One for all and all for one, right?"

"Uh-huh? Whatcha need?" Christine put her pen behind her ear and sat back.

"Feel like ordering a pizza tonight?"

"Sure. My place? If you're willing to slum it."

Julianna winced. "Your place is not a slum."

"It's nothing like the condo you live in."

"At least you pay for it yourself. I still live off Daddy's money. Anyway, your place works fine for me. See you around six," Julianna said, walking back out.

JULIANNA SHOWED UP WITH TWO small pizzas and a bottle of wine. They sat in the living room, choosing the couch over the dining room table. Christine got up to get a napkin and her phone chimed in a text. When she returned, Julianna was holding the phone up and pointing it at her.

"Is A.G. Austin?"

Christine looked at the text displayed on the screen, which read, *Thanks again for last night. Waiting for you to find me a new hit. Don't take too long.*

"Yep, that would be him."

"What happened last night?" Julianna said, sitting upright, her eyes wide.

"Nothing, really. He got locked out of his car near my apartment and needed a place to crash. It was three in the morning, so I went and picked him up and let him stay for the rest of the night at my place." Christine took a sip of her tea like this was no big deal.

"And you didn't call me?"

"For what?"

"I'd have come right over," Julianna said, her voice husky.

"For what possible reason?" Christine asked.

"What do you think?" Julianna asked.

"It wasn't a booty call, Julianna."

"It could have been," Julianna said, and then she scrunched her eyebrows. "Unless you've called dibs. Have you called dibsies?"

Christine shook her head as her phone chimed again.

Julianna grabbed her phone to see the text message: *Hey, Chrissy. I wrote a new song and want your opinion. I'll send it to you tonight if you have time.*

"He calls you Chrissy? You hate Chrissy. Nobody calls you that. You insist on Christine."

Christine rolled her eyes. "I've asked him not to, but he doesn't listen."

"How can you be so calm? Text him back!" Julianna was salivating.

"I will." Christine was playing it cool. "If you'll give me my phone back."

Christine took her phone and texted Austin: *Okay. Send it.* She paused, not sure if she should tell him she'd found some songs for him, too. She didn't want to be pushy, but she couldn't save the company with songs he wrote himself. It had to be songs from her company's songwriters. This added stress was going to drive her crazy. She decided not to push anything yet.

"So, have you?" Julianna asked.

"Have I what?" Christine was so deep in thought about songs she forgot the question.

"Called dibs. And it's not just me asking. It's driving Phoebe crazy that people are talking about you and Austin. She thought she'd be the one to land a singer."

"What is this? High school? She needs to chill. I've never understood how someone as nice as you can be besties with her. Don't you find her cold?"

"I've never told you the story?"

Christine shook her head. "You just said you'd met in college and she always had your back."

"My first day at college I had some girls being rude to me in the café line. They were making nasty comments about how short my skirt was. And it was short. But come on—I was eighteen. I tried not to listen, but it's hard to ignore words like 'slut.' Then I heard another girl say, 'Excuse me, but I'm going to cut in front of you now. You're welcome to bash my clothing all you want. And for the record, I own the word "slut."' It was Phoebe. She told me I needed to pledge her sorority and she'd be my big sister and protect me from nasty people. I commented on how nice she was and she said, 'Make no mistake. I'm not nice. But I'm fiercely loyal to my friends, and when you need it the most, I'll have your back.' And she always has."

"I can't argue with that. And to answer your question, no, I haven't called dibs."

"Why aren't you interested? He obviously is."

"No, he isn't," Christine said.

"CMT night, he invited you to his house." Julianna sat back and crossed her arms.

"I was the only woman in the car. Of course I'd win."

"He called you when he needed help."

"He'd been with another woman. He was escaping. Although he doesn't seem the type who would be bothered by multiple women in one night." Christine put her finger in her mouth and faked puking.

"What if he *is* interested? Will you go for it?" Julianna leaned forward, rubbing her hands together.

Christine shook her head.

"Why not? You never date. At all. Anyone."

"Pot, kettle. I don't see you with a guy right now. We both know this town sucks for finding men. Even waiters and Uber drivers are trying to be singers, songwriters, or musicians. And I don't really want to date any of those."

"But you have a chance with Austin Garrett," Julianna said, throwing her hands up.

"I have a *chance* to ruin a great business opportunity. Bad move."

"Why do you always have to be so in control?" Julianna asked.

Christine took a deep breath and let it out slowly. "Because it's the only way I feel safe."

"Safety is sometimes overrated," Julianna said.

"Not to me." Christine stood and took their plates to the kitchen.

Julianna followed. She leaned against the kitchen cabinet and stared at Christine. "I know you had a bad experience in high school that you never want to talk about. And I respect that. I really do. But it's been more than a decade. Maybe talking would help."

Christine threw her head back and looked at the ceiling before looking at Julianna. "A couple of guys, big guys, harassed me one night. One of them, well . . . he was very aggressive." Christine turned away and washed her hands, trying to stall so she could think about how to word what had happened.

"Aggressive how?" Julianna asked, touching Christine's shoulder and turning her back around.

"He grabbed me and kissed me. He squeezed my breast, hard, then my butt. He . . . I really don't want to talk about this." Her eyes misted. She blinked to clear them.

"Did you talk to your parents? A school counselor?" Julianna asked.

"Heck no. That would have made it worse. I just had to survive the last few months of high school and get out of there. I told a few people in college. Most just shrugged it off as 'guys will be guys.' One or two girls seemed to understand how I felt."

"Christine. You were sexually assaulted. That's not something guys just do. Most guys wouldn't dream of doing such a thing."

"I know they wouldn't. And it wasn't a sexual assault. I had my clothes on. Nothing happened."

"Seriously? Is that what you've been telling yourself while

deep down knowing differently? He touched you, Christine. In places he shouldn't have. He forced himself on you."

Christine took a deep breath. "I know. But it was before #metoo went viral and I thought it was just me. Like it would never happen to someone prettier or cooler than me. It was easier to not think about it and hope the memory would go away."

"But it didn't go away."

"No. It didn't. It never does. The reason I don't like being called Chrissy? They chanted at me, 'Chrissy is a sissy; Chrissy is a sissy.' It became the chant of the high school anytime I walked by a group of people who didn't like me. I'm getting used to Austin calling me that, and in some ways, it's starting to help heal the pain. But the memories are always there."

"Christine, I don't even know what to say."

"There's nothing to say. Moving on to another conversation, as I'd like this one to be over . . . I have not called dibsies. Have at it. I just want him for his talent. The truth is . . ."

"Yes?" Julianna said.

"I can't stop thinking about his tour manager, Matt."

"So, even after more time with Austin, you're still interested in his tour manager? Seriously? You have a shot at the hottest guy in Nashville," Julianna said.

"I think Matt's hotter."

"Then go for it," Julianna said, holding up her hands and shrugging.

"Not that easy. Risk versus reward. He might not like me and then I've embarrassed myself and potentially messed things up with Austin. Then I lose on both fronts," Christine said.

"Or, Matt likes you, you start dating, it solidifies your relationship with Austin, and you win on both fronts."

Christine grabbed her head with both hands. "This is making my head hurt. And that horrific stroll down memory lane didn't help either. Mind if we call it a night?"

"Not at all. I'm sorry to dredge up the painful past. But I'm kind of excited to think about your crush on Matt. This could be fun," Julianna said.

"Or not. Unrequited crushes suck," Christine said.

"True. But we don't know that it's unrequited. I'll see you tomorrow at work. And remember, I'm a phone call away. In good times and bad."

"Thank you." Christine hugged Julianna, and Julianna hung on for a second longer than usual. "Love you," Julianna said.

"Love you, too."

While rinsing out their glasses, Christine thought about how her life had changed since high school. As a kid, she had fantasized about working with songwriters in Nashville. She'd beg her parents to take her to every country concert that came to their local theatre. She'd google every song she liked to see who'd written it. She got to where she could listen to a song on the radio and name the writer without even looking. She understood their musical and lyrical styles. Even when she worked in promotions at a radio station, a job she'd gotten right out of college and loved, she knew it wasn't her true calling. She'd even convinced the station manager to put on songwriter nights, and twice a year, she'd hosted a Nashville songwriter's concert. The audience loved hearing the songs from the perspective of the people who'd created them.

A songwriter she knew had tipped her off to an opening for an entry-level position at Hit Songs Publishing. She applied and they made her an offer. Two weeks later, she packed her bags and left for Music City. She could still remember her first time walking down Music Row and looking at the huge MCA Records sign, the Warner Records building, and the Starstruck Entertainment offices. As she entered the building for Hit Songs Publishing, she'd closed her eyes and told herself to always remember that moment. It was a dream come true. She'd spent years building a life for herself and was proud of what she'd accomplished. But she did want someone to share it with. She just didn't want to waste her time with the wrong men. She had tried that a couple of times in college, attempting to make something fit that wasn't right. She'd been left feeling empty and regretful. She wanted a man, but she didn't *need* a man.

Like most young girls, she had fantasized about one day being chosen by a star. She'd live the life of the rich and famous, grace magazine covers, and be the envy of women worldwide. But in reality, that's not what Christine wanted. She yearned for something more normal. The older she got, the more she realized she didn't crave glitz and glamour, which might be why she migrated toward the songwriters more than the singers. Sure, Austin was a gorgeous star on his way to being very wealthy. Yet it was Matt she felt a connection with, Matt she was attracted to. She felt a sense of comfort near him.

She shook her head. It really did hurt. She hadn't had this much to think about in a long time, if ever. She got ready for bed and slipped under the covers. These thoughts would all be there tomorrow. Buried deep in her blankets, she went to sleep, the comfort and warmth enveloping her.

CHAPTER THREE

As Christine sat in her office, chai latte in hand, chatting with Julianna, the door flung open and Austin walked in. "Chrissy. What's up?" Austin walked past Julianna without looking at her.

Christine sat in shock. Nobody walked past Julianna without doing a double take. Most asked for her autograph, assuming anyone who looked like her had to be famous.

"Austin, meet my friend Julianna. Julianna, meet Austin."

"Nice to meet ya, Julianna."

"The pleasure is mine," she said, shaking his hand and using her most sultry voice.

Christine scoffed.

His gaze returned to Christine. "Found me some tunes?"

Christine sat up straight. She needed to sell this, and sell it hard. The future of the company was in her hands, and it all hinged on Austin cutting a song from Hit Songs Publishing. Sweat formed on her forehead, but she pretended it wasn't there. What is it they say? Never let them see you sweat? She had to play it cool. She forced a big smile.

"I did. I went so far as to go through an old box of cassettes."

"God, I love that. Those old forgotten songs can be gems."

"I have a handful to play for you. Want to grab a seat?"

"I'd rather listen in my own environment. Can I take them with me?"

"Of course. I can put them on a drive or send you MP3s. Do you have access to Box?"

"Slow down, Miss Technology. Just send them to my phone. That's how I like to listen. Cruising around. Don't most people listen to the radio in their cars?"

"That's what they say," Christine said.

"Then that's what I'll do. What are you doing this weekend?"

"Um, nothing. Why?"

"How about coming on the road with me? I'm the opening act on a run with Jackson Williams. I'll be playing in front of more than twenty thousand people a night. It would help you understand me even better if you saw me perform and were a part of it. You can watch how the audience reacts from the stage to get my vantage point. Ride the bus. You've already seen me in my underwear, so why not?" He smiled.

"You saw him in his underwear?" Julianna stared, wide-eyed. Christine shrugged.

"It wasn't my finest moment," Austin said. "What do you say, Chrissy? You up for a road trip?"

The offer had been on her mind since he'd mentioned it on that first night. Christine could think of nothing worse than jumping on a tour bus with a bunch of guys. She'd heard the stories of bus life and wanted no part of it—the women, the parties, the disgusting smells, and the noise. But she knew what it would mean for the company. Quality time listening to music with Austin meant a better shot at having him choose one of her songs. Every plugger she knew would give anything for this opportunity. Why would she pass it up?

"Sure. I'll go."

"Cool. Matt will get you the details." He turned to leave, reaching to shake Julianna's hand. "Nice to meet you, Julie."

Julianna's eyes opened wide and her mouth dropped open. Christine could tell she was shocked. Nobody forgot Julianna's name, or face, or body for that matter.

"It's Julianna," she said.

"Right. Catch ya later, ladies." He sauntered out the door while Christine and Julianna watched him leave.

"Damn. He looks as good leaving as he does coming," Julianna said.

"Yep."

"So Matt will call you?" Julianna said.

"It's business."

"For now," Julianna said, making kissing noises as she left the room.

CHRISTINE REGRETTED SAYING yes to going on the road with Austin. Of course, it was important for Hit Songs Publishing that she fast-track her work relationship with him. And even more important after her talk with Rick. She'd have time alone with Austin to better understand what type of songs he was looking for. This could be the opportunity she needed. But the bus? She'd briefly met the band, and they'd seemed nice. She knew them by reputation. It was a small town, after all. They were talented songwriters along with being excellent musicians. And there was at least one other female, Alicia. The others on the bus would be complete strangers. She'd see Matt, which was a plus. But Matt would also see *her*—first thing in the morning.

She knew people would find it odd that she cared more about what Matt thought than what Austin did. Austin was the famous singer women screamed for and fought over. Yet it was Matt whose mere presence had made her stomach flip and her skin feel tingly. She'd felt giddy when he was around. And Christine was not known for being giddy. Having read many women's magazines over the years, she knew attraction released dopamine as well as other happy hormones she could never remember the names of. While she enjoyed Austin's company, and he lightened up her serious personality, it was being around Matt that made her feel warm inside. And now he was going to see her, first thing in the morning, with messy hair and no makeup.

CHRISTINE PULLED INTO THE strip mall, saw the blue awning with the words "The Bluebird Cafe" printed on it, and parked. The Grand Ole Opry was known as the most sacred place in Nashville, but in Christine's mind, the Bluebird was a close second. From Vince Gill to Taylor Swift, every artist who was serious about a country music career had shared their song-writing skills on this stage. And "stage" was a generous word for it. Considering it was a small room next to a laundromat, Christine was always amazed by the amount of talent that had graced this small café.

Christine walked in and looked for Julianna. She'd felt feisty when deciding what to wear and chose her favorite black leather jacket and aviator sunglasses. She had let her hair go wild and curly. She spotted her friend at one of the small round tables and grabbed the seat next to her.

"I'm sorry. That seat is being saved for—"

Christine's eyebrows rose in question.

"Damn, lady. I didn't recognize you at first. You're looking all cool, like you rode in on a motorcycle," Julianna said.

Christine busted up laughing. "If I was riding on a motor-cycle, I'd be riding bitch. It would scare me to death to drive one."

"Do they call it 'driving' a motorcycle?"

"I have no idea. I love bikes but can't imagine being in the driver's seat."

"So, are you packed for the big weekend?" Julianna asked.

"What was I thinking? What happens if I need alone time?" Christine asked.

"Alone time?"

"Yeah, you know. Like, I need to go to the bathroom."

"Then you go. The bus has a bathroom," Julianna said.

"What if I have to *really* go?"

"Oh. Then you ask the bus driver to pull over. You can't do that on the bus."

"If I ask him to pull over, everybody will know what I need to do," Christine said in a whiny voice.

"Pretty sure they all suspect you poop like the rest of the world."

"But they don't know when," Christine said, her voice getting louder on the word "when."

"I'm sure they will suspect that at some time during your three days together, you will poop. It's not like you have a choice."

"Sure I do. Sort of. If I'm on a liquid diet. What doesn't go in won't have to come out."

"Good luck with that," Julianna said.

"The upside is, I'll probably lose a few pounds," Christine said, striking a sexy pose. Julianna snapped a photo.

"That, my friend, is your new Tinder photo."

"I don't have Tinder. Do I look like I'd have Tinder?" Christine asked.

"When you wear your black leather jacket and let your hair go all long and curly, you kinda do."

Christine waved her off while thinking that was one hell of a compliment.

"Maybe Matt's on Tinder and you can swipe right," Julianna said, picking up her phone and pretending to swipe right.

"Or he will see me on Tinder and swipe left, or whatever someone does when they aren't interested," Christine said.

"Geez. How did I never notice how negative you are?"

"'Cause you've never known me to be interested in a guy. My limited experience has not been positive," Christine said, shaking her head.

"I get you had a really bad experience. Horribly bad. But, Christine, most men are decent guys. They'd never hurt a woman or force themselves on her. Did you get any creepy vibes around Matt?"

"None. Not the slightest bit. He may be the hottest, most normal guy I've ever met in this business."

"Trust your instincts."

"Please don't say anything to Phoebe about my crush on Matt. She'll just tease me about it."

"Won't say a word."

Phoebe showed up right as the music started and all conversation ended. The great thing about the Bluebird was that people actually came to hear the songs, not to talk over them. Christine missed the last name of the guy who had just been introduced but caught that his first name was Justin. He mentioned being from across the pond, which was unnecessary as his English accent gave him away. His music was simple, staying within the three-chord progression of traditional country songs, but his lyrics were deep. These weren't songs about partying, drinking beer, and driving trucks. He got to the heart and soul of family, with the verses going from grandparents to parents to his life and what they'd taught him. His voice was deep and always on key. She made a note to get his last name and contact information. Country music had once been known for its ability to tell a story, but it had started to get away from that as newer styles proved successful with the audience. Justin's songs told stories that had the audience close to tears at times and laughing at others. The two best emotions for a song.

THE NEXT DAY, CHRISTINE PACKED her clothes. She went with sweatpants and a tank top to sleep in. She'd be comfortable and fully covered. After that, she struggled. Should she go cute with a little dress, business with a blazer, or casual with jeans and tops? She didn't want to overpack, but she also wanted options. She added two pairs of jeans, two tops, and a baby-doll dress. She put on a black leather jacket and a pair of boots. Both would go with all the outfits.

She met at the designated Kroger parking lot at 8:00 p.m. They had a twelve-hour drive and needed to load in at ten in the morning. Add in some fuel stops and they'd be right on time.

"Chrissy. You made it," Austin said.

"I did. There's a lot of people here," she said, mentally counting heads as people loaded luggage into the compartments under the bus. She knew a standard tour bus had twelve bunks.

"Three band members, Alicia, a sound guy, a guitar tech, Matt, a bus driver, me, and you."

She counted ten people, and eight of them were guys. It was an incredible amount of testosterone.

"One day, I'll have two tour buses. But for now, we're all squeezed on here. But we have room for you."

She stepped onto the bus with her oversized backpack and looked into the lounge. There were couches on both sides of the bus, each facing a flat-screen TV. One of the guys was channel surfing. Another was putting food and drinks into the fridge in the kitchen area while two sat across a table from each other playing cards. Alicia sat on a couch with her feet propped up on a box. Her baseball cap sported the famous Rolling Stones tongue logo. She looked up and gave Christine the peace sign. "Nice jacket," she said.

"Thanks. Nice hat." Christine hoped she and Alicia could form an estrogen bond. Women in the industry needed to stick together.

She noticed a closed door and assumed it was the bathroom. Then she walked through the lounge into the center area that held the beds. There were twelve, two rows stacked three high on both sides of the bus. Austin offered her his bed since it was a bottom bunk and, apparently, they were the best. She felt guilty taking it and said she'd be fine in the top bunk—until she tried to climb into it.

"What if I fall out?" she asked.

"You won't," Austin assured her.

"How do you know?"

"I don't. But nobody else ever has, so I have to assume you won't, either." It was a weak guarantee, but she nodded anyway.

"Are you sure you won't take my bunk?" Austin said, pointing to it.

Christine imagined what all had gone on in that bunk and gave an internal shiver. No soap was strong enough to get all that out.

"Nope. I'll be fine up here," she said, patting the upper bunk. "Is there anything else I need to know?"

"Yes. If we stop in the middle of the night, you know, to gas up or whatever, do not get off the bus without someone knowing about it."

"But if it's the middle of the night, I won't want to wake anyone," Christine said, reasoning it through.

"The driver doesn't do a bunk check. You'll get left behind. If you can't find the bus driver to let him know, the signal is to leave a roll of paper towels on his seat. That lets him know somebody got off the bus."

"Do people really get left behind?" Christine asked.

"Hell, a superstar once got left behind. Trust me, use the paper towels. It works."

"Got it." Christine prayed she wouldn't need to get off the bus. She couldn't fathom being left at a truck stop somewhere.

Another door at the far end of the bunk area caught her eye.

"The back lounge is through that door," Austin said. "I'm sure you remember the closet of women's clothing." He chuckled. "There's another small bathroom and a couch in there. Use whatever you need."

"Thanks." She didn't want to think about any recent additions to the closet.

They returned to the front lounge, and Christine met the few people she didn't already know. The bus driver, Al, peeked his head into the front lounge where everyone was packed in tight. He addressed Christine directly. "Now, little lady, I'm not sure what you know about being on a band bus, but we don't go number two in the toilet."

Christine's eyes darted from the bus driver to Austin to Matt and back to Austin, who stepped in to save her.

"I'm sure she'll be okay."

Christine smiled with relief.

"I told her to poop before bus call."

"You what? No, you didn't." She looked at the band and then the bus driver. "I didn't . . . I mean . . . he didn't. I . . . um . . ." Her eyes briefly met Matt's before she looked away in humiliation.

"Long as you don't poop on the bus, we're good. Let's go," the driver said. He hopped into his seat and started up the rig.

Christine sat down, horrified, while Austin fell onto the couch roaring.

"Asshole," Christine mouthed.

"Welcome to the road, Chrissy!"

The guys fired up the movie *Jackass Number Two*, and as the movie played, they yelled things like "gross," "freaking disgusting," and "dude, that's fucked up" while Christine sat in her corner trying to appear like she was enjoying it while nearly throwing up.

Alicia fit in like one of the guys. She high-fived the others at the most disgusting parts, and when there was a scene that included a guy getting overturned in a port-a-potty, she laughed so loud she snorted. Christine tried to laugh with her, the whole female bonding thing, but it came out more like a smirk.

Christine heard a door open and then close, and a guy walked into the lounge from the back of the bus. His wrinkled T-shirt read SHART HAPPENS. His sweatpants had a food stain as well as a couple of holes, and his hair stood up in all directions.

"Dudes, I just left an epic fart in the back lounge."

"Shit, man. I've got a guest on board. Chill," Austin said. He looked at Christine. "This is Ralph, our sound tech."

Ralph reached over to shake her hand, and Christine wished she was wearing a glove. "Christine," she said.

"*Woo-hoo!* We've got a chick on the bus," Ralph said, causing Austin to groan.

"Excuse me. You always have a chick on the bus," Alicia said.

"Where?" Ralph asked, looking past her.

Alicia flipped him off.

"My name's not really Ralph."

"Then why do they call you that?" Christine asked.

"'Cause he's always ralphing up something: farts, burps, and God knows what else. He's a one-man show," Matt said.

"I see. Nice to meet you," Christine said, thinking it really wasn't.

Ralph wiggled his way between Cat and Matt, causing them to groan. The movie resumed, getting more disgusting with each segment.

When her gag reflex could no longer handle it, Christine stretched her arms, gave a fake yawn, and announced that she was going to bed. She briefly stopped in the bathroom, only went number one, brushed her teeth, and climbed into her upper bunk. She was still getting settled when Matt came in.

"You have everything you need, Christine?" His voice gave her chill bumps.

She peered out from the bunk to see him standing below her. Crazy thoughts of him jumping into the bunk with her flashed through her brain. Where had that come from? She shook her head to clear it and return to reality.

"I'm good. Feeling a little awkward, but I have everything I need."

"I'd feel uncomfortable on a bus full of women, although they probably wouldn't be watching *Jackass* movies."

"No. We'd be knee-deep in *Love Actually*," she said.

"True confession? I love that movie. Hell, I love chick flicks. But don't tell the guys."

"Your secret is safe with me."

He bid her good night, and she watched him walk out the door.

The lights were off, the door was closed, and the room was pitch black. And it was cold. Christine snuggled down in the comforter, and with the road passing underneath the wheels and the bus gently rolling, she fell into a peaceful sleep.

CHAPTER FOUR

C hristine woke and sat up, hit her head on the ceiling, and fell back to the pillow. "This is like being in a coffin," she said to herself. She hit the overhead switch and turned on a small light, found her purse, rummaged through it, and did her best to apply a little makeup. She wasn't a vain person in general but didn't want raccoon eyes if she was going to run into guys first thing in the morning.

She climbed out of her bunk and joined the parade of half-awake bodies heading out of the bus. The tour buses and trucks were parked in a gated lot behind the venue. The gate had a security shack and two guards were already posted. The lot was a mini concrete city with a basketball net in one corner and a kiddie pool in the other. One of the crew guys had already set up a workout area with benches and weights. She saw two women on mats doing yoga outside one of the buses. She envied their energy and vowed, once again, to find a fitness regimen she could enjoy.

She found Matt at the security check-in. Austin was still sound asleep, so Matt led her to the "touring ladies' dressing room."

"You're lucky Jackson's tour sets aside a separate room just for the ladies. Not all of them do."

"Then where do the women go?"

"Unisex bathrooms."

"Ugh. No offense, but most of you guys can't aim at all. You leave the floor filthy."

"Yep. Guilty as charged."

She waited for her turn to get a shower and use the facilities. One glance in the mirror told her that her makeshift makeup application had been a failure. She tried to hurry, knowing others needed to clean up, but the hot water cascading down her back and through her hair made her want to stay. She lingered a few extra minutes before drying off and dressing. Next came the hair. First, the anti-frizz gel, followed by twenty minutes with a blow dryer and fifteen minutes with a flat iron. And then a quick prayer for clear skies and low humidity. Forty-five minutes later, she emerged.

The backstage area was large and confusing. A sign said "Everything" with a finger pointing to the right. Matt had told her to meet him in Jackson Williams's production room. If she didn't want to get accosted by security guards, she needed credentials to walk around backstage.

After making a few wrong turns, she found it. Matt motioned with his hand for her to come in. Two long tables faced each other and six people sat around them typing on computers. Starbucks cups sat by their computers along with remnants of other vices from cigarettes to gum to Skoal. Matt introduced her to the various members of Jackson's production staff, including the tour manager, tour coordinator, Live Nation rep, production manager, and security guards. They all looked up and greeted her with a smile.

"If there's anything else you need, let me know. I assume Matt showed you where the ladies' dressing room is," Rachel, the tour coordinator, said.

"He did. Thank you. I had a nice shower."

"It's a perk having a ladies-only room. Anytime you need it, or anything else, please feel welcome."

Christine appreciated the sentiment but felt like she was in the way. This was a major production. Tori was typing on her computer, Drew was stuffing envelopes, and Jake took a phone call. Christine thanked them for their hospitality and turned back to Matt, bumping into him. Chill bumps raised on her arms. She smiled. Something about this man made her feel both comfortable and stimulated.

He handed her two laminates. One was All Access for Austin and one was All Access for Jackson.

"Why both?"

"Austin's identifies who you're with. Jackson's allows you access backstage," Matt said, his musky scent dancing around her nostrils.

Focus.

"Makes sense."

"Austin will probably sleep until noon, so you have a couple of hours . . ."

With you? Christine imagined the two of them roaming the grounds holding hands.

"Catering is open if you want breakfast, or I can ask a runner to go get you something. I have one about to go to Starbucks if you need anything." Matt ushered her out of Jackson's production room, the crew's polite *nice to meet yous* trailing behind them.

"I'd kill for a chai latte," she said to Matt, very aware of how close he was.

"I think we can handle that without a murder charge," he said, putting his hand on her back. She reached around and placed her hand over his. Their eyes met. Was he feeling what she was? She thought maybe he was. Then he broke eye contact and took his hand away. Maybe he wasn't.

"Our production room is down this hall," he said. They walked into a much smaller room with one round table and two chairs. A single light bulb hung from the ceiling, and there was a floor lamp in the corner that didn't work. The floor tiles were cracked and the walls needed a new coat of paint.

"Cozy," she said.

"That's a nicer word than I would use. Feel free to kick back in here. Sound check is at three o'clock. Otherwise, I'm just getting things set up this morning." Matt laid out his computer, files, and envelopes.

"Can I help? I know very little about the touring world but would love to learn."

"Sure. When you're the opening act's tour manager, you're a one-man show. I'll take the help." Matt gave her a stack of tickets, meet-and-greet passes, and envelopes. Directions were printed on the envelopes explaining where people needed to line up to meet Austin. Matt then gave her a list of names designating who got tickets, who got passes, and who got both.

Christine stuffed the envelopes accordingly. She was meticulous, not wanting to mess up. After she had checked and cross-checked every item, she handed them back to Matt. It was eleven o'clock when Austin stumbled into the room.

"What's up, Matt? Chrissy?"

"Christine," Christine and Matt said in unison. Her eyes met Matt's. He seemed to really get her. It was as if he knew the name thing was important to her, so it was important to him, too. That had to mean something.

Austin grinned. "How about we go to the bus and listen to some songs?"

"That's what I'm here for. Matt, I think I have everything taken care of."

"You're the best," he said.

She blushed and then felt stupid for it. A woman shouldn't blush over a simple statement, even when it comes from her crush.

"Thanks for your help. I like this one, Austin. Can we keep her?" Matt leaned back in his seat and put his hands behind his head. He looked so sexy. Like he was just waiting for her to sit on his lap. Her stomach did a flip and her heartbeat raced. The feeling spread to areas south. It was something she hadn't felt in a long time.

"Hands off! She's mine," Austin said. He wrapped his arm around her shoulders. His eyes danced, making it look like a joke, but she wasn't sure it was.

Christine's head snapped around.

I'm his? Is that how he and Matt saw her?

"Yeah, yeah. Aren't they all," Matt said.

Christine wanted to argue the point of Austin's ownership but didn't know how. She didn't want to offend Austin or make it sound like she preferred Matt. In her head, she responded with, "I'm no man's property." She even saw herself doing the finger wag, but felt it was like saying, "Oh no you didn't." In her head, neither fit. Besides, the opportunity to speak up was gone. Matt had turned back to his computer, ending the discussion.

Austin and Christine had just gotten settled in the back lounge of the bus, ready to listen to some of Austin's new songs, when a text caused her phone to chime.

It was from Phoebe. *Are you out with Austin?*

Christine replied, *Yes. How'd you know?*

Phoebe texted back, *Socials are blowing up again.*

She pulled up Austin's accounts and saw a comment from AGFan: *The video awards date is with Austin again. And she's on his bus. I don't get what he sees in her.*

AUSTIN4Ever replied, *I just saw that pic too. WTH?*

AGFan said, *I don't get it. He could have anyone. Why her?*

AUSTIN4Ever said, *Have you seen her thighs?*

Every comment was like a knife sawing through her. She regressed to her teenage self and the negative feelings came rushing back. She shook them off. She was a successful, professional, adult woman. She needed to act like it and rise above this.

A third person, COUNTRYFANGIRL, said, *In fairness, she's not fat.*

Well she ain't thin! AUSTIN4EVER said.

Christine clicked on the link to the pictures. In one photo, she was getting off the bus in her big ol' sweatpants and oversized T-shirt. Her hair was twisted up in a sloppy bun. Not a cute Victoria's Secret model sloppy bun, either. It was a hair-sticking-out-all-over-the-place sloppy bun. The next photo showed her walking beside Austin. She looked better after a shower, but whoever had taken the picture must have been sitting down. It was taken from a lower angle, making her look like she had elephant thighs. Her legs weren't twigs, but they weren't that large, either. They were solid, average thighs.

Someone out here had taken these. But who?

"What's wrong?" Austin asked when he looked at her.

She showed him her phone.

"This again?" he said.

Christine nodded.

"What is wrong with people? I'm going to tell them they can all go to hell." He grabbed his cell phone and started typing.

"You can't."

"Why not?"

"Because you're Austin Garrett. If you do that, you'll lose fans. Just leave it alone. It's not a big deal." Christine had to think of Austin's career and the fact that hers was tied to it.

"Bullshit it's not. It's a big freaking deal if people are posting crap about you."

"Please, let it go. You'll only make it worse. It'll die down." She continued pleading with him until he put his phone down.

"Let's listen to some music," she said.

"I'm letting Matt know about this," he said, texting his tour manager.

Christine stared at him, willing him to let it go.

He exhaled slowly. "Okay. Here are the three songs I like the most. Two came from you and one came from another publisher. Three different themes and all different tempos," Austin said.

Christine held her breath. Her anxiety level rose. If he chose the other publisher's song, it could be eight to ten months before she could pitch to him again. Did Hit Songs Publishing have ten months to wait? She needed him to cut one of her songs but didn't want to steer him. An artist had to pick the best song for their personality and sound. If that song wasn't hers, she'd have to accept it.

He scrolled through his phone, connected it to the sound system, and played the three songs. Just like she did in her office, Christine silenced her phone, set it aside, and gave all her attention to the music. She intimately knew the two songs she had pitched but wanted to hear them in a different environment, along with the third song. Sometimes music was perspective, and this would give her some. She didn't say anything until the final chords of the last song faded.

"I know I pitched it, but I really like the ballad. The message moved me. It's a story song, and telling a story is what country music is best known for. It's also what the format has been lacking in the last few years."

"So that would be your choice?" Austin asked.

Christine knew she had to be honest. "My only concern is that it doesn't have a chorus. It has three very strong verses."

"Is that a problem?"

"Sometimes a song without a chorus has a harder time making a good showing in market research. Since the chorus repeats two or three times, it's what listeners remember. And it's what radio programmers use to test a song with the audience."

"I still don't have a real sense of what the research tells a radio person to do. My label always waves me off when I ask and tells me to focus on singing and performing. They say it's their job to worry about research."

"They're right. But it's fair for you to want to know. The research tells a programmer if the audience loves, likes, or dislikes a song. The more they love it, the more radio will play it. If they dislike it, they play it less. A chorus usually sticks with the listener and causes them to be more familiar with the song, usually meaning songs with choruses perform better in research."

"Understood. But a great song can still research without a chorus, right?"

"It can."

"What's your gut feeling?"

"It's strong. And you repeat the title several times. That would stay with the listener. I like it," Christine said.

"Do any stand out as definite hits or absolute failures?"

"The midtempo is fun. I think it'll be a favorite with women, and they're our core audience in country music."

"And they love a song where the dude admits he screwed up and had to beg to get her back."

"Won't argue that." She paused before commenting on the song that wasn't hers. Truth was, she didn't feel it was as strong as the other two. And she could honestly tell herself it wasn't just because someone else had brought it to him. "The up-tempo about the party in the field with beer and chicks in Daisy Dukes isn't my favorite. It's been done to the point of being overdone. I know it makes for a fun video, but I think the audience is over that theme," she said. "And I know radio programmers are."

"Yeah, I kind of felt the same. I wanted to make it a different kind of party song, but it came out sounding like all the others. I couldn't find a way to give it a unique twist."

"There's only so much you can do with a kegger," she said.

"Good point. I'm not ready to make a decision yet, but I feel closer," Austin said.

Christine screamed internally. She had hoped to nail him down to one of the songs today. She couldn't show him her stress, though. It wasn't fair to put that on him.

Austin rubbed the back of his neck. He closed his eyes and winced with pain.

"You okay?"

"I must have slept wrong. My neck hurts."

"Can I get you something?"

"Would you mind massaging it? I can't reach it."

"Oh, well, sure. I took a massage class back in college. Got a health credit for it. It's been a while, but I can try."

Austin lay down on the couch and Christine sat beside him.

"Hold on." Austin sat back up and took his shirt off.

Christine tried to look anywhere other than his amazing abs—and shoulders, and back. And now she had to touch him. She started to massage his neck and shoulders. His body slumped. The muscles softened at her touch. She rubbed his head, knowing that sometimes helped her when she had neck pain.

Austin groaned.

"Does that hurt?"

"No." His voice sounded raspy.

Christine continued. She often got massages herself and knew what she liked. She tried to do the same for Austin.

Austin shifted. Then shifted again.

"Everything all right?" she asked.

"Yeah, other than I'm fucking hard as a rock." His voice dropped, giving it a husky quality.

"You do have some tight muscles."

"That's not the muscle I'm talking about," he said, shifting again. He rolled to his side and Christine couldn't mistake the muscle he was referring to. His sweatpants did nothing to hide the obvious.

"Wow." Christine said it without meaning to.

"I told you it was impressive." He gave her an Elvis-type smile with a full-on lip curl.

"Oh my. I didn't mean to . . . I mean, that's not what I was . . ."

"It's okay, Chrissy. You have great hands." He took her hand in his. He reached up and put his other hand behind her head, pulling her toward him. He paused, looking into her eyes before settling his gaze on her lips.

Her head was pounding with one thought. *He is going to kiss me.*

The door to the bus opened and closed, followed by footsteps. Nobody sneaks onto a tour bus. He broke off eye contact and looked at the door.

A female voice said, "Hello?"

Christine pulled away from Austin.

"Damn. Next time," Austin said.

"Uh-huh." She stood and straightened her shirt. "I should probably go."

"I'm going to give my boy a minute to go down, and I'll meet you in catering."

She stumbled out the door and ran into Alicia.

"Hey," Christine said.

"Uh, hey. Is Austin back there?"

"Um, yeah. He is. We were, um, listening to some music."

"Is Matt?"

Christine stood still. Matt! Her crush. And here she almost kissed Austin. What was she thinking? She wasn't thinking. Warmth spread across her cheeks. She opened her mouth to speak, but only her breath came out. She closed her eyes and shook her head.

"Hello?" Alicia said.

"Huh? What? Oh, sorry. No, Matt isn't here. Did you try production?"

"He isn't there. They said he was heading for the bus."

"I haven't seen him." Christine wanted to get away, be alone, and think. Had Matt come to the bus and they hadn't heard him? No. No way. The door squeaked and the floor shook every time someone came on. They'd have known. Unless they were so into the massage and near-kiss that they'd missed it. But no—she'd heard when Alicia came in. Christine needed to calm down. She left the bus and practically ran to the ladies' dressing room, happy to find nobody was in there. She sat on the couch and tried to call Julianna. She got her voicemail. When her text chimed a moment later, she jumped.

It was from Austin. *I'm in catering. Coming?*

Austin was probably unfazed by the whole thing. He kissed a different woman every night. Maybe more than one. It meant nothing to him. She would try to match his nonchalance.

She texted back. *Yep. On my way.*

After getting her food, she sat next to Austin while Matt had an altercation with two of the servers. He had a phone in his hand and was pointing to it and yelling. Seeing him made her heart beat a little faster. He was in his standard black fitted T-shirt. His jeans molded to his body in all the right places. She chastised herself. How could she almost kiss Austin one minute and have her heart flutter over Matt the next? What was happening to her?

Christine looked back to where Matt stood and pointed to him. "What do you think is going on over there?" she asked Austin.

"No idea. The crap that guy puts up with is ridiculous. I can't keep up with it," he said.

They finished eating and Austin left to take a shower.

Christine walked over to Matt. "Everything okay?" she asked.

"I just had to fire two people."

"Why?"

"I'm hesitant to say anything, but they had pictures of you on their phones. I think they were the ones posting things about you."

"Do they even know me? Why would they do that?"

"They said they'd seen other people do it and were just having fun," he said. His lips thinned and he gave a huff.

"Fun? This is fun for people? What kind of low-life idiot considers this fun?"

"Let it out, Christine. Wish you'd said that to their faces."

Christine paused and gave herself a moment to gather her wits. "Thank you for asking them to go. Maybe now it'll stop. I just don't understand why someone would do that to a complete stranger."

"People suck. That's why."

"Good point. What's next on our agenda?" Christine put her hand on Matt's arm. It was solid, muscular. She was slow to let go.

"We wait. We rush, we wait, we rush, we wait. That's life on tour. Three o'clock is the witching hour," Matt said. "Then it's balls to the wall."

Christine nodded.

"Oh, sorry. Was that offensive?"

"Was what offensive?" Christine asked.

"The balls-to-the-wall comment. And now I've said it again," Matt said.

"I'm not a prude," Christine said, a bit put off.

"And now I've offended you by trying *not* to offend you. How am I doing in the 'trying to impress Austin's new friend' department?"

She put her hand back on his forearm. "You're doing just fine."

MATT WAS RIGHT ABOUT THE time crunch. First, Austin did a sound check, then a TV interview. At 4:15 p.m., he met with someone from the local newspaper, followed by a couple of bloggers. He had just enough time to grab dinner before his label rep brought the radio program director, Grover, onto the bus to hang out. Christine shook his hand but did her best to stay out of the way, slinking into the corner by the fridge. These were important people in an artist's career.

"Dude, you need to leave early tonight. The last time I was in town, you nearly killed me. Not many people can drink me under the table, but you did," Austin said.

Grover snorted. "Hell, my wife drank you under the table. How'd a guy like you get to be such a lightweight?"

"Whatever. You take drinking to Olympic-size levels," Austin said, but his grin showed his affection for Grover.

"I'll go easy on you tonight," Grover said, giving Austin's arm a light punch. "I'm loving the music you're bringing. A lot of artists start to slack off after a hit or two, but you're bringing your A-game every time. You have the makings of a superstar."

"From your lips to God's ears, my friend. Thanks for supporting my music. You were the leader on all three songs. And everyone knows you aren't a pushover."

"When it's real, and it's great, it deserves to be heard."

"Crown Royal shot before you go?" Austin asked. "A toast to great music being played onstage and on the radio."

"Hell yeah. Let's do it."

Matt poured two shots of whisky. Grover and Austin knocked them back, but Christine noticed that Matt abstained.

"You don't drink with the guys?" she asked.

"Not until after the show. Too much can go wrong."

"Ever the professional," Christine said. "That's one thing I understand."

Matt looked at his watch. "How about a quick photo?" he asked the guys.

Grover and Austin posed with their shot glasses held high.

"That's my cue to leave," Grover said. "I know you have a meet and greet. Can't wait to see the show. And I do have to leave a little early tonight, but I'll stay until the end of your show."

"Come back after I get offstage and do one more shot with me."

"You got it."

Matt escorted Grover off the bus. Christine knew local security sometimes hassled people who weren't with the tour, and she admired Matt for making sure Grover got safely back out front.

"You were great with him," Christine said to Austin. They were still on the bus.

"Y'know, when I first started doing this, everybody warned me about radio. Some artists aren't big fans of radio guys. And I get it. If they weren't playing my music, I might have an attitude, too. But they've played my songs, and I've had hits and always found them to be cool. I've swapped cell numbers with a lot of them, and we text frequently. It's all been a good experience for me."

Matt walked back onto the bus and pointed at his watch. "Fan meet and greet in fifteen."

"And this is what artists live for. The fans," Austin said.

Christine went along to watch Austin meet his fans. They were mainly females dressed in tight jeans, short skirts, crop tops, and cowboy boots. She knew most of these young women were hoping they'd get asked back to the bus. And one of them probably would. She often wondered if it bothered them the next morning, or a week or a month later. Then again, maybe she was projecting how she'd feel. She couldn't judge women who just wanted to have guilt-free fun. Men did it all the time. Why shouldn't women? She tried to guess which one would make it to the after-party. She didn't know enough about Austin to know his type, but she bet it would be a blonde. Blondes did seem to have more fun, as the saying went.

Austin greeted each one with a handshake, sometimes a hug, and always a big smile. He listened attentively when they spoke, making solid eye contact. Even though he only had about thirty seconds per person, they all left looking happy. Some girls could barely speak and others were crying. Christine had been there herself. It was hard not to get tongue-tied and, in some cases, emotional when meeting an artist you admired.

And then there were the few who wanted Austin to autograph various body parts, promising to get the autograph tattooed.

"They would really get a tattoo of his signature?" she asked Matt.

"You know you've made it when they want to tattoo your autograph. We see it all out here."

Matt asked her to hold the spare Sharpies, and when their fingers touched, she felt it down to her toes. "I'll be back. Hold on to these in case he needs a fresh one." His eyes met hers, and time didn't move until he turned and left.

With Matt out of the room, Christine focused on Austin. She was happy watching him with his fans until she heard two young women talking as they walked by. She swore she heard one of them say, "That's her. The one they keep posting comments about." Had any of her cyberbullies come through the line, or was she just being paranoid? She shook it off, choosing not to let it bother her.

IT WAS SHOWTIME. CHRISTINE WENT to the front-of-house soundboard, which was located in a gated area in the middle of the audience. This was where the sound guy controlled a large panel that determined volume, balance, and everything sonic. It would offer the best sound in the arena. Christine showed her laminate to the security guard and stepped into the square enclosure. She was careful not to trip over the wires that were attached to a large soundboard. She couldn't imagine being responsible for unplugging the show. She shook at the thought. A videographer sat on a riser behind her and she stepped out of his way. The view was somewhat obstructed by the fans, but she felt safe.

Imagining what twenty-five thousand people looked like was one thing. Standing in the middle of them was another. It was a sea of people, all moving and talking. It reminded her of an ant colony. The excitement leading up to the start of the show was palpable. The fans couldn't stand still. Some sang Jackson's songs, others kissed their partners, while others randomly yelled, "Yee-haw!" They were stoked and ready for the music to begin. As it got nearer to Austin's stage time, the crowd got louder and rowdier. When the band took the stage and played the opening notes, the audience welcomed them with an eruption of shrieks. Christine knew Austin was standing to the side, just out of sight. When she thought the crowd's volume could get no louder, he ran onto the stage and proved her wrong.

Austin had thirty minutes to capture the crowd. In Christine's opinion, the opener had the hardest job. The audience was there to hear the main act, or maybe they wanted to hear the middle act. But the opener had to reach out from the stage, tap them on the shoulder, and get them to pay attention one by one. Austin did it. He made the show into his personal party, which they'd all been invited to. He pointed to them, engaged them, and never stopped moving. He kept his eyes on the audience until they couldn't take their eyes off him. The crowd hung on to every note he sang. They were spellbound. Christine was caught off guard by a weird sense of pride. She was now part of this. She wasn't just a behind-the-scenes worker—she had an active role. This was a first, and she had to fight back a tear as she savored the moment.

Matt walked past, his shoulder brushing hers. He stood in an open spot behind her, and her whole body tuned in to him. Every nerve ending came alive, shocking her. She'd convinced herself she didn't have normal hormonal reactions. She'd never felt the feelings other women had described. Not after what happened to her in high school. But she couldn't deny Austin's effect when he almost kissed her. And her reaction to Matt was even more electric. Maybe her experience in high school *hadn't* left her unable to respond to a man. She'd felt almost robotic with the couple of guys she dated in college, afraid to lose control. But there was nothing mechanical about what she was feeling now.

As Austin wound down his last song, Matt whispered something in her ear about coming to the stage with him. She nodded and followed. Walking through the crowd, she could barely move. Claustrophobia kicked in. Guys in sleeveless T-shirts were sloshing beer and stumbling her way. Random people tried to high-five her, and one woman reached for her All Access pass, forcing Christine to push her arm away. Matt turned around and made eye contact before reaching for her hand. She grabbed his and held on tight. He pulled her close as they made their way through the jungle of human limbs that were spilling drinks and fist-bumping friends. When they made it backstage, she breathed a sigh of relief. They released their hands simultaneously. She had been so focused on surviving the crowd that she hadn't taken a moment to enjoy the feel of his fingers as they laced through hers. But her hand held his warmth, and she subconsciously raised it to her lips.

"That was scary," Christine said, her eyes wide.

"It gets worse. Hang out in the pit when Jackson takes the stage. Those fans have been tailgating since two."

"Maybe I'll listen from the side of the stage."

"Safe bet. Let's go to the bus and hang with Austin until Jackson goes on." Matt put his hand behind her back, so slight she could barely feel it. She leaned back into it.

"Okay," she said, hearing the huskiness in her own voice.

They joined Austin and his band for a post-show toast, and five minutes before Jackson took the stage, they left the bus. The lights flickered, the intro music notched up a few decibels, and so did the audience's screams. It was time. Jackson was taking the stage.

Austin took her literally *on* stage to watch the show. The lights went out, the smoke poured from the stage machines, and Jackson got into a backstage elevator that allowed him to jump high onto the stage riser right as the opening notes to his first song started. This was the moment twenty-five thousand people were waiting for—the moment their favorite singer appeared onstage, ready to rock their world for the next seventy-five minutes.

Jackson kicked it off with a rocking up-tempo song. The pyro shot into the air and was so strong the heat felt like a bonfire. Standing onstage gave Christine a different perspective. The energy coming from the fans was unbelievable. They sang loud and howled louder, reaching out to try and touch him. She was standing to the left of the drummer, whose hands were a blur as his sticks flew across the drums. Every time he hit the kick drum, she felt it in her chest. The bass player stood back-to-back with the lead guitarist, as they leaned against each other for full effect. The band rocked the house.

"If it's this incredible just standing here and watching it, I can't imagine what it's like for Jackson and his band."

"I know. I can't wait 'til I'm headlining," Austin said.

"What?" Christine leaned closer so she could hear him. He put his hand on her back, yelling in her ear, repeating what he'd said.

She put her hand on his shoulder and yelled back, "I can't, either."

She grabbed her phone to take some pictures, forgetting she still had Austin's social feed up. She knew better than to look, but she did anyway.

AGILY: *OMG! She's on stage with AG watching JW. WTF?*
CTRYFN: *Did he just nuzzle her ear?*
AGILY: *Oh, gross. Tell me he didn't!*
CTRYFN: *I don't get it. What does he see in her?*
AGILY: *Who knows? Maybe she can suck it like a Hoover. There's got to be something we're missing.*

She wanted to look into the audience and flip them off. But if she did, it would be the next photo posted. Someone out there was watching her. Screw them. They didn't get to ruin her evening. She switched her phone to camera and chose to ignore the cyberbullying. She plastered a big smile on her face. *She* was the one onstage with Austin. She had worked hard and gotten to this moment. She vowed to enjoy this experience no matter what anyone else thought.

Jackson sang his hits. She counted twelve, thirteen, fourteen, all the way up to twenty number one hits, and he hadn't even played them all. He was the reigning Artist of the Decade. She knew it took a village to raise an act to this level. There was a record label, manager, publicist, producer, musicians, songwriters, song pluggers, and radio. But even with all those people, it wouldn't work unless the artist had the "it" factor to be a star. At any given time, there were only about eight superstars in the format. And he was one of them. She wondered how many people had pitched him songs over the years. She'd never met him. She usually pitched to newcomers and didn't get to hang out with artists of his caliber. Maybe tonight she would.

The concert ended with Jackson cracking open a beer and spraying it on the people in the pit. His fans loved this personal moment with him. They were sharing his beer with him. That's what friends do. In that moment, they became his friends.

"Let's get out of the way," Matt said as Jackson, his band, and crew started to leave the stage. Everyone moved fast once a show was over. They wanted to tear down the set, which would take hours.

Matt led her and Austin back to the dressing room. Austin cracked a beer and offered one to Matt. Christine smiled as he accepted it. He'd abstained the entire evening, but now his work was done.

"Want to meet Jackson and his wife, Bella?" Austin asked Christine. "They should be in the vibe room by now."

"Duh," she said, excited to meet two of the hottest stars in the business.

Austin took her hand and led her to where they were standing.

"Bella, this is Christine. She works for Hit Songs Publishing," Austin said.

"Hi, Christine. Nice to meet you."

"You, too. My friend Julianna follows you religiously on socials and mirrors your style. She loves everything from your braids to your makeup and clothes. She's gorgeous like you. Even your name means 'beautiful.'"

"Aw, thank you. That's so sweet," Bella said, giving Christine a hug.

Austin tapped Jackson's shoulder.

"Hey, Jackson. I want you to meet Christine. She's the plugger who found 'Promises to Me.'" Christine was momentarily shocked at Austin's use of her given name, twice.

"Well, damn. Maybe I should be calling you for songs next time," Jackson said, shaking her hand.

"Hands off, man. She's mine."

Without acknowledging Austin's comment, Jackson looked at Christine. He put his hand to his ear in a "call me" sign. Then he laughed and lightly punched Austin on the shoulder. "Just messing with you. Great show tonight. You're the perfect artist to get the crowd going. You'll be middle slot before you know it."

"Thanks, man. Can't ever thank you enough for this opportunity."

Jackson turned back to Christine, reaching out to shake her hand. "Nice to meet you," he said, acknowledging her before turning to greet others. She was impressed.

"He seems so down-to-earth. So normal for a superstar," Christine said.

"He is."

"The first time I heard his debut single, I was sold. Then, when he released his second single . . ." Christine continued naming Jackson's hit songs.

"If we go through every song he's ever released, we're going to miss the rest of the party." Austin gestured to the room full of people.

Christine looked around the room, recognizing Jackson's band members.

"His whole band is in here. It's so rare that a touring band is also the studio band, but they're on every album. Best band in the business," Christine said.

"That's why they're called The Bad Ass Band."

A young, stunning blonde walked past, and without uttering a word, Austin turned and followed her.

"And Julianna wonders why I don't want to go for you," Christina said aloud.

She came off her concert high as her standard awkwardness began. She'd never felt comfortable at parties, and this was no different. She wandered over to the snack table. She popped a couple of peanuts in her mouth, realizing she hadn't eaten in hours. She looked for Matt but didn't see him. The production crew still had to tear down the equipment and probably couldn't join the party until later. Austin's band members had come in and were mingling. She didn't see Alicia but knew she was counting money and merchandise and then had to load everything back in the truck.

A loud laugh got Christine's attention. She turned around. It came from a tall, pretty woman with long black hair. The sound was infectious. Her smile never ended, and when she talked, she used her entire upper body. Her hands moved nonstop, back-patting the people around her and gesturing to accompany her words. She flipped the bird twice and clapped her hands at something funny. The people around her stared like she was the only person in the room. Christine felt like they were at two different parties. Just once, she wanted to be the life of the party. She never was in high school. Even in college, she had been happier playing games in the dorms with her friends than going to frat parties. But now, she was in an industry that thrived on events. She could learn from this woman. She walked over to where Austin was talking to the blonde and tapped his shoulder.

"Who's the girl over there?"

"Brandy, Jackson's record rep. Come on—I'll introduce you. She's a trip." He told the blonde to wait for him and walked Christine over to where Brandy was standing.

"Brandy, this is Chrissy. She works at my publishing company. Chrissy, this is Brandy." They shook hands.

"It's Christine," she said, wondering why he'd reverted to Chrissy after twice introducing her as Christine.

"I'll see you two later," Austin said, returning to the woman he'd been flirting with.

"You seem like you're having the time of your life," Christine said.

"Aren't you?"

"Not like you are."

"That's 'cause you're not doing it right. Come on." Brandy grabbed Christine's hand and pulled her to the liquor table. "First, we do a shot of Fireball."

"Oh, I'm not sure that's a good idea." Christine shook her head, remembering how fuzzy Fireball had made her the last time.

"Which is why you're not having as much fun as I am." Brandy handed Christine the shot and counted to three.

They slammed it down.

"One more."

Christine started to protest but thought, *What the hell?* And took it.

They slammed down number two.

"Now, you need a weed cookie. You eat those?" Brandy reached into her purse, brought out a cookie, and broke off a piece. She handed it to Christine.

"Uh, yeah. I'm not gluten free." Christine took the piece of cookie and ate it. She wasn't sure how it would help, but the cookie tasted good.

The music got louder and the people got friendlier. Her body moved in perfect time to the rhythm. She'd never been much of a dancer, afraid to move too much, but tonight her body was in tune with the beat. The music seemed to speed up and slow down all at the same time.

As two crew guys walked past Christine and Brandy, Christine grabbed one of them. "Dance with us." She put her hand over her mouth. Had she just invited a guy to dance with her? When one of them stepped behind her and put his hands on her hips, she bent down and did a little hip move.

"I think I just twerked," she said to Brandy. "But I'm not sure. I've never twerked before." So this was what fun felt like? To let go and not worry who saw you. To dance like nobody's watching.

"Having fun?" Brandy asked.

"I've never, ever had this much fun. Ever."

Slowly, the room cleared out and there were only a handful of guys left. She and Brandy were still dancing, and when the song got bluesy, Christine became frisky. She jumped up on a coffee table, unbuttoned her shirt's top button, and began to do a striptease.

Austin walked in as she was on the second button.

"What the hell?" Austin's mouth hung open and his eyes widened as he stared at the debacle unfolding in front of him.

"Austin, come dance with me," Christine said, reaching for him.

He didn't move.

Matt came into the room, looked at Christine, looked at Austin, and ran up to her. He pulled her off the table, buttoning the few buttons she had undone.

Christine swatted his hands away. "Matt! Dance with me. I'm having fun." She wrapped her arms around his neck and kissed his cheek.

"What did you give her?" Matt asked Brandy, trying to pull himself away from Christine.

"She gave me Fireball and a wheat cookie. And I'm having so much fun," Christine said, twirling around in Matt's arms, almost falling.

He steadied her and raised his eyebrows at Brandy. Austin was now at their side.

"Wheat cookie?" Matt asked Brandy.

"I said 'weed.' Apparently she misheard," Brandy said, shrugging her shoulders.

"Austin. I had Fireball . . . am having sooooo much fun!" Christine let go of Matt and tumbled into Austin.

He caught her and chuckled. He raised his eyebrows at Brandy.

"What? She said she wanted to have as much fun as I was having." Brandy smiled.

Christine broke loose from Austin's clutch and hugged her. "Best night ever, Brandy."

"See! Lighten up, dude," Brandy said.

"She's wasted," Matt said.

"Totally," Austin said.

When Jackson and his band came back in, Austin looked at Matt. "Would you get her to the bus, please?"

"Consider it done. Come on, Christine. We're going to the bus," Matt said, wrapping an arm around her like a shield.

"Party's over?" Christine pouted.

"Yep, party's over."

Christine turned to high-five Brandy, but she had moved on to talk to other people. Instead, she started singing Little Big Town's hit "Girl Crush."

"Stop singing and let's go," Matt said.

Matt took Christine out of the venue and brought her onto the bus. Cat was in the front lounge playing a video game.

"What's up, Catmandu?"

Cat raised his eyebrows at Matt.

"Jackson's record rep gave her Fireball and a cookie," Matt explained.

"Two shots of Fireball. And a wheat cookie," Christine said in a slurred melody. "You should try it, Catmandu."

"Wheat cookie. Any chance she means weed cookie?" Cat asked.

"I'm pretty sure the answer to that is yes," Matt said, wrestling Christine back to the bunks.

"Freaking hilarious. Let loose, Christine."

"Later, Catmandu."

Matt attempted to lift her into the top bunk. When that didn't work, he escorted her to the back lounge. Even in her current condition, Christine knew what the back room meant. She'd heard numerous stories about the sexcapades that happened in there. Sober Christine would explain that she wasn't that kind of girl. Party Christine thought it seemed like a great idea.

She grabbed Matt's face and planted a kiss on him.

"Slow down there," Matt said, unwrapping himself from her arms.

"Come on. Just a kiss." Christine tried to kiss him again, and he gently pushed her away.

"I'd love to kiss you. But I don't think this is the time or place," Matt said.

"You guys. You're all talk. Always saying stuff like 'yeah, gonna take a chick to the back room and get me some.' Is it all talk, Matt? 'Cause I'm right here ready to give some." Christine went in for another kiss.

Matt pulled back. "You're wasted. I prefer my women to know who they are hooking up with."

"I know who you are," Christine said before giggling. "What's your name again?" She giggled louder.

"Nice."

"Oh, I'm just kidding. You're Matt," she wailed.

"Shhhh. Someone will hear you. I don't need Austin getting mad at me." He helped her to sit.

She pulled him down beside her and rested her leg over his. Then she straddled his lap. "Austin who?" She leaned down to kiss him again.

This time, Matt returned her kiss. It deepened, and with a groan of pleasure, Matt flipped her over and laid on top of her.

Christine wrapped her legs around his body and slowly unbuttoned her shirt.

Matt stared. He stopped saying "no" as he pushed her bra down and kissed her neck, her chest, and her breasts. She moaned and grabbed the back of his head, begging for more.

Austin's voice broke through the sounds of their kissing.

"Christine, we have to stop," Matt said.

"Why? No one can hear us. And even if they can, nobody cares," she said.

"I care. Stay here." He got up and left the room, leaving the door open. Christine peeked out.

"Hey, Matt. How's Christine?" Austin asked, hugging the blonde chick draped on his arm.

"She's okay. I've got her in the lounge. There was no way she'd make it into her bunk."

"Damn. I was going to use that room. Oh well. We can fit in my bunk, can't we, sweetheart?" Austin nuzzled the woman's neck.

"Whatever you want, Austin Garrett," she said.

Christine rolled her eyes.

"Can you keep an eye on Christine tonight?" Austin asked.

"Of course," Matt said.

Christine watched Matt reach into her bunk. He grabbed her pillow and blanket and started walking toward her. She fell onto the couch and pretended to be asleep. She knew Matt wouldn't do anything with her now that Austin was on the bus, and she didn't want to be turned down again. Matt came into the back lounge, put the pillow under her head, and covered her with the comforter. He sat down next to her, pulled her legs into his lap, put his head back, and fell asleep.

CHAPTER FIVE

hristine opened her eyes. She was alone in the back of the bus. Her head pounded and her throat was parched. What the heck? She'd only had two shots of Fireball and a wheat cookie. She paused and questioned why Brandy had a wheat cookie. Oh God. Had she misunderstood and Brandy had said weed cookie? That made much more sense. How stupid to think she'd said "wheat." Christine had gotten drunk and stoned. She groaned, wondering what else she had done.

She concentrated hard, trying to remember. She recalled dancing in the vibe room with Brandy. Had she done a striptease? She had a vision of Matt taking her to the bus. She felt her entire body blush. Matt. Did she really climb on his lap and kiss him? Had she dreamt that she'd begged him to be with her, or had she actually been that bold? God, she hoped it had been a dream. Otherwise, she'd be mortified.

They'd already arrived in the next city, and she needed a shower. She left the lounge, made her way through the darkened bunkroom, opened the door to the front lounge, grabbed her suitcase, and left the bus. The touring ladies' dressing room was easy to find, and a hot shower helped her feel human again. She had no energy to go through the process of straightening her hair. Today it would be natural curls. She put some gel in it, then dried and styled it as quickly as she could. As she walked out of the room, she bumped into Matt.

"Christine. Good morning. How ya feeling?" He reached out for her.

Christine launched into the speech she had prepared. "I have no idea what got into me last night. I am so sorry. Can we just never mention it again?" She was so caught up in her embarrassment that she didn't notice Matt's smile fading away. "I thought she said 'wheat cookie,' but now that I'm sober, I think it was a weed cookie. I've never been stoned in my life. I just wasn't in my right mind."

Matt dropped his arms. "It's cool, Christine. Nobody knows anything, and I'll make sure nobody finds out."

"We can just pretend it didn't happen?" she asked.

"Of course we can. Not a big deal." Christine noticed a different tone in his voice. He sounded disappointed. She felt horrible that her antics had disappointed him.

"And please don't tell Austin." Christine was worried he'd fire her for being unprofessional.

Matt nodded and closed his eyes. "Yep. I won't tell him. I got it. It was no big deal."

"Thank you."

Just then, Austin came walking down the hall. Wearing a smile, she turned toward him.

"What's up, girl? Have fun last night?" He grabbed her up in a hug.

She squealed. "Remind me to never come out here again," she said.

"Oh, hell yeah you are. Dancing queen." He put his arm around her and they walked away, leaving Matt behind.

WHEN SHE RETURNED HOME FROM the tour, Christine met Julianna and Phoebe for a songwriter's night at Exit/In. With its concrete floor and metal pillars, it always reminded Christine of a frat house. It smelled slightly of beer at all times, like the alcohol had sunk into its pores.

Social media was lighting up, again, about her and Austin. As much as Christine tried to ignore it, she couldn't. Especially one post that looked ominous: *I'm seriously tired of seeing that ugly bitch's face everywhere AG is. I'm ready to hunt her down and take her out.*

Christine put her phone down, air escaping through her lips. "This is scary. Why are people threatening me?" she asked.

"They want what you have," Phoebe said.

"That's never happened to me before."

"Well, it's happening now," Julianna said.

"I can't imagine anyone will follow through on it. It's just crazed fans mouthing off," Phoebe said.

"Let's not forget that fan is short for fanatic," Christine said.

"Good point." Julianna nodded.

"And nobody has any idea who's doing it?" Phoebe asked.

"Not overall, but we did catch two of them," Christine said.

"What?" Julianna asked.

"Austin's tour manager, Matt, was in catering and happened to walk past two of the servers. He said they were early twenties, a guy and a girl. They were giggling and looking at photos. He saw they were of me and assumed it was on Twitter or Instagram. Then he realized it was on their phones. They had taken the photos."

"They should be fired," Phoebe said.

"They were."

A new singer-songwriter took the stage for her thirty-minute set. She wasn't a seasoned performer and some of her onstage moves were awkward. She kicked her leg out and slapped her butt, causing the ladies to look at each other with raised eyebrows. However, her voice was strong, she sang on key, and there was something about her that kept their interest.

"She has potential if she gets the right team behind her," Julianna said when the show was over. "I think I'll give her my card."

Phoebe paid the bill. The friends hugged and went their separate ways.

When Christine got to her apartment complex, she walked up the stairs and found a note taped to her door: *Yo, bitch. Back off from Austin Garrett or answer to me.*

She spun around, her heart racing. Shivers ran up her back. Was someone watching her? She unlocked the door and entered her apartment, bolting the door behind her. She took a picture of the handwritten note and texted it to Austin. *Hey. This is getting scary. Do you have some weird ex-girlfriend? Have you pissed off some chick?*

He replied, *I've pissed off a lot of them.*

Christine texted back. *That doesn't help. Maybe I should keep a low profile where you're concerned for a while.*

His response: *Fuck that. Ignore them.*

This was taped to my door!

That got Austin's attention. *Oh shit. How do they know where you live?*

How should I know? But I'm scared.

Come here, he texted.

Where?

My house.

Why? she texted.

I have security. Nobody will get past the gate.

I don't know where you live.

He texted her the address and said, *Pack a bag and get over here. At least I'll know you're safe.*

Okay, be there soon.

Christine thought about calling the police but knew they couldn't really do anything. No crime had been committed. The ultimate catch-22.

Austin's house was in a ritzy neighborhood, but when she arrived at the black wrought iron gate, she realized it was the smallest dwelling on the block. Assessing it before she passed through the gate, Christine guessed it was over five thousand square feet. It looked to be two stories, but there could also be a basement level. It was all brick. The garage had three bays and a bonus room on top. Christine knew it took time in the music industry to start making money. If you'd written a hit song—and Austin had written his first two—it could take a year to get the payoff. She also knew banks in Nashville would loan money based on the fact that you had written two hit songs and your mailbox would soon be filled with royalty checks. Three hit songs and you could demand a pretty high price for your concerts. Austin Garrett was not wealthy, but he was on his way. And a house like this proved it.

She texted him to say she was out front and the gate opened. She drove in, and within thirty seconds, the gate closed behind her.

Austin was waiting out front wearing jeans and slippers. He didn't have a shirt on. He directed her around the house to the garage.

She parked inside. Nobody would know she was there.

"Let me see the note," he said the minute she stepped out.

"Don't you believe me?"

"Of course I do. I thought I might recognize the handwriting if I looked at it up close." She showed him the note, but he shook his head.

"All I want is a shower and a bed. I'm emotionally drained right now," she said.

"Let's go in. There's a bit of a chill in the air."

"You're half-naked. Put some clothes on."

"Yeah, yeah. Thanks, Mom," he said, leading her into the house.

"You don't have any tattoos, do you?" she asked.

"None that you can see," he said with a smirk.

"I'm being serious. It's rare for a guy your age not to."

"I wanted them when I was younger. I was determined to get one as soon as I was old enough. But I saved every dollar I made so I could play gigs. I had to pay for equipment, instruments, gas, the band, and sometimes hotel rooms. There were out-of-town gigs we played where we didn't even make enough to cover our travel expenses, but I wanted to reach a new audience. I kept finding clubs farther and farther away that would let me play. It got expensive. Spending money on a tattoo didn't make sense. Then, when I had the money, I realized I was one of a few guys who didn't have one. I decided to hold off. It's almost rebellious to not have ink. I guess we have that in common, huh?"

Christine didn't answer.

"Hold on, now. Are you telling me you have a tattoo?"

"I'm not telling you anything," Christine said. "Where's a guest bedroom?"

"Lower back? Tramp stamp? I bet it's on your butt. I can see you taking a dare but refusing to let it be seen. Bottom of your foot?"

"You can quit guessing and tell me where I can take a bath and go to bed."

"You know I won't give up, but I'll let it go for now. The upstairs bedroom on the left has a full bath. There's all kinds of girly bath oils and stuff if you want to use it." He pointed in the general direction of the bedroom.

"Should I ask why you have girly stuff?" Christine raised an eyebrow.

"Probably not. It'll make me look like a male whore."

"But aren't you?"

"Of course."

Christine rolled her eyes, making him chuckle.

"Make yourself at home. I'll be in my studio. The kitchen is to the right and bedrooms are upstairs. The gate is closed and locked and the security code is set on the house. You should have nothing to worry about."

"Thanks, Austin. I appreciate it."

"Hell, it's because of me you're going through this. You don't owe me any thanks." He grabbed her suitcase, took it upstairs, walked down the hallway to the left, and showed her the bedroom. "My room is down the other hall, so you have plenty of privacy. I'll leave you in peace, unless, of course, you want my company." He stood there, no shirt on, body to die for, offering what so many women wanted.

"I would, but geez, there's something about being threatened that just takes the wind out of my sexual sails."

"Just let me know if that wind changes direction." He kissed the top of her head and went back downstairs.

Christine stood in the hall thinking about his comment. She was flattered. He'd offered twice now. And twice she'd said no. Not because she was a prude or because she didn't think it would be fun, or great, or any number of adjectives that could be used to describe Austin. She just knew it wouldn't last. And she didn't want a one-night stand. Flattered as she was, she knew part of her allure was that she kept turning him down. Christine wanted something more. She wanted it all. Smart, stable, sexy, and dependable. A vision of Matt came into her head. Those were all characteristics she'd use to describe him. A shiver ran through her.

Christine took a hot bath and admitted to herself that she enjoyed girly soap. She made sure to use a brand-new bar that was still in the box. She wasn't a germaphobe but drew the line at sharing soap with Austin's flings. With her bath taken, teeth brushed, and jammies on, she sank into the soft mattress in

Austin's spare bedroom, impressed at how clean and crisp the sheets were. He probably used a cleaning service.

She felt safe. After the threatening posts, and then finding the note on her door, she was grateful to fall asleep without worrying.

SHE WOKE EARLY, TOOK A SHOWER, and dressed for work. She tiptoed downstairs in case Austin was still sleeping and found Matt in the kitchen.

"Oh, hey. I didn't expect to see you here." She felt awkward around him because of her drunken night. She had a vivid vision of straddling his lap and kissing him. It stirred something in her that didn't resemble guilt. She fought the urge to straddle him right there in Austin's kitchen.

"Christine? I didn't expect to see you, either. I guess . . . well . . . I guess I shouldn't be too surprised, huh?"

His tone carried an edge that Christine didn't understand. Unless he was still angry about her drunken escapade. Maybe she should apologize again.

"For the record, there were no cookies consumed last night. Wheat or weed. I don't need to do anything else stupid. I apologize again for that night," she said.

He stared at her, opened his mouth, and then closed it. What did he want to say? She was about to ask when Austin came strolling into the kitchen in a pair of sweatpants, sans shirt.

"What's up, Matt? I thought you were coming over at nine," Austin said.

"No, I changed it to eight. Remember?"

"Hmm. And I agreed to meet that early?"

"You did. You don't remember?"

"No, but it's cool. I heard Chrissy get up and it woke me, so it's all good. How'd you sleep?" He surprised Christine by giving her a quick hug from behind and a kiss on her cheek.

Matt turned away, focusing on his iPad.

"I slept well. Thanks again for inviting me over. I'm going to head to the office. Matt, good to see you again."

"Yeah, you, too," Matt said, not looking up from his iPad.

Christine headed for the door, and Austin followed her to her car.

"If you get any more notes or threats, let me know."

"I will."

She drove straight to work, where Julianna was waiting in Christine's office.

"Um, did you spend the night with Austin?"

"How did you know?" Christine asked, throwing up her hands and plopping on her chair. "I thought I was careful."

Julianna held up her phone and there it was. Social media already had a photo of her car pulling up to Austin's house.

"Someone's stalking me." She told Julianna about the note and why she'd stayed at Austin's.

"Next time, come to my place. Did you call the police?"

"No. What can they do? Nothing happened. It's just a note and an idle threat." Christine shook her head and it drooped down to her shoulders.

"At least they can put it on record," Julianna said.

"True. Maybe I'll report it later today. Right now, I have music to listen to. I refuse to let this rule my life." Christine grabbed her headset, signaling that Julianna should let her get to work. She tried listening to music, but her mind was somewhere else. All she could think of was the nasty messages splayed across social media. She never thought she'd be the kind of person people paid attention to. She had always been invisible, at least until she befriended Austin Garrett. Was it worth it? She had to wonder.

He was heading out to the West Coast for a four-week tour. She wouldn't see him for at least a month. Maybe things would calm down and get back to normal during that time. She could only hope.

TWO WEEKS LATER, CHRISTINE WAS surprised at how bored she'd become. On the one hand, she'd received no new notes and nothing was circulating about her on socials. Not one photo. But she had a new barometer for what was exciting. Road trips, crazy phone calls from Austin, and seeing Matt all added up to fun. And hope. Every time she saw Matt, she hoped he'd give her some indication he was interested. Something she could latch on to, turn around, and make something out of. She knew she'd never be the aggressor unless she was drunk—and she had no intention of that happening again. But if he gave her any hint of interest, she would follow his lead.

The month dragged on with no communication from Austin, aside from the few times he sent her songs for feedback. She answered honestly and gave her opinion, and she took the opportunity to send him a song from Hit Songs Publishing. She didn't want to push him, but the weight of Rick's words remained on her shoulders.

She watched Austin's posts and could see he was having a great run. She initially resisted the temptation to follow Matt, not sure she needed the extra anxiety that social media can bring. But she missed him so she started following him on Instagram. He didn't over-post and share every moment of his life. He mostly posted before-show photos of empty venues and invited fans to come to the concerts. There were also some photos of him and Austin doing guy things. They went fishing one day and rode scooters another. What she didn't see, much to her relief, was a bunch of women. She didn't realize she was holding her breath and waiting to see Matt with some buxom twenty-two-year-old until she had scanned about thirty photos without seeing any. She exhaled.

THE DAY AUSTIN WAS DUE BACK in town, a Monday, Christine checked her phone every fifteen minutes. She knew she could text him but didn't want to seem needy. She was disappointed he didn't call her the minute he arrived. Then she chided herself for being an idiot. She wasn't his girl or his bestie. She was just his song plugger.

She lay in bed that night, looking through Matt's Insta account. He'd posted a photo of a road sign announcing that Nashville was five miles away and captioned it "Home sweet home." There was no picture of a woman waiting for him.

Christine scrolled through his other photos and found one she had missed. It was of him and the crew guys playing basketball at one of the venues. Matt was wearing gym shorts. His calf muscles were well-developed. She wanted to run her hand along them. He was sweating and his hair stuck to his face . . . he was sexy as hell. She took a screenshot and saved it. Then she worried someone would see it and deleted it. She could always look at his account if she wanted to see it again. She knew she would.

When her phone went off at midnight on Wednesday, she grabbed it so fast it fell on the floor. She heard a man yelling and picked up the phone.

"What?"

"Chrishy! I need help."

She sat up in bed. "Austin? What's wrong?" Her voice carried a tinge of panic.

"I'm stuck. I need you to come get me."

"Where are you?"

"I don't know. But there are dancing naked people all around me."

"What? Are you in Nashville?"

"I was at the Tin Roof, but I left. Everyone was too drunk for me."

Christine wondered how drunk they could have been if they were too drunk for him. "Where did you go after the Tin Roof?"

"Don't know. But there are naked people all around me. They look happy. And the guys have really big dicks."

"Austin, what else do you see? You're not making any sense."

"Naked people. Dancing naked people. Please come get me." The call disconnected.

"Austin? Austin? Are you there? Damnit!" She pulled up Julianna's number and called her.

"Christine? What's wrong?" Her voice was husky with sleep.

"Austin called. He was drinking at the Tin Roof, and now he's somewhere with naked dancing people. Is there a nudist colony in Nashville?"

"Not that I know of. Maybe he's at a strip club," Julianna said.

"That would make more sense than a nudist colony. But he said men were there, too," Christine said.

"Men?"

"Yes. Men with big penises. Naked dancing people all around him."

"Oh, God. He's on the circle."

"What?"

"The traffic circle on Demonbreun Street. You know—the statue of the anatomically correct dancing naked people."

"And it's walking distance from the Tin Roof. Geez. I can't believe I didn't figure that out myself."

Christine was always shocked by the bigger-than-life bronze statue of naked people happily dancing on the circle at Music Row. Children rode past there. Naked breasts, vaginas, and penises were on display for all to see.

"Okay, I have to go get him," Christine said, crawling out of bed.

"Is Austin dancing naked with them?" Julianna asked.

"God, I hope not," Christine said.

"God, I hope so. I'll meet you there," Julianna said.

"No. Do not show up. Go back to bed."

"No way in hell I'm missing this. See you at the naked people." Julianna hung up before Christine could protest further.

Christine threw on her sweats and an oversized T-shirt and darted out the door. The drive that took nearly an hour in rush-hour traffic only took fifteen minutes at midnight. She parked her car on the side of the street and was running to the center of the circle when Julianna pulled up. Together they found Austin passed out underneath the sculpture. His left shoe was off, his white T-shirt was stained with dirt, drool fell from the side of his mouth, and he snored—loudly.

Julianna busted up.

"What is so funny?"

"He's right under a huge naked penis. That was his last visual before he passed out."

"And there he is. Heartthrob to tens of thousands of women." Christine shook her head.

"I'd still do him," Julianna said.

Christine opened her mouth to say something and changed her mind. Why bother? Stars had a greater appeal than mere humans. She stooped down next to Austin and shook him.

No response.

"Austin? Wake up. It's Christine."

Nothing.

"Julianna, let's try to lift him."

"Okay." Julianna reached down for his feet as Christine lifted his shoulders.

He barely budged.

"He's out cold," Christine said.

"Ya think?"

Another car pulled up and parked at the circle. The driver threw on the flashers and stepped out. Christine's stomach clenched as she recognized Matt. Here she stood in oversized sweats, a baggy T-shirt, and no makeup. Julianna, of course, looked like she'd just stepped out of Victoria's Secret, still wearing her tight pink sweatpants and a black tank top. Her hair was in a sloppy bun with just enough tendrils dropping down to shape her beautiful face.

"I think I'm going to throw up," Christine said.

"Why?" Julianna asked.

Before Christine could answer, Matt walked up. "He called you, too?" he asked.

"Yep. I'm glad you're here, though. We can't lift him. He's dead weight," Christine said.

Matt looked at Julianna and then Christine. "And she's here why?"

"Moral support?" Christine said, more as a question.

"There's nothing moral about this," Matt said with a derisive snort.

"I didn't know you'd be here and didn't want to come out alone," Christine said, feeling defensive.

Matt nodded. "I'm so sorry you've gotten mixed up in all of this."

"It's okay. It's been boring without him around. He adds excitement to my life," Christine said, looking away from Matt and back at Austin.

"I'm sure he does. I get it. Kind of."

"What do we do?" Christine asked.

"Let's get him up." He walked over to Austin's left side and Christine went to the right.

"Can I help?" Julianna asked.

"Sure. Grab his hands and pull him up while we push," Matt said.

Between the three of them, they got Austin to a standing position. They half walked, half dragged him the few feet to Matt's car and dumped him in the back.

"Christine, would you follow me to his house? I'll need help getting him in," Matt asked.

"Sure."

"We may have to stay over. I don't think he should be left alone," Matt said.

"Okay," Christine said.

"I can come," Julianna said with a spring in her heels.

"Thanks, but I think we can handle it," Matt said.

Julianna crossed her arms and stood with one foot in front of the other. Her head was tilted and she looked at Christine with widened eyes. Christine saw it for what it was. She wanted an invitation. But Christine couldn't overrule Matt. Christine mouthed, "I'm sorry."

"Fine. See you tomorrow, Christine?" Julianna asked.

"Yeah, see you then. Thanks for coming." Christine gave a brief nod, barely acknowledging her friend. She was too focused on the fact that she'd be spending the night with Matt. There'd be bedrooms, not just bus bunks. And with Austin sleeping off his drunkenness, it would just be the two of them. The possibilities were endless.

They arrived at Austin's house and Matt keyed in the gate code. After they parked in the driveway, Christine helped him get Austin into the house. He was barely able to sit up, but Matt suggested they not let him sleep for at least an hour.

"Let's get some coffee into him and then put him in the shower," Matt said.

"Okay."

"In the morning, we'll give him Pedialyte. But until then, let's keep an eye on him through the night. The guy can drink a lot, but he may be drunker than I've ever seen him."

"Pedialyte?"

"You'd be amazed at its restorative abilities," Matt said.

"The things I've learned since being with Austin." Christine shook her head.

"I'd rather not think about it," Matt said.

They forced coffee into Austin, and when it seemed like he could stand without falling, Matt decided to get him into the shower.

"Can you help me get him out of these jeans?" Matt asked.

"I think I'll let you handle that yourself."

"Three's a crowd, huh?"

Christine wasn't sure what Matt meant, but when he started unbuttoning Austin's pants, she didn't stick around to find out. She headed down the hall.

"If you need me, I'll be in the bedroom to the far right of the hall," she said.

"Got it."

The sound of the shower filtered down the hallway before Austin started yelling, probably due to the cold water hitting him. Matt was yelling something back. Eventually, the noise abated. It had been an hour since they'd arrived, and between the coffee and the shower, she figured Matt would feel comfortable letting Austin go to sleep.

Christine got ready for bed and tried to relax. But she couldn't. Matt was right down the hall. Should she go into his room and make a move? Would he reject her? Was it worth the risk? Had he remembered her drunken night fondly or had she disgusted him with her come-on? So many questions she didn't know the answers to. With him right down the hall, she needed to know, and there was only one way to find out.

She got out of bed full of confidence, but it dissipated a moment later, and she crawled back under the sheets. She wasn't prepared for something like this. She imagined all the seductive things she could say. "As long as we're both here, would you like some company? I can think of a few ways to occupy our time." Or maybe, "Is that bed big enough for two?" Ugh. Even she could tell how stupid that would sound. It wasn't in her nature to be bold or aggressive toward a man. She needed to channel her inner Phoebe, but she didn't have an inner Phoebe. Not without weed cookies, anyway.

Thoughts kept running through her mind until she couldn't stand it any longer. She got out of bed and, as quietly as she could, made her way down the hall to where Matt was sleeping. His door wasn't closed tight, and she pushed it open far enough to peer in.

"Christine?" Matt propped himself up on his elbow, the sheet falling away and exposing his bare chest. Christine's vocal cords seized up and she couldn't think of a thing to say.

"Come in," Matt said.

She walked into his room and stood in a pose that she hoped was sensual. But she knew she looked ridiculous. She tried a hair flip, but her fingers got tangled in her curls.

Matt stared at her. It was now or never.

All the things she had wanted to say suddenly refused to come out of her mouth. She stammered while Matt looked at her with squinty eyes. She assumed he was trying to make sense of why she was standing in his bedroom. Hell, she was trying to make sense of it.

"I'm sorry. I thought I heard something. I worried Austin had gotten up and fallen." Christine could hear how lame that sounded. Even to herself.

"I didn't hear anything. Do you want me to check on him?"

"No, I'm sure he's okay. I may have dreamt it. It's been a strange night." She felt foolish.

"Kind of the norm with Austin," Matt said with a chuckle. The moment was quickly sliding down into being awkward. Too awkward.

Christine took a step toward the bed. She was trying to muster all her confidence when she blurted, "Okay, then. Good night." She turned and practically ran out the door.

"Uh, good night, Christine."

She sprinted to her room, closed the door, leaned against it, and silently screamed. *I'm such a dork*, she thought. She climbed into bed, then tossed and turned and stared at the clock as it laboriously made its way around the night. *Damn it. Why can't I be the type of woman who takes what she wants?* She punched the pillow, beating it like it was an assailant who had attacked her. Slamming back against the bed, she drifted to sleep around four, only to find herself wide awake three hours later.

She met Matt in the kitchen, and without saying a word, he slid a cup of coffee in her direction.

"How's Wonder Boy?" she asked.

"Fine. I checked on him half an hour ago and gave him some Pedialyte. He thanked me, told me to thank *you*, and now is sleeping it off."

"Lucky him. I think I slept a total of three hours," she said, not able to look at him.

"I worried about him, too," Matt said.

"Huh?"

"You couldn't sleep for worrying about Austin, right?"

"Oh, yeah. Of course. What else would it be?" She looked down at her coffee mug and hoped her cheeks weren't as red as they felt.

Matt walked to the sink, rinsed his mug, and set it in the dishwasher. He reached for Christine's as she drained the last few drops and handed it to him.

"I've got a meeting at the management company in an hour, so I've got to run. Are you okay?" Matt asked.

"Yeah. I have to get going myself."

Matt stared at her for a moment, causing her to raise her eyebrows at him.

"Aren't you going to stick around?" Matt asked. "Make sure Austin doesn't need anything?"

"Hell no. I think we did our time, don't you? Like you said, he's fine. Trust me, texts will blow up if he needs me," she said.

Matt continued to stare at her, his expression blank.

"I'll see you around, then, huh?" he said.

"I hope so." Christine watched him leave.

This moment had played out in her head numerous times during the night. They'd meet in the morning and joke about parenting Austin. He'd reach out and touch her hand, thanking her for being such a good friend. The touch would become a caress, which would lead to a hug, followed by a long, slow kiss. Christine stamped her feet in frustration.

She trudged up the stairs, grabbed her purse, hastily made the bed, and headed home.

CHAPTER SIX

Christine moaned in her sleep. The pain was working its way into her subconscious. She was being stabbed in the stomach again and again, and she tried to fight back, but her arms felt heavy and she couldn't lift them. She woke up, eyes wide, short of breath, looking around until she realized the source of her pain. She cried out and slammed back onto the bed. "Eve had to eat that damn apple, didn't she?"

She got out of bed, headed for the bathroom, grabbed some Midol out of the cabinet, and reached under the sink for a box of tampons. It was empty. "Argh." She rummaged through her purse, her backpack, and finally, her suitcase before finding one lone tampon.

"Just what I want to do on a Sunday morning. Go to the drugstore."

She didn't want to leave the house but had no choice. Wearing a sweatshirt and a pair of outdated mom jeans, she headed for her car. The upside was that she didn't know anybody who would be awake at this hour on a weekend.

She passed the drugstore and headed for Target. There, she could grab a Starbucks for her troubles. Whoever decided to put Starbucks inside of Target stores was secretly her hero.

She pushed her cart through the feminine product aisle, stocking up on tampons in three sizes along with Lightdays panty liners. A few rolls of toilet paper and some paper towels rounded out her morning shopping. Stifling a yawn and dreaming of curling back up in bed, she had just started unloading her cart at the checkout when someone called her name.

She shook her head and whispered, "Welcome to hell," before turning around to see Matt coming up behind her. She closed her eyes. "Please, God, make him go away."

"Hey, I thought that was you. What has you up so early?" Matt asked.

She raised her eyebrows and gave a little shrug. She motioned to the conveyor belt. No sense trying to hide the obvious.

"Oh. Uh, sorry." Matt's face registered numerous shades of pink and red.

"It's a fact of life, my friend. At least for those of us lucky enough to be born with a uterus."

Matt smiled. Christine blushed. Yep, she had it bad.

"And why are *you* up so early? It completely negates my thought that I could get away with baggy pants, sweatshirt, and no makeup. Only in Nashville. Country music's fishbowl."

"You always look great, Christine." Matt's voice was sincere, but Christine rolled her eyes anyway. She knew what she looked like.

"We just got in from last night's show," Matt said. "Before I crash for the afternoon, I figured I'd pick up some items."

"Austin mentioned having a three-day run this week. I totally forgot. I haven't talked to him much since the drunken night with the naked dancing people. He's sent numerous texts saying thank you."

"Yeah, one doesn't get over a night like that easily. Unfortunately for me, I can neither run nor hide," Matt said.

Christine grinned before turning toward the clerk and paying for her purchases. Once her unmentionables were safely tucked in a bag, she relaxed.

"I know you're exhausted, but I was going to grab a Starbucks." She pointed to the one in the store. "You up for it?"

"Absolutely. I'll meet you over there."

Christine's face lit up as she walked over to get in line. She had just ordered her chai latte the way she liked it (tall, no water, nonfat milk with an extra pump of chai) when Matt joined her.

"You like it strong, huh?"

"Like my men," she said. "Lame, I know."

He ordered a regular coffee and said, "Extra hot." Then he looked at Christine and said, "Just how I like my women."

"God, can we both be this pitiful?" she asked.

"We can, and we are." He nudged her shoulder, and she realized that even though she looked like a bum, she was enjoying this casual repartee.

They got their drinks and settled at a table in the back.

"How's song plugging going?" he asked.

"Going well. My relationship with Austin has helped me become more popular amongst other singers. Lynda Bell wants me to go on the road with her next weekend. She wants me to pitch her some songs."

"That's awesome. She's doing pretty well, right?"

"Her first album netted two top-ten songs and a top five. I hear she's on her way to a New-Female-Vocalist nomination. Who knew being late for the awards would be such a good thing for me?"

"Goes to show. Ya never know." Matt tipped his cup in a toast. "How's the social media glare?"

"It's slowed down for now. I think if I stay away from Austin, I'll be fine. But is it fair for me to let go of a good thing because of stupid stuff like that?"

"Is it really a good thing? You've seen him on the road, heard his antics. There aren't many secrets on a band bus."

"He's a mess, but yes, it's a good thing. So, we will see. Maybe the next time I'm out with him, nobody will say anything. It should be old news by now. I can always hope. What about you? How's tour managing?" She took a sip of her chai, looking at him over the rim of the cup. She could tell he was one of those guys who had no idea how sexy he was. She'd watched women flirt with him in the meet-and-greet line. Some were blatant, asking what he was doing after the show. Others were more subtle, putting a hand on his arm or giving him a long hug to say thank you. He'd respond politely and get right back to doing his job. She'd mentioned it to Austin. He'd shrugged and said Matt never seemed to notice chicks coming on to him. That made him even more attractive to Christine.

"With Austin's band, it's not just Austin who has fans. The whole band has their own groupies. And trying to manage that is like nailing Jell-O to a tree. I keep thinking if I hang in long enough, they're bound to grow up, fall in love, and get married. But hell, that could take years—decades, even. I'm not sure I can make it."

"You know you can. Those guys love you. I can see it. They treat you like you're one of them."

"Thank God. Could you imagine if they didn't?"

"How did you end up as Austin's tour manager?"

"It was a random meeting. I went to college for business and got my MBA. I worked as a stockbroker and did very well. Was on the fast track, making a lot of money, and single with no kids. Everything was going toward retirement 'cause I had no one to spend it on. But I was bored out of my mind. I was nearing my mid-thirties and having an early midlife crisis. All I needed was a sports car."

Christine had a quick visual of him looking hot in a Corvette. She said, "How'd you meet Austin?"

"A friend of mine works for a radio station and had a dinner appointment with him. He invited me. I liked Austin's music but also his personality. He didn't take himself too seriously and wasn't trying to act like the coolest guy in the room. Yet he was clearly the coolest guy in the room. After my friend left, Austin and I stayed and talked over a pitcher of beer. I told him I envied the life he was living, he asked about what I did, and we were both equally impressed. He knew he couldn't pay me what I was making but offered me a percentage of future earnings, which had the potential to be huge."

"More than huge. It was a risk, but what a payoff," Christine said.

"So, here I am. No longer tied to a desk every day and trying to keep these guys from having too much fun while they're out there. It's a balance."

"And what about you? Do you have any fun out on the road?" She wanted him to say no but was afraid she'd have to sit through stories about his own groupies.

"Only when pretty women drink Fireball and eat *wheat* cookies," he said, causing Christine to inhale her chai tea, sending it down the wrong pipe. She grabbed a napkin and coughed until her eyes watered.

"Sorry. I guess I shouldn't have brought that up," Matt said. He handed her another napkin.

"No, it's fine. It just caught me off guard."

Her comfort level dropped a notch at the memory of that night. The way he broke eye contact and focused on his coffee made her think he was also a little uncomfortable. They finished their drinks in silence and both stood at the same time.

"Thanks for inviting me. This was nice," Matt said.

Christine fished through her brain for something to say that would bring the levity back. "Well, I'd invite you back to my apartment, but considering my purchases . . ."

It worked. Matt cracked a smile. He looked down at his feet, then up at her. "Rain check?"

"Definitely." She could barely contain her excitement that he'd alluded to something happening in the future. It was nothing concrete, but she knew she'd hear that word in her head at least a thousand times and mull it over, picking it apart to see if there was hope.

They walked outside, and he followed her to her car, leaning in for a quick hug before saying goodbye. He smelled like the tour bus, which wasn't exactly a fresh, clean smell, but it wasn't a bad odor, either. She kind of liked it.

She arrived home and put a load of laundry in. A hot shower helped lessen her cramps. After a quick cleaning of the apartment, her errands were complete. She spent the rest of her Sunday lying on the couch, reading a Jodi Picoult novel with a heating pad on her stomach, and pausing every couple of pages to repeat the words "rain check."

GOING ON THE ROAD WITH LYNDA was a lot different from touring with Austin. To begin with, they weren't on a tour bus, but in a full-size van. And unlike Austin's bus call the night before the show, allowing everyone to sleep the whole way to the venue, Lynda's van call time was six in the morning. With a seven-hour drive in front of them and a three o'clock sound check, they'd have to haul some ass to get there.

They had crammed every instrument and suitcase into the back of the van and onto the last bench seat. That left two bench seats, the driver's seat, and shotgun. With three band members and a tour manager, every seat was taken. The band members took turns driving.

"I'm sure you'd rather be touring with Austin on a nice bus," Lynda said. She looked down, staring at her hands. Christine always marveled at the insecurity of some artists. In her mind, they had it all. The looks, the talent, oftentimes the money. The things she yearned for. Yet they were as human as everyone else.

"No, this is great. I appreciate you asking me to find songs for you. It's nice to think from a woman's perspective again."

Lynda's head popped back up and her eyes brightened. "I didn't think of it that way."

"Is Lynda Bell your real name? It's very country," Christine said.

"I know, right? Like I should live in Mayberry or something."

"Your music is more rocking country than classic country. It's a nice dichotomy."

"Which is why I like the name. My last name is Bellot. I shortened it."

"It works."

Christine learned a lot about Lynda on the drive. She had a sister and brother, and her parents were the perfect couple. She'd graduated high school and earned a music scholarship to her local college, but, after studying for two years, decided to chase her dream. She could always go back to college, she'd said, but she was only young once, and now felt like the right time to go for her career. She moved to Nashville, started hanging out with other singers and songwriters, and got the attention of the right manager, who set up a showcase for some labels. After that, she was signed. Not an atypical story of most artists who were signed to a label, but she was part of the small percentage of dreamers who got that far.

The van didn't have nearly the comfort of the bus, but Christine meant what she said. The opportunity to spend quality time with an artist was invaluable. So often, she knew an artist from their previous music and interviews but didn't know them personally. You couldn't hide much while traveling in a van, and Christine was happy to see that Lynda's easygoing public persona, put together by a publicist, no doubt, matched her real personality.

Christine put her headphones on and dug into the ten new songs that writers had recently sent her way. She always listened to each song at least half a dozen times before forming an opinion. Some songs hit her upside the head the minute she heard them. Other songs were like a slow, subtle message working their way into her subconscious and not letting go. Both types had the ability to be huge hits.

Three gas and bathroom breaks later, and having eaten more truck stop snacks than anyone ever should, they were close to the venue. She'd noticed two things about guys when it came to truck stop food. They loved caramel candies and beef jerky. Three of the guys bought multiple kinds of jerky and then traded them during the rest of the drive. The odor was an assault on her nasal passages, but she got a kick out of hearing their deep conversation about something she considered so mundane. The sweet barbeque flavor was the winner. Lynda went the healthy route with fruit. It wasn't easy being an artist on the road trying to eat healthy. Christine gave in to the lure of M&M's, telling herself she needed a sugar rush to get her through, but the truth was that she liked M&M's.

They arrived at the venue, a big field surrounded by food stands, and parked. They piled out of the van and stretched. Christine looked around, taking in the surroundings. There were multiple booths set up, and huge signs touted everything from chili dogs to bratwurst.

"Where are we?" Christine asked.

"The Rocky Mount Sausage Festival," the tour manager, Tim, said.

"The what?"

"Don't make me repeat it. Please." Tim took off for the stage, saying he was in search of the local production team.

"Anyone up for something to eat?" Lynda asked.

"Any chance of a burger?" the drummer asked.

"I'm going out on a limb and saying no," Christine said, as they headed for the stands.

Half an hour later, deeply regretting the chili dog with onions, Christine called Julianna. She needed to vent.

"I'm living the glam life. I'm at a sausage festival," Christine said.

"Oh, awesome. I do love a good sausage fest," Julianna said with a lift in her tone. "Anything look good?"

"Seriously? You've been to one of these?"

"Hell yeah. Every chance I get. It's like a smorgasbord."

"Of nothing but sausages," Christine said incredulously.

"And that's what makes it so delightful. What looks good?" Julianna asked.

"Well, I tried the chili dog, and it was okay, but I should have left off the onions. I guess the bratwurst doesn't look bad."

"Huh?"

"The hot dogs and bratwurst. Didn't you ask me what looked good?" Christine asked.

"Hold on. You're actually at a sausage festival?" Julianna asked.

"Duh. That's what I said."

"I thought you meant you were surrounded by guys," Julianna said.

"Well, there are a fair amount here, but what does that have to do with a sausage festival?"

"Christine!" Julianna's voice bellowed into the phone.

"What?"

"A sausage festival is another way of saying you're in a place with a lot of dudes," Julianna said.

"I don't get it."

"Urban slang. Sausage fest. Sausage, meaning penis. Sausage fest equals penis fest, meaning a festival of hot men." Julianna's voice gave away her exasperation.

"Gross," Christine said.

"Don't knock it 'til you tried it. Gotta run. Enjoy a sausage for me," Julianna said.

"That's disgusting," Christine said as the call disconnected. "Sausage fest. Seriously?"

Despite the long van ride, the dusty venue, and being surrounded by hot dog stands, Christine and Lynda spent quality time listening to songs Christine felt would be perfect for her. Due to Lynda's contemporary look and her rocking guitar style, Christine wanted the songs to have more of a country feel. It was okay to have a certain amount of pop or rock elements, but when listeners turned on a country station or streamed a country song, they wanted to know there would be enough country elements in the song to keep them happy.

"I never lean toward that sound for me, but now that you explained it, I hear how it would work with my style," Lynda said. "My rock edge can come through, but the song tells a story, and that's straight-up country."

"That's the plan, and I think it'll work. These songs we picked, they're solid with that thought in mind," Christine said.

"You have a fantastic ear, Christine."

"Thank you. As a teen, I'd listen to songs for hours, focusing on the writing technique. Like a lot of people, I assumed every artist either wrote their own songs or they paid to buy songs from writers. I had no idea that people were paid to write songs and a career like song plugging existed. The idea of taking a song and finding a singer who wanted to record it was foreign to me. When I realized there was such a thing, it was a dream come true."

"What a find you were for Austin. It's amazing how it just takes one artist to create an 'it' factor for someone."

"What do you mean?" Christine asked.

"You're the new 'it' song plugger. All the artists are talking about you. You've taken Austin Garrett from new artist to star, and he trusts you implicitly to find the right songs for him. Everyone wants a song plugger like that. The male artists are holding back because they feel like you're Austin's girl, but I figured what the heck. You can't very well give chick songs to Austin, so why shouldn't I give your ears a go. And I'm so glad I did."

Lynda left to change into her show clothes. Christine was speechless. She'd never been the "it" anything. She had been a nerd in high school, teased when she wasn't being ignored. She was studious in college, nowhere close to being the life of the party. Now here she was, nearing thirty, and somehow she had the it factor. She had no idea how it had happened but knew the music business was a fickle friend, and you had to grab the ring when it presented itself. It didn't always come around twice. This time, it had come around in a beautiful, talented package named Lynda. Lynda had dark-blonde hair that fell below her shoulders. She had the body of a woman who worked out enough to stay in shape but who didn't seem opposed to a chocolate bar if the mood hit. Lynda was a perfect combination of gorgeous enough to make men swoon and down-to-earth enough not to threaten women. It was harder to break into the industry as a new female singer than it was as a male. It had become the enigma of country radio. Program directors and consultants battled the fact that songs by females did not research as well as songs by males. Nobody could firmly put their finger on why, but it had become a challenge for females to break into star status. Lynda was beginning to break through that barrier, joining the ranks of artists like Lainey Wilson, who had taken country music by storm with her authentic music and bell-bottom-country theme.

Lynda's show started and Christine walked out into the audience to get the full effect. The sound quality backstage didn't do her justice. Lynda was a talent. Christine already knew that, but seeing her live made that belief even stronger. She stood out because of her ability to play electric guitar. Very few females could shred a guitar and take the lead. Lynda was one of them. When she played a guitar solo, the audience hushed. Fans brought out their phones to record her. People moved closer to the stage, their eyes focused on her fingers as they ran across the guitar strings. Her voice was lower than most females. She didn't have the range or ability to hit the high notes, but she sounded like melted butter. It warmed you. The mix of her mellow voice and rousing guitar playing made her a unique artist. Lynda would be an incredible client. Christine planned to nurture the relationship.

BY THE TIME CHRISTINE ARRIVED back home on Sunday, Lynda had put a hold on two of her company's songs. A hold wasn't a guarantee that Lynda would record the songs, but it meant she wanted to. And as long as everyone involved in the creative process agreed, from her producer to the label's artists and repertoire person, it would move from a hold to an actual album cut. And maybe, if Christine and the songwriters were lucky, a radio single. It wouldn't be enough to save the company, but would add favorably to the bottom line. Christine emailed her boss, who immediately replied with praise and appreciation.

"The sun is shining, Christine. Bail that hay," she said to herself.

She sifted through a weekend's worth of mail, wondering why she even bothered to get mail anymore. She paid her bills online, and, other than communications from her mom, who was Hallmark's best friend, all her correspondence came via email or text. Even thank-you notes were sent through email. So, she was surprised to see what appeared to be a personal letter with her name and address handwritten on the front. She tore it open and gasped.

I strongly suggest you continue going on the road with Lynda and never go out with Austin again. You are pushing your luck and pushing my limits. You've been warned.

Her hands started shaking. She tried to remember the communications law course she had taken in college. She was sure it was a federal crime to threaten someone through the mail. When she grabbed her phone and googled it, she found she was right—it was a federal crime. She smiled to herself. She had something concrete to give the police. As scary as that was, she knew if they ever caught the person, she could nail them with a serious penalty.

For the first time, she felt empowered. "I've got you now," she said. After double-checking that she had locked and bolted her door, she climbed into bed, turned off her light, and fell asleep.

CHAPTER SEVEN

Christine stopped by the police station on the way to work and handed over the letter. She stood with her arms crossed, a smug smile on her lips. "This makes it a federal crime, right? We can do something now," she said.

The officer read the letter, gave a brief nod, and jotted down some notes. Not exactly the hard-core response Christine had hoped for. Her smug smile dissolved. The officer made it clear that until they had some idea of who was making the threats, there was little they could do. They encouraged her to be careful, watch her surroundings, keep people around her, and always lock her doors.

She drove to work feeling defeated but determined to go on with her life. While shuffling through her stack of songs, Christine did her morning ritual of choosing songs that needed an immediate listen versus those that could wait.

Her phone chimed.

It was a text from Austin: *Party at my house this Saturday. Bring hot friends.*

Christine was glad she didn't have a crush on him. A guy like Austin was always looking for the next exciting thing, the hot friends. Even if he did seem to find her attractive, he still wanted her hotter friends to come along. It's just who he was.

How do you know I'm not busy? she texted back.

Are you?

She was tempted to say that she was in fact very busy. But he'd know she was lying. *No,* she texted.

See you around eight. And thanks again for helping me a few weeks ago. You saved me from embarrassment.

Only because I haven't posted the photos. Stay on my good side. Christine smiled as she hit SEND.

I plan to.

Next, she group-texted Julianna and Phoebe. *Party Saturday at eight at Austin's house. Want to come?*

Their responses came in so fast it was like their fingers were already poised over their phones.

I'm in. TY, was Julianna's reply.

Hell yeah, was Phoebe's.

Most likely, Christine would be the designated driver since she couldn't trust the others not to tip back a few. At least she wouldn't be standing at the party alone. She wondered if Matt would be there. A vision of him flashed through her mind with the word "rain check." She considered asking Austin but couldn't think of a way to do it without raising suspicion. She could text Matt, but that would seem weird, too. She wished she could talk to someone who knew him. But they worked on two separate sides of the industry and she didn't know anyone close to him. Still, she banked on him being there, which kept her excited all week.

THE MUCH-ANTICIPATED SATURDAY night had arrived. Christine put on her best pair of Miss Me jeans, her favorite fitted shirt, and a pair of boots. The boots added three inches to her five-foot-seven height, and she felt tall. Too tall. But she liked how the boots gave her butt a lift, so she left them on. She tried to calculate Matt's height. He had to be at least five-foot-eleven, so she wouldn't tower over him. She'd be close to eye level. And if the eyes were the windows to the soul, maybe she could lift his shades a bit.

Julianna's condo was closest, so she went there first.

"Thanks so much for asking me. This is exciting. I've never been to a singer's house before." Julianna plopped herself in the shotgun seat and buckled her seat belt. She had on a cute pair of leggings, tucked neatly into boots with a four-inch heel. Christine's feet hurt just looking at them. Julianna's shirt fell right below her thighs and flowed freely. The V-neck enhanced her generous D-cup breasts. She smelled faintly of perfume. Christine thought it went against nature to have natural D-cup breasts with a size three waist, not to mention long, thin legs up to her neck. She must have been first in line that day in heaven when requesting all the best body parts. Christine tried not to compare her body to Julianna's. That was a rabbit hole she'd spent too much time in and was making a conscious effort to stay out of.

"Think Phoebe will wear anything appropriate?" Julianna asked, raising her knowing eyebrows.

"Appropriate for what?"

"Good point." Julianna grinned.

When they pulled up to Phoebe's, she came waltzing out in five-inch fuck-me pumps and a short, tight dress. Christine could swear she saw her friend's panties. At least she was wearing them. Phoebe opened the back door and climbed in behind the driver's seat.

"Damn, Phoebe. It's a house party. You may be a tad over-dressed," Julianna said.

"I plan to score big tonight and am bringing my A game," Phoebe said. "Anyone have an issue with that?"

"Not me," Julianna said.

"May the force be with you," Christine said. She caught Phoebe's eye roll in the rearview mirror.

They arrived at a fashionable eight fifteen, parked the car, and walked up to the door. Christine rang the doorbell and a few minutes later, Austin opened it.

"Chrissy. What's up, girl?" Austin wrapped his arms around her, lifted her off the ground, and gave her a twirl. She caught Phoebe staring, eyes wide, mouth open.

"These are the hot friends you requested. Julianna, whom you've met, and Phoebe." Christine pointed to each one and Austin shook their hands.

"Good to see you ladies. Come on in. Chrissy, you know where everything is, so grab some drinks and make yourself at home." He stood back to let them pass before someone yelled his name and he excused himself.

"Mark my words, girls. I will get in those tight-ass jeans of his," Phoebe said.

"Please, Phoebe. Attractive as you both are, I don't need the visual," Julianna said as Christine led them to the kitchen.

The girls each grabbed a beer while Christine took a water. They stayed close to one another, anchored by comfort, until they started recognizing people. Phoebe and Julianna chatted up a woman Christine had never seen before. Christine recognized Austin's band members and some of his crew and went up to greet them.

Fifteen minutes later, they made their way back to the entertainment room. Some people were shooting pool, others were playing darts, and a few yelled at a baseball game on TV.

Christine saw a familiar face and walked up to Austin's merchandise manager. Alicia's brown hair was in a ponytail, mostly covered by a baseball cap turned backward. She was more cute than pretty. She was shorter than Christine by a couple of inches, but while Christine had a fuller figure, Alicia had a taut, muscular body that was slender and athletic. Christine had watched her haul boxes of merchandise and was shocked by her strength. The few times Christine had helped her, she struggled to lift the same boxes Alicia raised with ease. Her mode of dress was jeans, black combat boots, and a T-shirt, usually touting some rock band. Tonight, it was Green Day.

"Alicia, how are you?"

"Hey, Christine. Good. You?"

"No complaints. Just another Saturday night in Nash Vegas."

"Yeah, you'd think after being on the road with these guys I wouldn't want to party with them when we're home. But they're kinda like my family."

"How's merch moving?"

"Great. This tour has been good for Austin. He's outselling the middle act nearly every night. We're discussing a whole new line for the upcoming single. He's so amazing. His career just keeps getting hotter."

"He's definitely on his way, isn't he?" Christine looked over at Austin; he was doubled over, chuckling about something. He didn't seem to have a care in the world.

"Yeah, he is," Alicia said, also looking at him. "I'm off to the bathroom. You only borrow beer, y'know?"

"See you around."

Christine spotted Matt. Her body tingled and the word "rain check" reverberated through her head. She was raising her hand to wave when she saw an attractive brunette grab his arm. The way he leaned into her and the casual way she touched him caused Christine to pause. They were together. She was still staring when he looked up and saw her. Their eyes met and Christine gave a little half-wave before turning around. Her chest constricted. She couldn't inhale but kept exhaling. She forced herself to breathe deeply and count to ten as she searched for her friends.

Two guys were talking to Julianna. They talked a bit too loud, possibly from the alcohol, possibly because they were chatting with a beautiful woman. She caught Julianna covering her mouth as she yawned, clearly uninterested in the conversation. Phoebe, on the other hand, was quite animated, smiling with her perfect white teeth and talking to everyone in the room who was standing remotely close to Austin. Christine watched in amazement as Phoebe made her way past each person, their eyes trained on her until she left their side to get one person closer to Austin. It took some time, but she managed to finagle a spot right next to him and start working her magic. She said something he couldn't hear, and when he bent down to have her repeat it, she wrapped her long fingers around his neck and whispered into his ear. He laid his arm around her tiny waist and she moved in closer.

Focusing on her friends had brought her breathing under control and taken her mind off Matt—until he appeared right beside her. "Hey," he said.

Christine's head whipped around. "Matt. I didn't see you walk up," she said.

"Not drinking?"

"I'm the designated driver."

"Make them take an Uber. You should be able to have fun, too," Matt said.

"If I remember, the last time I imbibed, I practically assaulted Austin's tour manager."

"Yeah, well . . . that was a night to remember, huh?" He smiled. "I confess I was thinking about it the other night."

Christine's eyes grew wide. "Really? Why?" She hoped the answer would be that, despite her being drunk, it was the best kiss of his life. Or something along those lines.

Matt opened his mouth but was interrupted by the brunette's arrival. He kept his eyes on Christine, and she returned his stare. Then, the brunette touched his arm.

"Uh, Christine, this is Cait. Cait, this is Christine."

"Hello, Christine. I've heard great things about you," Cait said.

Christine wanted to walk away but knew it would be rude. "I can't imagine what you've heard." She looked at Matt, worried it was about the Fireball-and-cookie night.

"I may have told her about the dancing naked people fiasco," Matt said.

"Ah, yes. Quite a night," Christine said.

"Matt," Austin yelled. "Come here."

Matt excused himself, leaving Cait and Christine alone. Christine regretted not having a drink. She needed something to relax her. She had this sudden odd fear she was going to blurt out her feelings for Matt. She wished Cait had left with him. Their eyes moved around the room, the conversation stalled, and they stood there.

"So," Cait finally said. "Matt told me you're a song plugger."

"I am. And you?"

"I work in banking. Loan officer. Nothing exciting," Cait said.

"Exciting can be overrated. For example, dancing naked people," Christine said with a subtle motion of her hand.

"True, but you have better stories."

"How do you know Matt?" Christine asked, dreading that the answer would confirm they were a couple.

"He came in for a loan when he bought his house. We became friends," Cait said. Christine latched on to the word "friends." Maybe that was it. Like she and Austin were friends. Maybe nothing romantic was going on.

Cait started talking again. "We go out from time to time. Nothing serious yet. But it's been nice. Who knows, right?" Cait shrugged.

Christine was glad she hadn't eaten. If she had, she was sure she'd have vomited right there in the foyer. "Rain check" had just become a rainstorm.

"Ya never know," she said before Matt returned.

"I swear, Austin relies on me for every detail necessary to live his life. He'd forget his pants if I wasn't around to remind him to wear them," Matt said.

"Job security," Cait said with a laugh.

"True that," Matt said.

Christine didn't want to be a part of this threesome any longer, and when she noticed Phoebe walking toward the bathroom, she took the excuse to talk to Austin.

"Nice meeting you, Cait. Later, Matt."

Christine was falling apart inside. She knew she had no right to be angry. Matt hadn't come on to her that night. She had come on to him. But still, he had kissed her back. Then again, he had also stopped things from going any further. Now she knew why. He had a girlfriend. She groaned as she approached Austin.

"What's with the groaning?"

"Oh, was that my out-loud groan?"

He reached his arm around her shoulders and gave her a side hug just as Phoebe emerged from the bathroom. Phoebe glared at Christine when she saw her spot had been taken. She turned her back and joined Julianna, who was casually looking at her watch. Sometimes, it was difficult to find the right mix of people, no matter how cool you were.

"Thanks for the invitation, but I'm going to gather up whoever wants to leave and head out," Christine told Austin.

"So soon? You've only been here a couple of hours. You seem a little unsociable. And taciturn."

Christine laughed so loudly that she started to cough. "Taciturn? What the hell?"

"I couldn't find any movies to watch a few days ago and ended up with *Pride and Prejudice*. I've been dying to use that line. It sounds so . . . I don't know. British."

"*Pride and Prejudice*. You're a Jane Austen fan?" Christine asked.

"I don't know. Who's she?"

"The woman who wrote *Pride and Prejudice*," Christine said.

"Maybe. Is she attractive?"

"She's dead."

"Oh, not so attractive, then. All I know is Keira Knightley's in it, and she has a rocking bod. And Mr. Darcy is the shit. I want to be like that dude. He's rich, cool, and in the end, he got the girl."

"Austin, you never cease to amaze me."

"I'll take that as a compliment. Have I convinced you to stay and party?"

Christine looked around the room, spotting Cait's arm resting lightly around Matt's waist.

"Nope. Two hours is my limit. Shy of Mr. Darcy walking in and sweeping me off my feet, I'm out of here."

"Okay. We'll talk soon. And you know, you can call me now and again. You don't have to wait to hear from me all the time."

"I'll remember that."

His comment cheered her up, making her feel warm and fuzzy, and a little gutsy. She reached up and kissed his cheek. He surprised her by dipping her down, disco dance style, and kissing *her* cheek. She giggled loudly. Christine never giggled. When she turned around, Matt was staring with an expression she couldn't read. She looked away.

She walked over to her friends. "Ladies, I'm out of here. You can leave with me or take an Uber."

"Oh, I'm totally staying," Phoebe said, barely glancing in Christine's direction as she left to take up her spot beside Austin.

"I'm ready to go, but what about Matt? Don't you want to make your move?" Julianna said.

Christine pointed to where Matt stood with Cait, her arm resting casually around his shoulders.

"Oh, Christine." Julianna reached for her hand. Christine snatched it away.

"Don't. I'm barely holding it together, and any affection from anyone will send me over the edge."

Julianna nodded. "Okay. Let's get out of here."

Christine looked across the room to where Matt was. She lifted her right arm and wiggled her fingers at him.

He looked over at Austin, with Phoebe's arm around him, staking her claim. He looked back at Christine and shook his head. He started to walk toward her and she put her hands up and stopped him with a shake of her head. She couldn't talk to him any more tonight, knowing he was leaving the party with another woman. She just wanted to get out of there. Cait turned around and looked between Matt and Christine. Christine bolted out the door.

THE NEXT MORNING, CHRISTINE lay in bed, cuddled in her sheets, not wanting to move. Her eyes felt puffy, probably from her crying jag. Christine rarely cried, but last night, her heart had felt broken. She allowed herself to wallow until she fell asleep. All she wanted to do was stay in bed.

Her cell phone went off. "Oh, come on. It's Sunday." Granted, she should probably be in church. She used to go every week. Her faith hadn't changed, just her habits. She leaned over and focused on the tiny print on her phone.

It was from Austin. *I couldn't sleep. I need a song and want more to choose from. Do you have anything new to play me?*

I do have one I think you'll really like, Christine said, knowing exactly what song she could play him. It had just come in from one of their writers and she had taken it before any of the other pluggers could get it. She had meant to mention it at the party but was derailed by seeing Matt with another woman.

He said, *Want to grab a bite?*

Sure, why not, she texted back. After watching Matt with Cait last night, she needed a win, and maybe this morning would give it to her.

I'll call you later. Maybe we can get brunch somewhere.

Okay.

THEY MET AT THE PANCAKE PANTRY, and Austin put in his earbuds to listen to her song. After one listen, he was humming along.

"I like it. It's got a solid lyric and the melody is memorable," he said.

"Mid-tempos tend to do well. It has the potential to research with the audience, which radio will love," she said.

"There it is again. The word 'research.'"

"I know. Music used to be about a gut reaction. About passion. Writers would pen a tune that an artist loved, and the record label would get excited and decide to release it. They'd take it to radio, who would also get excited, and they'd play it and run it up the charts. Now everything is put into a formula where we poll a few and ignore the masses."

"And all we want to do is write songs and sing," Austin said.

"And all I want to do is work my songs and get artists to cut them," Christine said, hoping Austin would take the hint.

"And then you deal with artists like me who make you wait for their answer on those songs. I swear I'm not trying to be difficult. I just need the right follow-up to 'Promises to Me.' It was so big and I can't afford to miss," he said, taking a bite of his pancake.

"I know. I can be patient. But feel free to give me that good news anytime you want."

He laughed as if she was joking. She wasn't, but she couldn't tell him that.

They finished their coffee and walked out to their cars. As Christine got closer to hers, she noticed a piece of paper stuck under the windshield wiper. "Why would I get a ticket in a parking lot?" she said.

Austin reached over and pulled the paper out of the wipers.

He read the note. *Yo, ugly bitch. Stay the hell away from Austin or plan to pay.*

Christine frantically looked around, expecting someone to jump out and attack her. "Someone was this close to us? They know my car?"

"This has gone too far. You have to let me do something about it." Austin's face turned red, and his hand formed a fist. He saw a man getting into his car and said, "Hey! Hey, you. Did you leave this note on my friend's car?"

The guy flipped him off.

"Austin, the person is probably long gone. And I doubt it's a guy. Why would a guy be jealous of me?"

"I understand fans can get a little possessive, but this has gone too far. I should have stopped it months ago."

"How? What can you do? Nothing that won't make it worse. Just let it go."

Austin cursed under his breath.

"Please, Austin. For now, just ignore it. It's bound to go away."

"You've been saying that for months. It ain't going away, sweetheart. I'm telling you, if it keeps up, I will do something. Have you made a police report yet?"

"Yes. I turned in the letter I got in the mail and documented the rest of what's happened. I'll add this to it." She put the note into her purse.

"Good. Don't let up."

He hugged her goodbye, tucked her into her car, motioned to lock the door, and walked away. Christine took a couple of deep breaths and waited for her hands to stop shaking before starting the car. She kept an eye on the rearview mirror, just in case someone was following her. When she turned onto her street, there was nobody behind her. She rushed home, ran up the stairs, and looked right, left, and behind her before unlocking her door and slamming it shut. She leaned against it, shaking on the inside.

CHAPTER EIGHT

Julianna sat on Christine's desk, pleading with her not to commit career suicide.

"I don't care how good it is for my career. I can't take the threats anymore. They come to my home, leave things on my car. It's not just cyberbullying. It's too close for comfort. I can't hang out with him anymore."

"I get it. I do. But geez, Christine. Are you really going to break all ties with Austin?"

"From a business perspective, no. There's no way I can step back from Austin as a client. I need him and Hit Songs needs him. From a personal one, let's see. Matt has a girlfriend so I've got a broken heart to deal with, and Austin is directly tied to it. Remember when I said that was my fear? If I mixed business and pleasure, it could get awkward? Well, here we are. My fear was real. And just to make things more fun, I get to have the fear of physical pain or death thanks to a stalker. So, yeah, I'm going to break all personal ties."

"These are bound to be empty threats."

"And what if they aren't? What then? You can write on my grave, 'but she was on a career roll.'"

"Not funny, Christine." Julianna crossed her arms and pursed her lips.

"Do you see me laughing? Every part of my life has stress."

"Something going on at work?" Julianna asked. "Something I should know about? I've gotten a couple of vibes from you and Rick. Is it all in my head?"

Christine thought about telling her what Rick had said, but they'd spoken in confidence. If he'd wanted the rest of the staff to know, he'd have told them. Since Julianna was his assistant and didn't seem to know, Christine could only assume he wanted to keep it quiet.

"Just the normal stress of getting songs cut."

"But you have Austin. Doesn't that make it easier?" Julianna asked.

"Only if he actually records and releases one," Christine said. If only she could talk about her daily concerns and the nonstop conversations she had with herself about how much to tell Austin and whether she should beg for his help or wait to see if it happened naturally.

"You know he'd choose your song if you directly asked him to," Julianna said.

"I can't. He's an artist and has to choose the best song for himself. And on top of that, I need to ask him to stay clear of me. How do I say, 'Hey, Austin, cut my song but stay away from me, please'?"

"Yeah, tough situation, for sure. I'm sorry, Christine. This sucks. It should be the best time of your life, and instead, some total bitch is ruining it for you. I wish I could find this person and put an end to it for you."

"I know, and I love you for that."

AFTER JULIANNA LEFT, CHRISTINE texted Austin: *Let's take a break for a while. Maybe the haters will go away if we don't feed them.*

He texted back, *That's crazy. Screw them. You're my friend.*

Please, Austin. For me. Let's try it my way.

Her phone went silent as she waited for a reply. Fifteen minutes became thirty, which turned into an hour. She kept checking her phone to find nothing. At the end of the day, she packed up and went home.

Two hours later, there was a knock on her door. She gave an involuntary scream, tiptoed over to the peephole, and looked out. Austin was standing on her welcome mat. She undid the three bolt locks and opened the door.

"This is stupid, Chrissy. Don't let them win." Austin barged in.

"It's not a matter of winning, Austin. It's a matter of me wanting to stay alive. What if this person is crazy and tries to hurt me? Or kill me? What then?"

"They won't. They just want to scare you."

"Yeah? Tell that to the people in the grave who've been killed by stalkers. I'm out, Austin. I need a break, and you need to give it to me."

"How long?"

"I don't know." Christine went into the living room and sat in the recliner.

"No," he said. "I disagree with this. I think we forge ahead and force them to accept our friendship."

She shook her head. "I don't understand why you want to hang out with me so much."

Austin sat on the couch across from her. "Why is it so hard for you to accept the fact that I like you?"

"Because cool guys like Austin Garrett don't like nerdy girls like Christine Matthews."

"Sure, they do. Don't you watch Hallmark movies?" Austin said, a sly grin sneaking across his face.

"I do. Shocked that you do. But life isn't a movie. And in the real world, the geek doesn't get the hotshot."

"Who the hell did this to you?"

"What do you mean?" She tried to appear defiant, but her voice quivered.

"You know damn well what I mean. Who made you feel this way about yourself?"

"Oh, Austin. It's not a story you want to hear." She got up and went to the kitchen, poured herself a glass of wine, and grabbed a beer for Austin.

He took it and clinked his bottle with her glass.

"I do want to hear it."

"Well, I don't want to tell it—or relive it. It's in the past."

"No, it's not. It's very much in the present. At least for you."

Christine took in a breath and held it while Austin stared at her. It was as if he was waiting her out. His eyes held compassion. Concern. And something more that she couldn't put a name to.

"Short *Reader's Digest* version? I was bullied. Of course, in hindsight, weren't we all bullied to some degree in grade school? But back then I didn't have a big social circle, so I thought it was just happening to me. In seventh grade, I went from being an average-sized kid to feeling gargantuan. I grew five inches in one year and my body filled out. While my friends were staying cute and petite, I was growing hips and breasts like a full-grown woman. I had the body of everyone's mom. And remember, this was all before fat shaming became taboo. Sadly, nobody seemed to have a problem with it back then. With my crazy, curly, unruly hair, I was called everything from ape-girl to Sasquatch. There was another Christine in our class, but she was Cute Christine. I was Ugly Christine. They found a way to differentiate us so nobody would confuse us. No guy wanted to say he thought Christine was pretty and have people think he meant me."

Christine paused. She had to think fast. She didn't want to tell him everything. She closed her eyes, not wanting to remember *that moment* but unable to stop it from coming to the surface. It was Senior Spirit Night and there was a big pep rally at school. Her parents had insisted that she go, despite her protests. They thought it would be a way for her to bond with classmates and have fun. It wasn't. She sat alone in the bleachers. The four guys sitting behind her were drunk. She could smell the beer on their breath. They harassed her, pulling her hair and calling her names. They talked about her like she couldn't hear them. She moved. They moved behind her. She moved again. They followed. It was a game to them. She wanted to get up and leave but was afraid to be alone in the parking lot. What if they followed her? She tried to ignore them, and when the rally ended, she got up and headed directly outside. But even with a crowd of people leaving, they still followed and encircled her. One of the guys was big, a wrestler, and he seemed to be the leader. "I bet you've never even been kissed, have you?"

Christine stayed silent.

"I'll tell you what. I'll take one for the team. I'll give you your first kiss."

The hair on Christine's neck stood up. Unbridled fear. The body reacts before the mind catches up. Why wasn't anyone else noticing this and helping her? Her classmates walked by, talking with one another, laughing. How could they not see what was happening in front of them? She thought about screaming but worried she'd make the guys mad. What would they do if they were angry? And her classmates still might not help her.

"Bryan, that's so gross. You're kissing Sasquatch?" said one of them.

"Just trying to do my civic duty and help the ugly one out. Can't only kiss the pretty girls, can we? What do you say, Christine?"

"I say no." She said it quietly but with conviction.

"No? You're saying no to me?" He gave a sardonic huff.

"I said no." Her body shook from the inside. Bile rose to her throat. She swallowed it, refusing to let them see how scared she was.

Bryan's cheeks reddened and his voice rose in pitch. "You're not only ugly but gutless. Scared of a little kiss, are we? Chrissy is a sissy. Who knew?" He punched the guy next to him, who nodded in agreement.

They chanted "Chrissy is a sissy" over and over.

Christine felt tears coming. She closed her eyes tight to keep them from falling, and when she wasn't looking, Bryan's big hands grabbed her, pulling her against his body. Her eyes flew open. She couldn't move. They always talk about fight or flight, but what about freeze? She froze. He brought his mouth down on hers and ground his lips against her teeth.

"Oh, yeah. Now she's getting it. Put the ol' tongue in there, Bryan," one of his friends yelled.

"Grab her big juicy tit," another voice said.

He'd tried to force his tongue into her mouth, but she'd clamped her lips shut. His hand squeezed her breast, hard. It hurt. She slammed both of her hands against his chest, trying to push him away, but he was so big he didn't move. Her brain couldn't catch up to think ahead of those brutes. She was smarter than they were, but this wasn't about intelligence. This was physical and raw and mean.

His friends circled closer. They were within a foot of her and Bryan, shielding what was happening so nobody else could see.

"Hey, Bryan. How about we move her to the shaggin' wagon and really show her what you've got?" one of the guys said.

"Yeah. It's not just his hands that are big," another voice said, laughing.

Laughing? They find this funny? Christine thought.

Bryan reached around and grabbed her ass, then snaked his hand under her butt, his fingers pushing at her vagina. She knew in that moment that she was a step away from being forced into his van and raped.

Anger kicked in and adrenaline soared through her body. She lifted her knee as hard as she could, rammed it into his groin, and dropped him to his knees.

"Fucking bitch," he said, grabbing his privates.

"Oh, shit," one of his friends said, chuckling into his hand.

"Back the hell off or you're next," Christine said, spinning around, looking at each of them.

They all retreated and let her through their circle. She ran to her car, locked the doors, and sped home.

After that, her nickname was Chrissy the Sissy. Nobody confused her and Pretty Christine again.

"You okay?" Austin said. "I lost you for a minute."

Christine looked up to see him staring at her, his brow quizzical.

"Um, yeah." She shook her head, forcing herself back to the present.

"How'd they do it? Differentiate you from the other Christine?"

"They nicknamed her Tina," she lied.

Christine looked Austin in the eyes. She had worked hard to bury Chrissy and become Christine again. And then Austin started using that awful nickname. He was slowly making the pain of it go away, like waves gently washing away tar from the sand. But the memories remained vivid.

"You're not in high school anymore. You're a grown woman with a beautiful body and a smile that warms people. And honestly, you've got a great rack."

Christine nearly spilled her wine. "Thank you. But I've seen your type. A lot." He had the decency to look embarrassed. "And I'm not it."

"You're so sure of that, are you?" he said. Before she could respond, he kept going. "So how did you get through those tough years?"

"My church youth group. My family went to a church in the next town, so I didn't go to school with any of those kids. The youth group was made up of a melting pot of people: brains, jocks, nerds, and even a pothead or two. But there was something equalizing about doing our confirmation class together, going bowling, or having a sleepover movie night. We didn't pay much attention to what each other did or didn't do in high school. At my lowest moments, I had them. And they got me through."

Austin sighed. "Geez, girl. I'd like to tear apart the people who made you feel this way about yourself. High school was a long time ago, y'know?"

"Do we ever get past those formative years when we're defined by our peers?"

"If we choose to. You need to choose it. Why do I hang out with you? Because I like you. I enjoy your company. When you do what I do for a living, you find very few people who don't want something from you. You can't tell reality from fantasy. Would people be my friend if I wasn't a singer? You don't pull punches with me. You don't swoon when I walk in the room. You treat me like a person. I believe you'd be my friend no matter what. And that means something to me."

This was why she wouldn't push him to record a song. Everyone wanted something from him. She couldn't be just one more. Christine closed her eyes. She wanted to open them and not be sitting across from Austin Garrett. She didn't want to make the decision to extricate herself from his life. She also didn't want to be afraid for *her* life. She opened her eyes. He was still staring at her.

"I would be your friend, no matter what. I like you, too. I care about you. You've been a fun, crazy addition to my life and have catapulted my career, but—"

"No but. Don't say it."

"But I can't live in fear. I need a break. And you need to respect that."

Neither said a word. Their silence overtook the room. Christine heard the ticking of her clock's second hand. She knew she'd give in if she spoke first, so she stayed silent. A minute went by.

Then, Austin stood. "Fine. We take a break. But damn it, it's not going to be too long. I don't plan on giving you up over some maniac."

"You may not have a choice."

"And professionally?"

"What do you mean?"

"Are you walking away both personally and professionally?" he asked.

"Of course not. Rick would fire me. But you know as well as I do that most pluggers do not become best friends with their artists. They have a friendly professional relationship, but they aren't necessarily friends. We are not the norm."

"So, you'll still send me songs. You won't pawn me off on a coworker?"

"Austin, there may be places in my life where I'm insecure, but my brains and work are not two of them. I'm damn good at my job. Rick would lose his mind if he thought I'd risk you going somewhere else. I remain your faithful song plugger."

"Would it change your mind if I said I'd cut one of your songs?" Austin asked, a grin on his face.

"It would make my year if you said that. But I'd still insist we take a break on a personal level. I have to," Christine said, holding her breath and hoping he was serious about cutting her song.

"Okay. We do it your way," Austin said, not mentioning her song.

Christine drew in a deep breath and let it out. Now wasn't the time to beg him to record it, no matter how much she needed it.

Austin reached for Christine's hands and pulled her up. He held her hand as they walked to the front door. He hugged her and she hugged him back. He ran his hands up and down her back, massaging it.

Christine melted. She longed for affection. She'd never been with a guy who she really cared about. And she really did care about Austin. He wasn't Matt and she didn't see a romantic future with him, but they were both consenting adults. And maybe he could help her forget Matt.

He read her body language, sliding his hands down to her lower back. He reached for her hair, turned her head toward his, and dropped a light kiss on her lips.

Instead of pulling away, she leaned toward him. She had a fleeting thought that she wished Matt were kissing her but willed it out of her head. Matt had a girlfriend. She needed to let that fantasy go.

Austin spun them around so her back was against the door, and she couldn't contain her moan when he slipped his tongue into her mouth.

She reached her hands under his shirt and felt his rock-hard abs. His body was perfect. She'd have to be a reptile not to want him. She tensed up, visualizing them both naked. She didn't have a perfect body. But he wanted it anyway. She relaxed for just a second until she thought about the next morning. The next day. The next week. In this moment, they were both emotional. This would be a night. She stopped kissing him.

He nuzzled her ear. "Why'd you stop?" he asked in a light tone.

"I'm not a one-night-stand kind of girl."

"I know."

"And you're not a commitment kind of guy."

He buried his face in the crook of her neck. "Maybe I can be."

"And most likely you can't. At least not now. You're just starting your career. You have women throwing themselves at you every night. Beautiful young women. This is not the time for you to be in a relationship."

He started to protest, but she stopped him. "This," she said, motioning between them, "is not a good idea."

He pulled back and looked her in the eye. "But you're the coolest chick I've ever met."

Christine's head snapped back. "Right. I'm the coolest chick."

"Like it or not, you are. I don't think I can stay away from you," Austin said.

"For now, you have to. My safety and sanity depend on it."

He held her face in his hands and stared at her. She stared back. He bent down and kissed her nose. With a silly grin and his best Arnold Schwarzenegger voice, he said, "I'll be back."

Christine snickered. "I hope you will."

Austin left with a salute.

Christine sank back in her chair and let the tears flow. *And there goes the best thing that's happened to me in years*, she thought. She thought of all she was giving up by letting Austin go. Sure, she'd keep the professional side of their relationship going, but his friendship had given her a confidence she'd never had before. And Austin was her connection to Matt. Even though he had a girlfriend, Christine still wanted him. She never thought the day would come when she'd be all googly-eyed over a guy. It wasn't her style. But here she was lying in bed and staring at Matt's socials just so she could look at him and feel closer to him. She put her phone down and fell into a fitful sleep knowing her exciting new lifestyle had just come to a halt.

THE DAYS WENT BY SLOWLY. A week felt like a month. Christine missed Austin. She also missed Matt. She had tried to stop thinking about him. It was the proper thing to do. Girl code and all. But she thought of him. Every day. Every night. The mind can make all the decisions it wants, but the heart doesn't always pay attention. Christine finally understood people's obsession with social media. She now lived on it, virtually fulfilling her hunger to be with both Austin and Matt. Matt never posted about Cait, and she now understood why he didn't post about other women. It would be disrespectful. He seemed like the faithful type. The main characteristic she looked for in a man. Yet it was also what kept them apart.

Like most artists, Austin posted about everything. She knew artists were encouraged to post often, and when they did it themselves instead of hiring someone, it made the fans feel closer to them. He was having a great run, playing festivals with multiple A- and B-level artists. All of whom Christine could be meeting and making important connections with.

Eventually, she shut down the socials. It made her have severe FOMO. She used to laugh when her friends expressed their fear of missing out. Christine was more of a JOMO person—she loved the joy of missing out, staying home on a Saturday night, reading a book instead of being at yet another industry event that was wall-to-wall people. She wasn't laughing now as she realized FOMO was real.

TWO WEEKS AFTER CUTTING TIES with Austin, while having a taco lunch with Julianna, Christine groaned.

"I miss him," Christine said. "He's like my crazy little brother who left for camp, and I miss his antics."

"Then call him," Julianna said.

"It's not that easy. I miss him. I don't miss being stalked."

"Maybe the person has given up," Julianna said.

"As long as I'm not seen with him. Maybe he's found someone to hook up with," Christine said. "That would help." She noticed a weird look on Julianna's face.

"What?"

"I didn't want to tell you," Julianna said.

"Just tell me."

"Phoebe saw him at Losers Bar this past weekend. He was drunk, and when he saw her, he unloaded about missing you and how he couldn't stand what was happening and so on. Phoebe said he was practically in tears."

"Let me guess. She consoled him the only way Phoebe knows how. God. I thought she was making a play for Chase Rice. Didn't she always say he was the most shaggable guy in country music?"

"I don't think that's the word she used."

"I'm trying to clean it up. Couldn't she just leave Austin alone? Did she have to bring it so close to home for me?"

Julianna said, "I'm not sure it was about you. She said—"

"I've heard enough," Christine said, waving Julianna off.

"It bothers you," Julianna said.

"I don't care what he did with Phoebe. It's not like that with Austin and me. But why does it have to be Phoebe? And now it'll be even more awkward when they break it off."

"How do you know they will?" Julianna asked.

"Odds are against them," Christine said. "She's just so . . . so . . ."

"Phoebe," Julianna said.

"Exactly. Oh well. Maybe the stalkers will back off now."

THE WEEKS MELTED TOGETHER. Christine chided herself, berated herself, and had long conversations with herself. She missed Matt and the opportunity to see him. And accidentally touch him. And pretend she had a chance with him. She had set aside her thoughts of having a physical relationship with him, but that didn't stop her from having an emotional relationship with him, if only in her mind. It was comforting to know she could have feelings for a man. She'd worried after her high school experience that she'd never allow herself to open up to a guy. Yet here she was in an emotional relationship with two of them—one as a friend and one as something more. It made giving them up that much harder. There was a constant battle raging in her head. Should she give in and reach out to Austin, knowing the cyberbullying and stalking could start up again? Or should she stay safe and remain at a distance? And if he was with Phoebe, wasn't she in the clear anyway?

Christine had a heart-to-heart with herself. She hadn't taken many risks in her life, but when she had, it paid off. Like when she stood up to her bullies that night. And although she had to endure their harassment, she'd never regretted dropping that guy with a solid groin kick. Maybe this was a time to be brave.

Christine was staring at her phone when Julianna walked into her office.

"You know, we haven't been to a songwriter's night in months. I know you're afraid to go out in public, but how long are you going to hide?" Julianna asked, sitting down.

Christine was still staring at her phone.

"What are you doing?" Julianna asked.

"Thinking about texting Austin."

Julianna grinned and nodded. "It's about time."

"He's with Phoebe, and maybe that will make the stalker leave me alone, right?"

"Only one way to find out," Julianna said, pointing to Christine's cell phone.

Christine sighed and texted Austin. *Hey. What's up?*

A return text came through in less than thirty seconds. *Chrissy. Is my exile over?* He ended with a smiley face emoji.

She shook her head and put the phone down. "I can't do this, Julianna. My stomach is in knots."

Her phone chimed again. *Don't ignore me. You know it's not possible. Six weeks is enough.*

"Seriously, Christine? You're going to wimp out?" Julianna came around her desk and read the texts with her.

The next one said, *Christine! Answer me, damn it.*

"He's not playing now," Julianna said. "He called you Christine. And he's using exclamation points. Guys don't use those."

"I know."

I just finished a meeting down the road and am about to be outside your office. We're going to lunch, Austin texted.

She replied, *What? No, we aren't.*

He texted back, *Yes, we are. Get your sweet ass out here.*

Sweet ass? He'd never used that one before.

"Have I mentioned that I am beginning to adore Austin Garrett?" Julianna asked.

Another text came from Austin: *I swear, Chrissy. I will walk in there and fireman-carry you out to my truck.*

You couldn't lift me, she texted back.

Don't bet on it.

Christine sighed. Maybe six weeks was enough. She typed, *Then come and get me!*

Julianna cheered.

When Austin walked into the office a moment later, Christine stood.

"Chrissy!"

She couldn't help but smile.

His eyes sparkled and his body practically bounced up and down. He was like a big kid.

She was just about to hug him when he picked her up and threw her over his shoulder. She screamed, hitting his back with her palms.

"Austin. What the hell are you doing?"

"Proving my point."

Julianna clapped and slapped Austin lightly on the back.

"Dude, I love your attitude," Julianna said.

Christine grinned. Maybe she wasn't as heavy as she thought. Austin had lifted her like she was a feather. He hadn't even grunted.

He set her down at the office's front door. She could feel how big her smile was.

"Uncle. I admit it," Christine said. "I've missed you. Where are we going?"

"Somewhere nobody in the industry will be—McDonald's."

Christine waved at Julianna and headed out the door. A moment later, she was climbing into Austin's truck.

He drove the mile down Broadway Street to McDonald's and pulled into the drive-through, where they placed their order and ate in his truck.

"Nobody will see us here," he said.

Christine sat sideways in her seat. "Okay, tell me what's been happening on the road. What have I missed?"

Austin filled her in, sharing the band's antics. "Nothing on the road changes, Chrissy. It's a party every night and a hangover every morning."

"And yet it never gets old."

"Nope, never."

"How's Matt?" Christine heard her voice go up a notch. Her face reddened and she looked down. She'd tried to sound nonchalant, like she was asking about any ol' person, but it didn't come out that way.

"And why do you want to know?" He gave her the side eye.

"Well, he's become, you know, a friend. I mean, I helped him on the road, and I miss him. I mean, I miss helping him."

"Uh-huh. He's doing fine. I know he misses your help. He's mentioned it a couple of times. Or maybe a couple hundred times."

"Really? Please tell him I say hi."

"I will. Or you could tell him yourself with this handy little thing called a cell phone."

Christine frowned. "Ha ha. And how's it going with Phoebe?" She'd gotten some updates from Julianna but wanted to hear it from Austin. She hated the idea of them together but refused to let anyone know it. Granted, she didn't want a sexual relationship with Austin herself, but he was still her special friend. The idea that he now shared something special with Phoebe made Christine feel less unique. But she'd never let on—if for no other reason than to make Phoebe think she didn't care. Christine refused to give her the upper hand.

"Fine. Sorry you didn't hear about that from me, but you asked me not to contact you unless it was business-related."

"You're right. I did."

"She hinted that she'd like to go to the CMA Awards with me. So, I guess I'm taking her."

"I'm sure she'll love that," Christine said.

"I need you to be there in case our song wins. I have six tickets, so why don't you take two? They're not in the first few rows where the artists sit, but they're on the floor, so they're good seats. Grab yourself a date and make a night of it."

Christine tried to envision who she would take and nobody came to mind. Literally, nobody. Well, Matt, but he'd already be there with Austin and maybe Cait.

"Thanks. That would be great. I'll see if Julianna can make it," she said.

Austin's brow bent down before his eyes opened wide and he smiled. "I didn't realize."

Christine raised her eyebrows.

"Didn't realize what?"

"You and Julianna. I mean, it's cool. Equal rights for everyone, y'know? And shit, girl, kudos. Julianna is about as hot as it gets."

"What in the hell are you babbling about?" Christine asked, staring at him like he'd lost his mind.

"You and Julianna. You're a couple, right?" he said.

"Huh? What in the world makes you think that?"

"I told you to bring a date and you mentioned Julianna. I never see either of you with dudes. You keep turning me down. I put two and two together."

"And you came up with five. We're not together, Austin. Although I have to be honest—I'm kinda flattered that you think I could score Julianna. Almost makes me wish I was," Christine said.

"Well, damn. That exciting visual was short-lived," Austin said.

"You're pitiful."

"Guilty as charged. You still want the tickets?"

"Oh yeah."

They finished lunch and Austin returned her to the office.

"Is our hiatus over?" he asked.

"We'll see. If socials light up about us being at Mickey D's, then it's back on."

"It won't. Nobody saw us, and I didn't tell anyone we were going." He leaned over to kiss her cheek. "I missed you."

"I missed you, too." She got out of the truck.

He called out to her. "See you soon, Chrissy."

Christine buzzed Julianna's extension when she got back to her desk.

"Want to go to the CMA Awards?"

"And yet another awards show. How many can one industry have?"

"Currently about five. Want to go?"

"Ugh. We always get shitty seats. I can't handle one more awards show where I'm so high up that my back is against the concrete wall. I think I'll pass, but thanks."

"Austin scored me two floor seats. I need a date, and sadly, you're it," Christine said.

"Floor seats? For real? I've never had floor seats. Consider me your date. So, how'd it go with lunch?"

"I don't know. I guess I'll give it a shot and see what happens. I've been watching his social accounts and fans seem to accept Phoebe. So maybe it's over."

"Let's hope."

"Oh, by the way, Austin thought we were a couple," Christine said.

"Huh?"

Christine explained the exchange she'd had with Austin.

"That's hilarious. God, if only we were. That would make things so much easier," Julianna said.

"I'm sure same-sex couples have the same issues as heterosexual couples," Christine said.

"Maybe. But I already know I like you. You're nice, and kind, and faithful, and you put people ahead of yourself. You'd make a great girlfriend."

"Could you design a resume and reference letter, say all of that, and send it to Matt? Please," Christine said.

"I'd do all that and more if it would make you happy."

"Love you."

"Love you," Julianna said.

CHAPTER NINE

"The first week of November is exhausting," Julianna said. "The general public has no idea." She and Christine were in the conference room, having just finished a meeting about the employee schedule for awards week. Since Julianna was Rick's executive assistant, she kept the master calendar. Christine enjoyed watching Julianna run the meeting. This was when her brilliance shined. It wasn't easy keeping everyone on track with multiple events and schedules. Julianna had a natural knack for organization, which tended to be in short supply in a creative industry.

"I know. They see the CMA Awards on TV and assume that's it. But the songwriter awards are every night leading up to it. BMI, ASCAP, SESAC," Christine said.

"Fun, but sucks the energy right out of ya," Julianna said.

"And this year is even more nerve-racking. 'Promises to Me' qualified for every awards show. It's nominated for three awards. It could go home with three trophies or zero trophies. The stress is in the not knowing. If only they told us in advance."

"Think of all the people who weren't nominated at all. They may not be stressing, but they didn't get the honor of being a finalist either," Julianna said.

"So true. I'm not complaining. I just want it to win so badly. It was a risk for Austin and me. And it paid off in so many ways. An award would be icing on the proverbial cake."

"You up for going to the mall and looking for dresses? If it does win, you'll want to have an award-winning look to go with that award-winning song. I figured we could make a day of it with mani-pedis," Julianna said.

"Why not? I assume Phoebe's going?" Christine's lip curled up in a snarl.

"She is. I wish you two would get along."

"She doesn't like me. She thinks I'm not good enough," Christine said.

"She envies you."

Christine guffawed so loud she snorted.

Julianna held up a finger. "First, you and I became close, making her feel there was a threat to hers and my friendship," she said. Then she held up another finger. "Second, you scored a friendship with Austin. He adores you. And she knows it. Hence, she's jealous."

"Phoebe doesn't have an insecure bone in her body," Christine said, arms crossed, lips pursed.

"You know, Christine, you weren't the only one with a rough childhood. Phoebe may not have been bullied like you were, but she had some tough teen years. Her parents were a train wreck and it affected her badly."

"At least I didn't become a mean girl," Christine said, but her voice was quieter, less emphatic.

"People handle things differently. You have your way, which is to be way more insecure than you should be. She handled it by becoming a block of ice that nobody can break down."

"You know, growing up, I used to pray for the cool kids to have a reason to be jealous of me. It's not as fun as I thought it'd be."

"Watch what you pray for. Let's focus on pretty dresses and getting our nails done. It always makes me happy."

"If only a pretty dress could cure the world of problems."

"It probably can. It's just that nobody has proved it yet." Julianna gave Christine a winning smile.

CHRISTINE, JULIANNA, AND PHOEBE met at the mall after work. Christine stood in the store in awe of the dresses her friends were buying—dresses that were formfitting, short, and had cutouts that gave glimpses of bare skin that would otherwise be covered. She hadn't tried on a single dress yet when Julianna rounded the corner with an armful.

"Your turn, Christine," she said.

"I'm good. I have a couple of dresses from the last few years."

"No offense, but I saw last year's dresses. You're trying these on," Julianna said.

"Fine. Give them to me." She ducked into a dressing room.

"Try the black one on first," Julianna said.

"Got it," Christine said, stepping into the black one.

She looked in the mirror. The dress was shorter than she was used to, but it swayed nicely above her lower thighs. It was light and airy, and it would be comfortable for sitting and walking while still looking elegant. The shoulders were open, revealing her smooth skin, with bell sleeves that ended in cuffs. There was only one problem. It was tight around her midsection. She frowned at her reflection.

"I can't pull this off. I don't have the abs for it," Christine said, refusing to come out of the dressing room. She shrugged out of the dress.

"Don't move and do not hang up that dress," Julianna said, rushing out of the dressing room area. She returned minutes later, sliding an item under the dressing room door.

"What's this?"

"Spanx. The secret weapon of practically everyone in town. Put it on, then put the dress back on. And don't give me an eye roll," Julianna said.

Christine knew Julianna couldn't see her, but she gave an eye roll anyway and did as she was told.

"Holy crap! I've heard about these but never believed they worked," Christine said, admiring the way her tummy had flattened under the dress.

"Yep."

"And there are no telltale lines," Christine said, turning back and forth in front of the mirror.

"Open up the door and let me see."

Christine obliged.

Julianna's jaw hung open. "Stunning, Christine. Absolutely stunning."

"Thanks." Christine blushed. She looked at Phoebe and couldn't get a read on her expression. Christine wasn't going to beg for a compliment. She turned to head back into the dressing room.

"It looks beautiful on you, Christine," Phoebe said.

Christine cocked her head and looked Phoebe in the eyes. She saw sincerity. "Thank you, Phoebe."

Christine chose two more dresses and made her purchase.

"Anyone up for a bite to eat?" Phoebe asked.

"I think I'm going to head home. Shopping is a bit stressful for me," Christine said. She knew that as a woman she was supposed to love shopping. But when you were tight on money and insecure with your body, it was a different experience.

"Are you sure?" Julianna said.

"I am. Thanks for including me in this girls' night out. It was more fun than I expected. Enjoy your dinner," Christine said.

Christine loved the black dress. As she drove home, she tried to envision a scene in which Matt would see her in it.

THAT SCENE CAME TO LIFE AT the BMI Awards, which was held the night before the CMA Awards to honor the songs and songwriters.

The ceremony was held in the parking garage of the BMI building. It took hard work to transform a regular parking garage into a glitz-and-glamour awards room. Workers spent days setting up a stage and lighting. The lighting is what made it special. Along with stage lighting for the performers, the room lights sparkled blue and red, giving a romantic ambience to the evening. Tables, draped with white tablecloths and adorned with floral centerpieces, were arranged to maximize the number of people who could attend. Bars were set up on both sides of the room, fully stocked with liquor served by tuxedo-wearing bartenders. Rick had purchased a table for his employees, and Christine and Julianna made sure to sit next to each other.

"How do they do this every year?" Christine asked Julianna, who looked stunning in a gold dress with a plunging neckline and a hem that fell perfectly mid-thigh.

"Transform a parking garage into the glitziest place in Nashville? I have no idea. They work on it for weeks. Look at those chandeliers. Probably cost more than most cars," Julianna said.

"My car for sure."

"Do you think 'Promises to Me' will win?" Julianna asked.

"I don't know. I hope so, but it peaked on the charts so late in the voting season it's hard to tell."

Austin sauntered in fifteen minutes before the awards started. Phoebe looked regal on his arm. The dress was a few inches longer than what Phoebe usually wore. She looked like a runway model. Austin saw them and led Phoebe to their table.

"Chrissy girl. Let me see that dress!" Austin reached down to pull Christine to her feet. He let out a slow whistle and turned her around in a circle. "Damn."

Christine beamed.

"The miracle of Spanx," Phoebe said, a grimace altering her face.

Christine chose to ignore her.

Austin reached out his hand to Julianna. "Good to see you again. You also look gorgeous this evening. Then again, when don't you look gorgeous?" He stared a little too long, his gaze dropping below her neck before reaching her eyes.

"Thank you, Austin. As do you," Julianna said.

Phoebe gave a loud throat clear.

"Huh? Right. I've got to go hunt down Matt. He's holding our seats. Come by our table later," Austin said, stealing another glance at Julianna.

Christine's stomach danced a jig at the sound of Matt's name. She watched Austin and Phoebe walk to their table. She saw the back of Matt's head but couldn't tell if Cait was with him.

"Is it my imagination or did Austin just flirt with me?" Julianna asked.

"He flirted. Wish you could have seen Phoebe's eyes. They were throwing darts."

"At me?" Julianna's eyes widened.

"Nope. At Austin."

Christine no longer felt nervous about the awards. Instead, she focused on the moment when Matt would see her in her dress.

"Promises to Me" did not win the award. Although Christine was disappointed, she was content that it had been nominated. So many songs were released in a year, and being among the top five was still worth celebrating.

"I'll be back, Julianna. Need a quick bathroom break."

Christine entered the bathroom and took a passing glance at a woman across the room. She was beautiful with long, flowing, curly dark hair and donned a dress very similar to Christine's. Christine looked away, envying the woman's svelte body, once again wishing she could look like that. She decided to steal another quick look and gasped. There was no woman across the room. It was a mirror. Christine had admired her own image. "Oh my God," she said. "I'm beautiful."

When she walked back to her table, she held her head a little higher. Her gait had more confidence and a smile filled her face.

"What happened to you in there?" Julianna asked.

"What do you mean?"

"You seem, I don't know, different. Like you went in as Clark Kent and came out as Superman."

"Make it Superwoman and I'll agree."

"Whatever it is, it's working for you."

Christine got a text from Austin when the after-dinner coffee was served: *Two people just left our table. Bring Julianna and come sit with us.*

Christine showed the text to Julianna, who shrugged. "Why not?"

Christine spotted Matt before he saw her and had to snap her mouth shut. He looked handsome in a black suit with a white shirt and gray tie. He was standing near the table, talking with someone she didn't recognize. It gave Christine a moment to get her breath back before he turned and saw her.

His eyes widened and he walked away from his conversation in mid-sentence. "Wow. Austin said you looked amazing tonight, but I had no idea."

"How red is my face right now?" Christine asked, giving an uncharacteristic titter.

"A few shades," Matt said.

"You look pretty darn handsome yourself."

The quick break ended, and they took their seats for the remainder of the awards. Matt pointed to the empty one next to him.

"Isn't Cait here?" Christine asked, trying not to sound hopeful or pitiful.

"I never bring dates to these events. I'm Austin's beck-and-call guy, and that can be painful for a date."

The table was built for six chairs, but they had squeezed in eight. This made for tight quarters, and despite her attempts to be proper, her arm brushed against Matt's every time she reached for her drink. His thigh touched hers, ever so slightly, and after she pulled back twice, giving him distance, she gave into it when his thigh touched hers for the third time. She even relaxed into it, subtle as it was. He didn't pull away. The touching heated her skin to the point where she thought of spontaneous combustion. Was that even a real thing? A few times, he leaned over to whisper something about the speech. Having his lips near her ear caused her to shiver.

"Are you cold?"

"No."

"You shivered."

She decided to be bold. "I have sensitive ears and you were practically kissing one."

"Should I apologize?" he asked. "In this PC world, I don't want to do anything unwanted."

"No apology necessary. At all."

He smiled. "Noted."

The next time he whispered in her ear, her breath caught in her chest. She was afraid to move. She wanted to look at him, but at the same time, she didn't want to.

He leaned in again.

"Christine?" His mouth was warm on her skin.

"Yes?"

"You can whisper back anytime you want."

She closed her eyes and counted to five. Matt moved away and Christine turned to face him, eyes wide open. "I plan to," she whispered.

Matt reached under the table and gently squeezed her knee before returning his hand to the top of the table.

Christine couldn't focus. Had Matt and Cait broken up? Had they never been a couple to begin with? Was he just being playful and flirty? Christine was happy and confused all at the same time. She decided to just be happy and enjoy the moment, whatever it meant.

When the event ended, she reluctantly stood, ending their proximity.

"Let's take some pictures," Julianna said.

"I want one with my girl Chrissy," Austin said, causing Phoebe to audibly gasp. Austin didn't acknowledge it, but Julianna nudged Christine, who whispered, "Behave."

Matt gave Christine her thrill of the night by handing his phone to Austin and saying, "My turn, bro." Matt put his arm around Christine, and she prayed he couldn't feel her tremble.

"Smile," Austin said, and snapped the photo.

"Now one with my date," Christine said, grabbing Julianna.

"And the fantasy continues," Austin said, causing Phoebe to slap his arm. "What? I can take a photo of all three of you and add you to the fantasy."

"No. Thank. You," Phoebe said.

They posed for one group photo and called it a night. It would be a long week, and they still had the big night to go.

CHRISTINE SANK INTO HER BED AFTER the awards and, snuggled amongst her comforter, relived every one of Matt's touches, accidental and otherwise. Her thoughts were interrupted by a text. Her heart flipped when she saw Matt's name appear on her screen along with the photo they'd taken. Her eyes were open, her smile looked natural, and she loved her dress.

She texted him back. *Great pic. Thanks!* She thought about adding, *We make a dashing couple*, but hesitated.

Then her phone chimed in a text: *We clean up nice.*

She replied, *Yes, we do. Nice seeing you tonight.*

She hoped he'd send at least one more text. Sending the last text in a conversation with your crush always sucked. You waited for a reply that never came. Luckily, that wasn't her experience tonight. He sent another text: *Always good to see you.*

She burrowed further under the covers. He'd said "always." That word had so much potential. Only certain things *always* happened. Like the sun rising in the east and the moon making a nightly appearance. Mom's hug making her feel safe. Important things held the title of always. She reached for her phone and looked one more time. *Always good to see you.*

Always good to see you, too, she thought, putting the phone away and falling into a peaceful sleep.

THE COUNTRY MUSIC ASSOCIATION Awards had arrived. This was the big night everyone had been waiting for. Once again, the Bridgestone Arena had been changed from a concert and sports venue into an awards arena. In front of the stage was an open section where fans stood and cheered. Behind them were seats for the artists, performers, and awards presenters. The other layers of seating held industry people and fans. Large screens were set up throughout the venue, projecting everything happening on the stage.

The usher escorted Christine and Julianna to their seats. "I like your friendship with Austin. It has great perks," Julianna said, sitting in her assigned floor seat.

"No obstructed view. Remember the year we sat under the scaffolding?" Christine said.

"I can't believe we paid for those tickets."

The show was in its second hour when the Single of the Year category was announced. Julianna grabbed Christine's hand when "Promises to Me" was mentioned as a nominee, and although Christine had made a promise to herself to never pray for work-related things, she couldn't help but whisper, "Please, God."

Two reality show actresses—Christine missed their names—were presenting the award. "And the winner is ... Austin Garrett and 'Promises to Me.'" Julianna and Christine leaped to their feet, their screams deafening. Grabbing each other, they jumped up and down, turning in circles.

The cameras panned to Austin. Phoebe had a death grip on him and was planting kisses all over his face. He extricated himself from her embrace and returned high fives and a couple of hugs on his way up to accept the trophy. He stepped up to the microphone. "Man, I don't know what to say. There are so many people to thank. First, I have to thank God for this life that I live. A big thanks to country radio for playing this song and making it a number one. I wouldn't be here without you. Thanks to my record label, my management, booking agent, and publicist. Thanks to the songwriters who wrote this incredible song and my band and crew who are there with me every night on the road. And I have to thank a very special woman who recently came into my life and took it to a whole new level."

The cameras panned to Phoebe, who had a camera-ready smile and well-timed tears tickling her eyelashes.

Austin pointed back to where he knew Christine was sitting, and the cameras tried to follow.

"Christine Matthews brought this song to me, and if it wasn't for her, I'd have never heard it until it was a hit for someone else."

The cameras aimed at Christine, and Julianna stood with her finger pointing at Christine's head. Suddenly, Christine's face appeared on the huge monitors.

"Chrissy, this is for us. Thanks again, everyone."

The camera cut back to Austin, waving his trophy high above his head as a woman escorted him to the backstage area.

"Damn! That is going to piss off Phoebe," Julianna said.

"Not to mention all my haters. Ugh. Why did he have to mention me?"

"Because you deserve it, and he knows that."

Christine sat through the rest of the awards show, restless by the end. Was there a party? Would she be invited? If it was Austin's party, she probably would. Did she want to be around Matt if he was with Cait? The thought of them together caused her stomach to churn.

Her phone chimed in a text. It was from Austin. *Congrats. We won that one together. Wish we could hang, but believe it or not, I have bus call. Show in California, day after tomorrow, and it'll take two days to get there.*

Christine typed a response: *Why would you accept a show right after the awards?*

His reply came in fast: *$$, girl! They offered to pay me twice my going rate. I like a good party, but hell, I like money more.*

You're smarter than you get credit for, she texted back.

Duh. I keep telling you that. I could have taken a flight tomorrow, but I want to celebrate with my road family. These people have been with me through it all the last few years.

I get that. Have fun. We'll celebrate when you get home, Christine texted.

Deal.

She showed Julianna the text.

"Now what?" Julianna asked.

"We could probably weasel our way into a party somewhere . . . or . . ."

"Waffle House?"

"Yes."

Decked out in their formal wear, they went to Waffle House and indulged on breakfast food, reliving the moment when Austin won. They hadn't heard from Phoebe and decided not to contact her until time had passed and she was less mad.

When she and Julianna parted ways and headed home, Christine believed that nothing could ruin her mood. It was a night to be cherished, recalled, and remembered. And she hated to admit it, but knowing Matt was on the bus heading to California with the guys, and not in another woman's arms, made it that much better.

She walked up the stairs to her apartment and stopped short when she saw a large cooking pot in front of her door. She fell against the wall, making herself as small as possible. Could someone see her? Were they still there? She peered at the object inside the pot. A stuffed rabbit? She crept toward her apartment, her eyes darting left and right while she kept her back to the wall.

"No. No, no, no." As she reached the door, she heard footsteps. She fumbled with her keys, trying to unlock all three locks as quickly as possible. Her hands shook, making it impossible to get the key into the little keyhole. "Breathe, Christine. Breathe." The footsteps were gone. Must have been a neighbor downstairs. She forced air in and out of her lungs and steadied her hands to unlock the door. She grabbed the pot, and, once inside, pushed the door firmly closed before bolting it. There was a note tied around the stuffed animal's neck.

Enough is enough. Tonight was the final straw. How did YOU manage to steal the limelight? Your hold on him ends now. No more warnings. When you least expect it, expect it.

She rushed through the house, looking under the bed, in the closets, in the shower, and on the deck.

Nobody was there.

She double-checked the outside doors and sat on her couch, still in her dress, shaking. She called Julianna.

"Someone left a cooking pot and a stuffed bunny on my doormat."

"Get out of there. Come to my place," Julianna said.

"I don't want to go outside. I'm afraid they're waiting for me." Christine ran through the house, pulling down blinds and triple-checking door and window locks.

"I'm on my way."

"Thank you," she said.

Julianna showed up in a pair of sweats with a backpack over her shoulder.

"I'm staying with you tonight . . . but, Christine?"

"Yes?"

"I insist you call the police."

"I already did. They told me if I didn't feel I was in immediate danger, I should come down to the police station tomorrow and file another report."

"Let's see the offending object," Julianna said.

Christine led her to where it sat on the kitchen counter. Julianna pulled the little stuffed bunny out of the pot. "It's like they found the creepiest-looking stuffed bunny they could. Its eyes are crossed and its whiskers are all snarled. And what's with its weird smile? Do rabbits even smile?"

"Why do creepy-looking stuffed bunnies even exist?"

"This is so 1980s. Come on. At least be original," Julianna said.

Christine hugged her. "I can always count on you."

"I'm starting to think this is more than just a superfan," Julianna said.

"I agree."

"Okay, I'm pouring us a large Baileys and we're watching *Love Actually*," Julianna said with a firm nod.

"Thank you," Christine said.

"I chatted with Phoebe," Julianna said while pouring their drinks.

"Was she pissed about him mentioning me?" Christine didn't say what she was thinking. *Could Phoebe have left the pot and bunny?*

"She didn't say. And I know what you're thinking. She didn't leave you a gift on your doorstep."

"I wasn't . . ."

"You were. Anyway, she raved about being backstage and how she bumped into so many stars. Then she asked me a million times if she looked pretty and thin when she showed up on the TV screens. Of course, I said yes. She looked amazing and bone-thin. Which, to her, is a compliment."

"You can't blame her. It's a pretty big deal," Christine said.

"Yeah, but you didn't ask me a million times how you looked when you were sitting next to him at the CMT Awards."

"I knew I didn't look thin. I saw it for myself. Why wear you out with it?"

"Not to mention you were hobnobbing with the elite while I was in the nosebleed section."

"That night started out so bad," Christine said, accepting the drink Julianna handed her.

"It did."

"But it turned out pretty good for me. Up until threats and bunnies in pots," Christine said, pointing to the stuffed animal.

"Pretty damn good."

"And it didn't turn out badly for Phoebe, either. I swear she could fall into a hole and come out wearing a diamond."

"She's that kind of person," Julianna agreed.

"I thought you were going to make a play for him," Christine said.

"Austin? Yeah, I was, but he needs to grow up a bit. He's super sexy, and honestly, I can tell he's a good guy by how he treats you. But like you keep saying, he's just out for a good time right now, and I'm getting beyond that. I'm twenty-seven. Time to think past being the party girl, y'know?"

Christine nodded as they took their Baileys to the couch. "That's pretty much what I said to him when he kissed me the night I asked him for a break."

"Phoebe's perfect for him right now. She told me they're free to see whomever they want when he's not in town as long as he sees her when he *is* in town. I couldn't do it, but she can."

"Not for me, but if it works for them, who am I to judge?"

"Wait a minute. Did you say he kissed you?" Julianna asked.

"Oops. Had I not mentioned that before?"

"Hell no you didn't. Spill it."

"I was saying goodbye and next thing I knew, my back was against the door and his tongue was expertly making its way around my mouth."

"How in the heck did you not say yes to whatever he offered?"

"I seriously considered going out with a bang. But he's not the commitment kind of guy, and I'm not the one-night-stand kind of woman."

"Maybe you should have been. Have you been with anyone since college?"

"Nope. I believe at this point I'm considered re-virginized. And look who's pointing fingers. When's the last time you got laid?" Christine asked, pointing at her.

"What year is it?" Julianna said, making a face. "It's been a good year and a half. Last time was with the physical therapist I met when I tore a hamstring doing yoga."

"Corey?"

"Cody. This is getting depressing. Let's watch the movie."

They cued up *Love Actually* and started singing along with the opening scene.

When the movie ended and they'd each had two Baileys cocktails and a shot of whisky, Christine was feeling little pain. She grabbed her phone, walked over to the cooking pot with the bunny, took a photo, and posted it to her socials. She tagged

Austin and included every hashtag she could think of to link his social accounts to her photo. She kept it short: *A boiling bunny? You can't be more original than that? Sooooo . . . 1980s.*

Julianna ran over. "Are you crazy? What are you doing?"

"Fruck them," Christine said, and then she started giggling. "He's right. It is hard to say when you're drunk."

"Christine!"

"I'm taking control. A guy who was in the army told me once that the craziest person in a fight wins. Bring it on, you crazy bitches. I'll be crazier."

Julianna held up her glass in a salute and retweeted Christine's comments. "Then I'll be crazy with you."

Half an hour later, Austin called. "What the hell is going on with you?"

"Your crazed fan left a cooking pot and a stuffed bunny on my doorstep. So, I called her out for her lack of origin, um, orinality. Um, her lack of . . ."

"Are you drunk?"

"Very."

"Christine, you're only going to incite the crazies with that post," Austin said in a firm voice.

"That's a very impressive word, Austin. Incite. To encourage behavior. Incite."

"What?"

"When I complained about being bullied, my teacher said, 'Well, Christine, did you do something to incite them?' What a bitch she was. I said, 'Yes, ma'am, I sure did. I showed up at school today.' Then I went home and memorized the definition of 'incite.'"

"Are you alone?"

"Nope. My hot girlfriend is here with me." Christine fell into a fit of laughter.

"Put her on the phone."

"He wants to talk to you," Christine said, switching to speaker and handing the phone to Julianna.

"Hey, Austin. What's up?"

"Okay, first, are you really girlfriends? Because if you are, I'm asking you—no, I'm begging you—take photos and send them. I swear I won't show anyone else."

"We aren't gay, Austin. Sorry. The only hot photo you're going to get is Christine and me in sweatpants on a couch watching movies."

"I have an incredible imagination. Send them."

"You're hard not to like."

"You've tried? Never mind. Is she okay? She sounds like she's losing it."

Christine held her fingers up in the okay sign. "Tell him I'm okay."

"He can hear you, Christine. This may have been the straw. She's going to the police again tomorrow."

"Are you staying with her?" he asked.

"Yes. This is a funny turn of events."

"What is?"

"Usually, you're the one everyone is holding together during drunken escapades."

"Ha. Ha. Thanks for being there with her."

"You got it. Y'know, she was my best friend before she was yours," Julianna said.

"It's not a contest, Julianna. Let's not make it one. We have Phoebe for that," Austin said.

"Damn, just when I start to not like you, I like you again."

"I do that to people. Can you at least sleep in the same bed and tell me about it?"

"Goodbye, Austin," Julianna said.

"BYE, AUSTIN!" Christine yelled from the couch.

"Later, ladies." Austin disconnected the call.

"Damn. I don't want to like him, but I keep finding myself doing it," Julianna said.

"Yep, he's like a stray cat. Welcome to my world."

Julianna plopped on the couch next to Christine. They posed for a selfie in their sweatpants and sent it to Austin.

He texted back, *That's a start!*

"*The Proposal*?" Christine asked, picking another of their favorite movies.

"Yes."

Half an hour into the movie, Julianna started talking.

"Christine, I have a confession. I can't stop thinking about Austin. Ever since that night he flirted with me at the awards. I mean, I know he's with Phoebe and he cares about you, but his call tonight was so sweet . . . Christine? Hello? Did you hear me?"

"Uh-huh. Austin. Sweet. Good night."

"Maybe I shouldn't repeat that when you're sober. Some things are better left unsaid," Julianna said.

"Mmmmmm," Christine said.

Partway through the movie, they fell asleep on the couch.

ON HER WAY TO WORK, CHRISTINE stopped by the police station and filed another report. They took her information and kept the letter, pot, and stuffed bunny. They also asked for a list of people who might have an issue with her.

"All of Austin Garrett's fans."

The police officer raised his right eyebrow—only his right one—fascinating Christine for just a second. They asked for Austin's phone number, and she hesitated before realizing it was the police. They could find the number if they wanted to.

She had avoided looking at any social media, not wanting to see what had been said about her, but once she got to the office, she couldn't stand not knowing. She pulled it up. It was worse than she expected. Christine had hoped that after seeing Phoebe on his arm at the awards, Austin's fans would move their anger toward her. Phoebe was strong. She could handle it. But the anger was still targeted at Christine. There was an entire thread stating that Phoebe was a plant, a hired date to take the attention off Christine, and that's why Austin mentioned Christine from the stage rather than Phoebe. Even Austin dating someone was not enough to make the haters quit harassing Christine. It made no sense. But when has irrational behavior ever made sense? By its very definition, it's not logical or reasonable.

Christine shut down socials. "Enough."

CHAPTER TEN

Christine ate a spoonful of delicious soup made with shredded chicken, Spanish rice, avocado, and tomatoes. She and Julianna were at their favorite Mexican restaurant. The waiter was unabashedly appraising Julianna, who didn't even notice.

"How are you holding up?" Julianna asked.

"Not well, honestly. I went to the doctor and got some Xanax. Every noise freaks me out. The neighbor's cat jumped from their deck to mine last night, and I nearly came out of my skin."

"I'm so sorry. There's got to be something more we can do."

"Not until we find out who's stalking me." Christine's phone rang and she put her finger up to motion for Julianna to hold her thought.

"Hello, Austin. What's up?"

Julianna mouthed, "Speakerphone."

Christine shook her head but then figured she had nothing to hide and hit the SPEAKER button.

"We're taking this shit international. We're going to Canada."

"That's barely international. You can drive there," Christine said.

"Not so. We need passports. That means it's in-ter-na-tio-nal."

"Fair enough. When is this world tour?" Christine asked, the sarcasm sneaking out of her voice.

"Don't be a hater, Chrissy. It's in January, and I want you to go with me."

Julianna put her hand over her mouth. Christine could tell she was chuckling by the shaking of her body. Christine waved her off but was smiling herself.

"You know I love being on the road with you and the guys, but it sounds bitter cold," Christine said.

"It will be. But if I have to be gone for almost two weeks, I want one person there who has the guts to call me an ass when I'm acting like one."

"Two weeks? I can't take two weeks off work. That's all the vacation I get for the whole year, and I prefer to spend it under a palm tree somewhere."

"I already called your boss and promised him you'd get first shot at pitching me music. He's banking on a hit coming out of this trip and some serious *cha-ching* for his company. He said yes, and you don't have to take vacay days."

"You shouldn't have done that without talking to me," Christine said.

"Nope, I shouldn't have. But I did. Niagara Falls, here we come."

"Austin, are you forgetting I have a stalker intent on harming me? Or at the very least scaring me. Going to Canada is a horrible idea."

"Your stalker is in America. In fact, appears to be in Nashville. I bet Canada is the safest place for you. Hell, I bet you're safer in Canada than you've been since you met me."

"Doesn't that strike you as an odd thing to have to say?"

"Yeah, a damn pitiful thing to have to say. But I wouldn't ask you if I didn't think you'd be safe. I can count on you, right?"

"I'll think about it."

"And I'll take that as a yes." He disconnected the call.

Christine sat staring at her phone until Julianna cleared her throat.

"I hate to be cold," Christine said.

"I know you do," Julianna said, a smile creeping onto her face.

"I don't want to go."

"I know you don't."

"But I probably will."

"You most definitely will," Julianna said.

"But I don't want to," Christine repeated.

"But. You. Will."

"But I will." Christine plunked her head down on the table.

"Look at the bright side. Matt will be there," Julianna said, causing Christine's head to snap back up.

"He has a girlfriend," Christine said.

"Yes, but he hasn't put a ring on it."

"Which doesn't make it right for me to make a play for him," Christine said, slamming down her spoon.

"All right, all right. But, Christine, you've fallen hard for him. And you think he's the one for you. At least give some thought to letting him know how you feel."

"Argh. Enough. I can't think about this right now. It's making my head hurt. Change the subject."

"If Austin's still with Phoebe when you leave for Canada, her head will go into a tailspin."

"And that scares me a bit."

"It's not her."

"Uh-huh."

"Christine. It's *not* her," Julianna said.

They paid their bill, left the restaurant, and got into their cars.

"Canada. In winter. You've got to be kidding me," Christine said, pounding her steering wheel before putting her car in drive and heading out.

Christine went home, thankful not to find any nasty notes on her door. She made a cup of tea and sat on her couch, staring out the deck doors. She wanted to sit on the deck, but being outside made her vulnerable. Anybody could see her. Looking at the outdoors would have to suffice for now. Even though she lived in an apartment complex, there was a tree line across the parking lot, and she enjoyed how pretty it was in the evenings. Fall in Nashville could go either way, weather-wise. It could be sunny and hovering in the seventies. Or, it could be ugly, near freezing, and rainy. So far this year, it had been warm.

Christine enjoyed a quiet Friday night, choosing to stay in, watch a movie, read a book, take a bath, and pamper herself. The hoopla of awards week was behind her and all of Nashville was slowing down, preparing for the winter break. When her phone rang at five o'clock in the morning, she dreaded what it meant. It was either her parents calling with horrible news or Austin calling with some dilemma. She bet on it being Austin. She looked at the caller ID and said, "Damn, wish I'd laid money on it."

She picked up the phone. "Austin, it's five in the morning."

"I know, but I need help."

"Are you drunk in some chick's apartment?" she asked.

"I am not. I'm stuck in Cookeville, and the bus left without me."

"I thought you were finished touring. It's almost Thanksgiving. Who tours this close to the holidays?" she said, turning on the light and shaking off sleep.

"We had a radio show last night in Roanoke and the bus rolled out at some crazy hour of the morning. The driver stopped at an all-night Walmart, and it woke me up. I decided to go in and get some snacks."

"And he left you? Didn't you leave the paper towels on his seat?"

"I did. It's not our regular driver. I guess nobody told him what the paper towels mean," Austin said.

"So, call him, or Matt, or one of the band guys."

"Oh, duh. Why didn't I think of that? Give me some credit for having a brain. I called them all. Except the bus driver. I forgot to get his number. Nobody is answering."

"How long have you been there?"

"About an hour. Those guys will arrive in Nashville and sleep on the bus until ten. They tied one on last night. It'll be hours before they realize they left me. You have to come get me."

"Call Phoebe. She's your girlfriend."

"Eh. I'd rather you come and get me," he said.

"Why?"

"That's a long time in the car with her."

"You're sleeping with her, for God's sake."

"True dat. And if we could have sex the whole way back from Cookeville, she'd be my first phone call. But we can't. I mean, we could, but it wouldn't be safe. Please, Chrissy. Come get me."

"Austin . . ."

"Chrissy . . ."

"Fine. Text me the address."

"Thank you."

Christine pushed the END button on her phone, turned the radio on, and started singing. Despite being in the music industry, Christine couldn't sing.

At all.

But alone in her apartment, she didn't care, so she sang at the top of her lungs.

"Chrissy!" Austin yelled. "Chrissy!"

Christine looked at her phone and saw it was still connected. "Austin?"

"Your phone didn't hang up. Nice Miranda song, by the way. See you soon."

Christine was horrified. He'd heard her sing? She made sure the phone hung up this time.

She padded into the kitchen, grabbed a mug, poured in some water and a tea bag, and popped it into the microwave. She chided herself. "What the heck, Christine? You could've said, 'No, I'm not driving out there on a Saturday morning.' 'No' is a word, and you're allowed to use it. Even dogs understand the word 'no.'"

She put on a pair of jeans, a T-shirt, and a ball cap. She brushed her teeth, washed her face, grabbed her purse and tea, and got in her car.

"Half a tank of gas. He's filling it up."

It was a pretty drive, despite the fact she was heading east and the sun was in her eyes. Here she was on yet another crazy excursion, compliments of Austin. She wondered what the last five months would have been like if she hadn't met him. She wouldn't have a stalker, for sure. But she also wouldn't have had the adventures of a lifetime. She'd still be holed up at work and in her apartment, afraid to open herself to a guy. It was good to start with Austin. It wasn't romantic, but it was intimate. In a different way. She recognized it as a step toward healing and not seeing every man as a potential threat.

Her GPS took her directly to Walmart, and at seven o'clock, she found Austin sitting outside the store. He was playing guitar and singing for about fifty people. She smiled.

When he saw her, a lopsided grin spread across his face. He finished his song and posed for about thirty selfies before sauntering to her car. "Thanks for coming." He opened the back door, threw in his guitar, and jumped in the passenger seat, then leaned over to hug her.

"You got off the bus with your guitar?"

"Huh? No. I got bored and bought a cheap one in there. I had a song idea I wanted to get down. But then people started showing up and recognized me, so I did a little impromptu concert. Ya never know when you're going to make a fan. Don't ever blow an opportunity."

"Do you have a degree in marketing or something?"

"And what if I do?" he said, looking directly at her.

"Seriously?"

"Never underestimate me, my friend. I studied marketing for two years before I was offered a publishing deal and left school. I can always go back and get my degree. And I probably will. But, hey, seriously, thanks for coming to get me. I called every one of those jerks and they either ignored it, slept through it, or had their phones turned off. I'd have sat there for hours."

"It's okay. You'd have done it for me," Christine said, realizing she meant it. He probably would have.

"Yep, I would. Or at the very least, I'd have sent Matt," Austin said, his eyes gleaming.

Christine's stomach butterflied when she heard Matt's name. "That sounds more like it," she said. She drove out of the parking lot and onto the highway, heading toward Nashville.

"So, tell me. Who's your favorite singer?" Austin asked.

"Promise not to laugh."

"Depends. Are you going to say David Cassidy or the Bay City Rollers?"

"How would I even know them?" Christine asked.

"I don't know. Some people grow up listening to what their parents liked. Maybe your mom couldn't get enough of *The Partridge Family*," Austin said.

"That's the reason for who I'm going to name. My mom dragged me to every Willie Nelson concert she could find, and I fell in love with him and his music. He's the number one reason I followed a career in country music. From my early teens, I was determined to one day meet him and work with a music company in Nashville. I used to go to every country concert our local theatre offered. I even saw Willie play there once when he did a private benefit for the children's hospital."

"Why in the world would I ever find that funny?" Austin

asked, reaching into the back seat and grabbing his guitar. He strummed a chord and belted out the opening lines of "Blue Eyes Crying in the Rain."

When the song ended, Christine shook her head and looked at him. "Austin, that may be the most beautiful gift anyone has ever given me."

He followed that up with "Angel Flying Too Close to the Ground," "Crazy," and "On the Road Again." Then he said, "I'd love to keep going, but your gas tank is on E. We need to stop."

"Oh, shit. I was so busy listening I wasn't paying attention." They both held their breath as the gas light blinked and the mileage monitor dropped down to ten miles, then nine, skipping eight to go to seven.

"If I'd wanted to walk, I wouldn't have called you," Austin said, a grin teasing his face.

"I can't believe I did this. I've never run out of gas. I'm always diligent."

"I bet you are. You still have seven miles. Have faith."

With five miles left to go, they saw a sign for gas at an exit two miles away.

"We're going to make it," Austin said.

Christine stepped on the accelerator, thinking if she ran out near the exit, she could drift closer on momentum. When she saw the turnoff, they both exhaled.

Austin jumped out of the car before she could put it in park. He didn't think twice about pulling out his credit card and filling up her gas tank.

"I need a Starbucks," she said when he was back in the car.

Austin asked Siri to find them one, then preordered their drinks and sandwiches. Ten minutes later, they were seated at a table. Austin took Christine's ball cap, despite her complaints about unruly hair, and pulled it down low over his eyes.

"Embarrassed to be seen with me?" Christine asked.

"Trying to save your sweet ass from more harassment."

Christine reddened. She should have known he'd never be embarrassed to be seen with her. "Thank you."

"I've got your back. Never doubt that."

"I don't."

When the barista called the names Chandler and Monica, Austin got up to grab their drinks and breakfast sandwiches.

Christine pointed at the cups when he sat back down. "Chandler and Monica?"

"Did you want me to say Austin and Christine?"

"No, but Chandler and Monica?"

"Can you think of two people who describe us any better?"

She thought about Chandler's character on the TV show *Friends*. He's a hard worker, quirky, lovable, and a bit of a frat boy at heart. Then she thought about Monica's character: type A personality, a bit OCD, takes life too seriously most of the time.

"Fair assessment," she said. Austin asked for an update on her stalker situation and apologized yet again for what she was going through.

They finished their sandwiches and were standing to leave when two young men approached their table.

"Aren't you Austin Garrett?"

"I am."

"Dude, I'm a huge fan. I wasn't sure it was you in that ball cap. I love your music. Caught one of your shows in Knoxville last year. You nailed it." The guy pumped Austin's hand up and down in an exuberant handshake.

"Thanks."

"And this must be Ugly Christine," he said, letting go of Austin's hand and waving to Christine.

Christine's eyes narrowed.

"What?" Austin said. Christine reached for his arm to hold him back.

"No offense. It's what everyone on social media calls her. I thought it was, you know, like, your shtick or something."

"No offense? Are you freaking kidding me? There's no way to take that other than as offensive." Austin had raised his voice, which made Christine nervous. Other people were starting to stare.

"Austin, please don't make a scene. It's fine."

"It's not fine, Christine. It's not fine at all. Look at her. Does she look ugly to you?"

Christine visualized how she must look: hair askew, baggy jeans, an old T-shirt, and no makeup. "Now might not be the best time to ask that, Austin."

Austin took a step toward the guy. The guy had a good few inches in height on Austin and at least thirty pounds. Christine did not want this to become a fistfight.

The guy's friend stepped up and grabbed his friend's arm. He said, "Come on—let's go. I think you did enough damage here."

The guy pulled his arm out of his friend's grasp but didn't argue. He turned and walked away, leaving Austin and Christine standing there.

"I have totally screwed up your life, haven't I?" he asked her.

"It has become challenging. Are you ready to go?"

"Yeah, I'm ready."

They traveled the rest of the way in silence. No more Willie Nelson songs, no more funny stories, just two people ready to be out of the car.

"Am I taking you home or to the bus?" she asked when they came into Nashville.

"The bus. Same Kroger parking lot. Thanks."

Christine prayed she wouldn't see Matt. She looked bad and felt worse. She just wanted to go home. She pulled up beside the bus, grateful not to see anybody.

Austin leaned back in his seat and looked at her.

"Don't try to say anything, Austin. There's nothing to say."

"You have no idea what that did to me."

"Yeah, well. It didn't do me any favors, either."

He unbuckled his seat belt, leaned over, and gave her a hug and a light kiss on the lips. "I'm sorry."

"I know."

He got out of the car and walked onto the bus. Christine knew Matt was behind the bus door. So close. She shook her head, put her car in drive, and went home.

CHAPTER ELEVEN

Shortly after the drive home from Cookeville, Austin left for his parents' house in Clearwater, Florida. With his tour over and Thanksgiving a week away, it was a good time for him to relax on the beach. Christine was happy to see him take the time.

She fell back into a routine of going to the office, listening to songs, contacting people who might record those songs, and having quiet evenings at home. Occasionally, she'd grab a bite to eat or watch a movie with Julianna. Austin called and begged her to visit. Christine missed him, but there was no way she would go.

She didn't mind the break from her cyber haters. What she really missed was the chance of seeing Matt. She was tempted to text him and see if he wanted to grab a cup of coffee since coffee was safe and didn't automatically mean a date. The temptation was so strong she had written out the text a number of times before deleting it. "Respect Cait," she reminded herself. "She has first claim."

A WARM SPELL HIT NASHVILLE the Friday before Thanksgiving; the forecast said it would be sunny and seventy-five. It would probably be the last time until spring. Christine decided kebabs on the grill sounded like a perfect—and safe—evening.

She parked at Publix, opened her car door, hit the lock, and accidentally dropped her purse on the ground. She was bending down to pick up the contents when her elbow hit the door and it closed. "No!" She looked inside at her keys, which were still in the ignition. "This ruins a beautiful day," she said.

She had just pulled up the Uber app to get a ride home and grab her spare keys when she heard a motorcycle pulling up close to her. She loved motorcycles. There was something slightly dangerous and exciting about them. This guy, however, was getting way too close. He stopped beside her and she sensed a familiarity. When he took off his helmet and shook out his hair, her heart stopped.

Matt rode a motorcycle? How did she not know this?

"Hey, Christine. Everything okay?"

"No. I locked my keys in the car. I didn't know you rode a motorcycle."

"Yeah. I rarely have time to, but today was so beautiful I couldn't resist. No spare key?"

"I have one back at my apartment. Big help, huh?"

"Here." He reached behind his back and grabbed a helmet. "Put this on and I'll take you there." He took her purse and stuffed it into the back compartment.

"I can't ask you to do that," she said while thinking about how awesome it would be to slide behind him and hold on.

"You didn't. I offered. And you're already wearing a black leather jacket. It's like you were expecting me."

She put the helmet on and climbed behind him. It was a tight fit and she tried not to focus on how close her entire body was to his. But it was impossible. He was right there, nestled between her legs.

"Hold on tight."

She wrapped her arms around him and inhaled, breathing his scent into her lungs. She was worried she might rest her head on his back and drift into la-la land. Or worse, nibble his neck. She restrained herself.

"Do you want to go straight to your house or ride around for a bit?"

"Even need to ask? Ride around." *And hang on to you the whole way*, she thought.

"Done." He took off.

Between the bike's vibrations, having her body pressed against Matt's, and his musky smell mixed with the smell of leather, Christine was overwhelmed by the sensations coursing through her body. A warm whirlpool of emotion circled through her stomach. Matt didn't seem to have a goal in mind—he just drove. He passed the expensive homes in the town of Franklin, and Christine looked at them with longing. She'd never been a pretentious person, but working in an industry with so much wealth made it difficult not to dream. Matt handled the bike with expertise, even when the road started winding. His sexy factor went up three notches.

He circled back an hour later and took Christine to her apartment. She was pleasantly surprised that he remembered where she lived since he'd only been there once, when the limo dropped her off.

"Do you want to come up and get water or tea?" she asked.

"Sure."

He followed her to her apartment and stopped cold when she shrieked.

"What is it?"

She pointed to the note on her door. "With Austin gone, my stalker has been leaving me alone. This was unexpected."

"What's it say?"

Christine grabbed the note and read, "'Glad to see you're not following him to Florida. If you know what's good for you, you won't.'"

Matt followed her into the apartment.

"How many of these have you gotten?"

"I lost track. Six? Seven?"

"Geez, Christine. This is nothing to mess around with." Matt walked through the apartment, looking in the closets, under the bed, and in the bathroom. Christine heard him move the shower curtain aside. Her heart fluttered at his protecting her. He cared. Matt came back out to the living room.

"All clear. Are you doing anything to protect yourself?"

"I put more locks on my door, and I've made the police aware of it. But unfortunately, there's nothing anyone can do until the stalker makes a move."

"I can't believe you're going through this." He leaned against the counter, and she wanted to lean into him. She didn't.

"It's absolutely surreal. But let's not ruin this beautiful day by talking about it. Okay?"

"Okay. You have a nice place."

"Thanks. It's the perfect size for me. And I like the view." Christine grabbed two bottles of water and handed him one.

He walked out onto her deck. "A grill. Use it much?"

"I was going to pick up something to throw on it tonight. Want to join me? I do owe you." She'd blurted the words before giving them a second thought. Now, she held her breath waiting for his answer.

He glanced at his watch, and she knew right then that he had plans. Probably with Cait. "I'd love to, but I can't tonight."

"Rain check?" she said. It was becoming a curse word to her. He probably didn't even remember saying it before.

"We're racking those up, aren't we?"

Christine grabbed her spare car keys, and after finishing

their drinks, they got back on the bike. The red lights she had hated hitting every morning came as a blessing because they gave her a few more minutes with Matt. At the second stoplight, he dropped his right hand to her calf and gave it a squeeze. The gesture was sensual, and Christine felt it shoot from her calf to her thigh and higher.

They arrived at Publix ten minutes later, and Christine reluctantly released her grasp on him. She took off the helmet and yelped as the clasp got stuck in her hair. She tried to free it but ended up tangling it worse.

"Hold on. Let me help you before you rip it out," Matt said, taking off his own helmet.

Christine's body tingled from having him so close to her. He gently freed her hair. "You have beautiful hair."

She felt the tears coming and turned away. "Thank you." Her voice was a whisper. Had he really said those words? The unruly hair that had given her nicknames like Sasquatch was something Matt saw as beautiful.

"Let me get your purse." He reached into the back compartment while Christine composed herself. She hit the button on her key fob and the car door unlocked. She retrieved her keys and jangled them in the air.

"Success."

"Christine . . ."

She didn't know what he was going to say and wasn't sure she wanted to. On the one hand, he might say something like, "If things were different and I wasn't already seeing Cait . . ."

On the other, he might say, "I get the feeling you have a bit of a crush on me, and as flattered as I am, you need to know I don't feel the same way." She didn't want to risk hearing either, so she interrupted him.

"Thanks for being my knight in shining armor. I'll see you soon?"

"You're welcome. And I hope so."

Christine turned away and started walking toward the store while she could still hold her head high. She turned back and caught him watching her.

CHRISTINE HAD A WONDERFUL Thanksgiving with her parents before returning to Nashville for the short time before Christmas break. Her mother was savvy enough on social media to know what was going on, but Christine downplayed it, knowing it would accomplish nothing other than worrying her.

Christine kept up with Matt's Thanksgiving activities on socials. He'd posted a few photos with family. She learned something about his personal life through photos of his parents cooking a turkey, his niece and nephew climbing on his lap, and his family playing flag football. The way he posed for photos by embracing his younger relatives made her think he liked kids. She tucked that morsel into the back of her heart. And he was apparently an avid fly fisherman. A photo of him wearing waders in a stream with the caption "Doesn't get any better" surprised her. She realized she didn't know much about him personally. She also knew he'd returned to Nashville thanks to his post of a sunset taken from a plane. He wrote, "Heading home."

She hoped to run into him. She made sure she had makeup on and looked her best every time she went anywhere—the mall, Target, Starbucks, or Publix. No more sweats and oversized shirts. She calculated the odds to figure out where he might be, knowing exactly how ridiculous that seemed. Two weeks later, she still hadn't seen him.

She confessed to Julianna one night while chatting on the phone. "I want to run into him so badly, but it isn't happening. It's a small town. How hard can it be?"

"Call him and say you want to get together for coffee."

"And what would be my reason?"

"To wish him a Merry Christmas? Duh. It's coffee. You're not asking him to get naked."

"Is that an option?"

"It would be in my book. But I know you, and as long as Cait's in the picture, you won't do it."

"Ugh. I hate my moral standards sometimes."

"Yeah, they are a tad annoying."

"What do I say?" Christine asked.

"Ask if he's finished his shopping yet. Maybe you'll get a hint of where he'll be doing it and when," Julianna said.

"Okay. Maybe."

"No maybe. Just freaking do it."

"Okay. I'll talk to you later."

"Let me know how it goes."

Christine hit the END button and decided to practice what she was going to say. It came in the form of, "Hi, Matt. It's Christine. I, um, just, you know, wanted to say Happy Christmas. I mean, Merry Christmas." *Geez, Christine. How hard is it to say "Merry Christmas"?*

Christine heard giggling and realized her phone hadn't hung up . . . again. She put it back to her ear. "You're still there, aren't you?"

"Happy Christmas? Seriously?"

"My damn phone. I think something's wrong when I hit END. It hasn't been hanging up like it should."

"Maybe Santa will bring you a new phone for Christmas."

"I need one. Austin heard me singing the other day."

"That's ugly. You can't sing worth a damn."

"I know. And now, so does he."

"Call Matt. And it's *Merry* Christmas."

"It's a good thing I like you. I'll call you later."

Christine lost the nerve to call Matt but decided a quick text wouldn't hurt. She texted, *Hey, just wanted to say Merry Christmas.*

She stared at the unsent text for five minutes. She double-checked the spelling, made sure there was nothing weird about how it sounded, and then berated herself for it. It was a simple *Merry Christmas*. She hit SEND, then waited and waited.

Three hours later, she texted Julianna. *He never texted back.*

Julianna asked in a return text, *When did you send it?*

Three hours ago.

Another text came from Julianna: *Give him time. Maybe he's at the movies or something.*

With Cait!!

Patience, my friend.

The next morning, Christine was drinking her tea and wrapping some presents when her phone chimed. It was a text from Matt. *Hey, Christine. I forgot to charge my phone and it died. I got your text this morning. Whatcha doing?*

She texted back, *Wrapping gifts. You?*

Getting ready to go shopping.

Yeah, I have some more to buy, too. Where ya going?

Galleria. You?

Same. Christine had no intention of going to the mall but would make the trip if Matt was going to be there.

If I don't run into you, text me and let me know where you are. We can say Merry Christmas in person.

OK.

Christine took a screenshot of the conversation and sent it to Julianna with an *eeek!* Julianna sent back a thumbs-up.

Christine took a quick shower, put on makeup and her favorite sweater, and left for the mall. She said a quick prayer to the relationship fairy that Cait wouldn't be with him and pulled into a parking space.

Christine didn't want to seem too eager, feeling like a chance meeting would be better than texting him right away. She tried to think like a guy and figure out where he might be. Sporting goods store, Hallmark, or one of the anchor department stores? The mall was a big place, and it was impossible to know. Forty minutes later, she was still wandering around aimlessly, not really shopping but trying to pretend she was.

"Christine?" She heard Matt's voice and then saw him coming her way, shopping bags in hand.

"Hey. It looks like you've had a successful venture so far." She pointed to his bags.

Matt glanced down at her empty hands. "You haven't been so fortunate, huh?"

Christine berated herself. She should have purchased something so it looked like she was here for the intended purpose.

"Uh, yeah. I only have my mom left to shop for, and she's always the tough one. A bit picky in her choice of clothes," Christine said, embarrassed at the bald-faced lie.

"I was about to grab a bite to eat. Care to join me?"

"I'd love to," she said.

They grabbed a table at the crowded food court and opted for slices of pizza.

"You'd think I get enough pizza on the road. It seems to be what every venue serves. But honestly, I just love pizza."

"Who doesn't?" Christine said.

"Have you heard from Austin?" Matt asked.

"Some texts. He wants me to visit, but I think it's a very bad idea, so I said no."

"It's unfortunate you have to hide your relationship."

"No wonder famous people get tired of all the rumors in rag mags and on the internet. People can make up anything they want."

"I'm a big believer in freedom of speech, but there should be a limit to freedom of lies," Matt said.

"Agreed. Especially now that I'm on this side of it. Where are you spending the holidays?"

"Back home with my family in Ohio. My brother and sister are still living there, and my parents love it when we're all together. Typical Midwestern family. You?"

"I'll spend it with my folks as well. Central Pennsylvania. There's something calming about going home and letting Mommy and Daddy dote on me."

"So true. Austin doesn't hit the road until mid-January, so I'll probably stay until after the first."

Christine felt a surge of hope at the realization that Matt and Cait wouldn't be together on New Year's Eve. She knew it was ridiculous. What was one night? But it was an important night in a relationship, so maybe they weren't that serious.

They finished their lunch and stood to throw away their trash.

"Here. I'll take that." Matt reached out and took her empty plate and cup.

"Chivalry. Such an attractive trait."

"Remind me to throw away your trash more often," Matt said with a wink.

They left the food court together and came upon Santa posing for photos.

"Shall we?" Matt asked, a twinkle in his eye.

"Seriously?"

"Oh, why not? Let's send it to Austin and make his head spin."

"Why would his head spin over a photo with Santa?"

"It'll drive him crazy that I'm here with you."

"You're as bad as my stalkers. He doesn't care if we're at the mall together."

"Trust me, it'll drive him crazy."

"All the more reason to do it. He certainly drives us crazy enough," Christine said.

They got in line to sit on Santa's lap. When it was their turn, Christine took the right knee and Matt the left.

"Ho ho ho! Aren't you a nice-looking young couple?"

Christine smiled.

"We sure think so," Matt said.

"And what would you like for Christmas?"

"A nice picture with Santa to send to our good friend," Matt said.

"That's very nice of you," Santa said.

"Smile," the photographer said.

At the last second, Matt reached out and put his hand on Christine's knee. She knew it was meant as another dig at Austin, but she was still thrilled. When they stood, her knee felt warm where his hand had been.

They thanked Santa and waited for their picture to print. It was perfect. They looked like an adorable couple posing for their Christmas photo. Matt ordered two. Once they were printed, he took a picture and texted Austin: *Hey, buddy, we sure do miss you. Merry Christmas.*

The reply was immediate: *You're fired.*

You can't afford to fire me, Matt texted back.

You're right. Asshole. Merry Christmas. Give Chrissy a hug for me.

I'll go one better and give her a kiss, too.

Suck it, Matt, Austin texted.

"Well, that was fun," Matt said.

"You have an ornery streak."

"He brings it out in me. I'm so glad I got to see you. Unfortunately, I've got to run. Shopping is finished, so I have to get home, wrap gifts, and start packing."

"I'm glad we ran into each other," Christine said, wishing the moment could last a little longer.

"Me, too. Thanks for texting yesterday. It was good to hear from you. Have a great time at home," Matt said, reaching out for a hug. His bags gently hit her in the back as she returned his hug.

"Same back to you, Matt."

He pulled back and then surprised her by kissing her on the lips. He didn't linger, but it was definitely more than a peck.

"Oh," Christine said.

"Sorry," Matt said, looking away.

"For Austin?"

"Sure. We'll go with that. Merry Christmas, Christine. See you in the new year!" Matt gave a little wave and walked off through the mall.

Christine watched him for a minute before ducking into the candle store. She needed a few minutes to regain her composure and could always use a new fragrance.

She was driving home when her phone rang. She hit SPEAKER. "Hey, Austin."

"Hanging with Matt while I'm gone, huh?"

"We ran into each other at the mall."

"Looked a little cozier than that."

"Jealous, Austin?" Christine said.

"Should I be?"

Christine paused. How much should she tell him about her feelings for Matt? Was she ready to share that with Austin? She didn't want to make their friendship awkward.

"Are you jealous?" She decided to put it back in his court.

"Hell yeah. You won't come hang out with me."

"You're in Florida. Matt is down the road."

"I offered to get you a plane ticket. You said no."

"I'm enjoying this lack of notoriety right now. Nobody is saying horrible things about me. It's a welcome reprieve."

"Haters gonna hate. Can't let it stop you."

"For now, it's going to stop me. If I flew to Florida to visit you, it would be nonstop harassment. Can't do it, Austin. Not even for you."

"All right. Not going to bug you. You still with Matt?"

"No. Hey, Austin. Have you given any more thought to the

songs you're cutting for the next album?" Christine rolled her eyes at herself. She hated asking. Under normal circumstances, she wouldn't. But potentially losing her job was not normal circumstances.

"It's all I think about. I'll see you when I get back?"

"Of course," she said, letting it drop. He'd tell her when he was ready, and she didn't want to push too hard.

"And Canada is still on?"

"As of now, yes."

"On that positive note, I'm going to go. Merry Christmas, Chrissy."

"Merry Christmas, Austin."

She hit END and started singing "We Wish You a Merry Christmas." Christine heard a sound and looked down to see her phone was still connected. Austin was yelling her name.

"Austin?"

"The phone never hung up."

"Oh, God. Did you hear me singing?" Christine said, feeling the embarrassment heat her cheeks.

"I did. Again. Your phone doesn't always hang up," Austin said.

"I know. I need to make a trip to the cell store."

"Chrissy?"

"Yeah?"

"Don't give up your day job. You can't sing worth a shit."

"Tell me something I don't already know. Bye, Austin."

"Later."

Christine hit END, making sure the call was disconnected, and then belted out "Jingle Bells."

She lay in bed thinking about Matt. She allowed herself to have hope. He'd wanted a Christmas photo with her. And he'd kissed her, although chaste kissing was not unusual in the music industry. He hadn't mentioned needing to buy Cait a gift or seeing her over break or for New Year's Eve. Could their relationship be over? Maybe the new year would bring an opportunity for Christine to be honest and tell Matt how she felt. Was she ready? For the first time, she thought she might be. Canada might be a good time for true confessions. *Yes*, she thought. *That's when I'll come clean.*

THE HOLIDAY BREAK ALWAYS SEEMED so long when it started and so short when it ended. Christine and Julianna were back in the office on January 2, sharing stories from their holiday. Christine's had consisted of staying with her parents, baking cookies, and going to church. Julianna had gone to Aspen where her parents had a condo.

While Julianna took a quick call, Christine scanned her phone. She had taken a social media break over Christmas and found it refreshing. Now she did a quick catch-up. She stopped cold when she saw Phoebe's post from New Year's Eve.

Julianna ended her call. "Is something wrong? You just went pale."

Christine turned her phone around.

"You hadn't seen that already?" Julianna asked.

"Nope. Took a break from socials during the holiday."

"Oh, Christine. I assumed you knew. I'm sorry."

"And the way Phoebe writes it. 'What a sweetie I'm dating. Austin flew Matt, Cait, and I to Florida to chill on the beach and ring in the New Year. Here's to the four of us. Cheers.'"

Christine looked at the photo again. "The four of them look quite cozy."

"You knew Matt was dating her."

"He made it sound like he was spending New Year's in Ohio. Maybe this was last minute, I don't know. But he was kind of flirtatious at the mall before Christmas. And he didn't mention her at all. I guess I was hoping it was over."

"Did he post about New Year's with her?"

"No. I looked at his account before I saw Phoebe's and didn't see anything. He never posts about her. I thought about telling him how I feel when we're in Canada. Oh well. Back to square one."

"There's still no ring on it. Keep hope alive. I'm jealous that they were in Florida. I hate Nashville in winter. If it's going to be cold, I want snow. Snow, I love. We get ice," Julianna said.

"I'll send pictures," Christine said, dread in her voice.

"You're really dreading this Canada trip, aren't you?"

"Yes and no. I know social media is going to go crazy again, and I'm just not ready for it. Do you know an entire Facebook thread claimed Phoebe and Austin were fake dating as a cover for him dating me? It went on and on about how she and I have been friends for years and planned the whole thing to keep the haters away. They say it's why I'm not more upset about them being a couple and why I'm still being seen out with Austin."

"Yeah, Phoebe mentioned it," Julianna said.

"Why is the public so brutal? Would it be that awful if Austin fell for someone like me?"

"Yeah, someone who is smart, pretty, and fun. Horrible," Julianna said with an eye roll.

"If only the world could see me through your eyes."

"Your world does. It's only you who doesn't." Julianna got up, blew Christine a kiss, and walked out the door.

CHAPTER TWELVE

Austin was the direct support act on the Canadian tour, a more prestigious slot than opening. His name would be a major ticket seller, and his time slot lasted a full hour. He needed a bigger crew and more equipment, so he traveled with two buses and a truck. This meant there was more room to spread out; the crew was on one bus and Austin, Matt, Christine, and the band were on the other. They met in the Kroger parking lot at four o'clock on a Monday afternoon, and an hour later, Christine was already looking at a social feed about news of her trip to Canada with Austin.

"How in the hell do they always know where I am?" she asked.

"Sometimes I feel like someone injected a GPS under my skin," Austin said.

"We meet the bus in the same public parking lot every time. It doesn't take a genius to go online and figure out our schedule. Anyone can see us," Matt said.

"Good point," Christine said.

The downside to the long bus rides was boredom. Christine could only watch so many movies and read so many books before she started going stir-crazy. It took two long, laborious days to make it to the Canadian border. The crew bus had gotten ahead of them by an hour and Matt told them to wait at the border. Christine, Austin, and the band were watching a movie when they heard Matt yell.

"Shit. Are you freaking kidding me?" He'd been taking a nap, and when he emerged, his hair was sticking up as if he'd tried to pull it out.

"What's wrong?" Kennedy asked.

"Freaking Stan. I know I was very clear about not bringing anything that resembled a weapon, toy or otherwise. He brings a toy gun that looks so realistic they pulled them over at the border. Idiot had it sitting out on the front seat. Border patrol couldn't miss it. They're searching the entire bus and have him inside being questioned."

"What do they think we're going to do? Take over Canada with a squirt gun?" Austin asked.

"Doesn't matter. Other countries think we're all crazy gun-toting rednecks."

"That's just plain unfair. Only half of us are like that," Kennedy said.

"I swear I'm firing that asshole when we get back home. Brings a squirt gun. What the hell?" Matt said before crawling back into his bunk.

When they reached the border, it took Matt two hours to convince the authorities they weren't loaded down with weapons. Border officers did a complete search of both buses, confiscated the toy gun, and eventually sent everyone on their way.

"Sorry about this, Matt," Stan said.

"Don't talk to me for at least three days," Matt said, and walked away.

Jerk move that it was, Christine felt a little bad for Stan. He'd just been hired as a guitar tech to tune the guitars and make sure the players had the right one in their hands for each song.

"Am I going to get fired, Austin?" Stan asked.

"Not as long as my guitars are tuned right," he said, and lightly punched his shoulder. "Matt will chill out. He's got a lot on him. Just give him some space."

Back on the buses, they continued toward Niagara Falls. Once they'd arrived at the venue, Matt pulled everyone in for a quick meeting. "I know we're all excited to see the falls, but first we take care of business. You know the routine—I don't have to tell you. After—and *only* after—we are set up and ready to go is anyone allowed to sightsee. Got it?" Matt said.

"Got it," everyone replied.

Christine turned in a circle, surveying the stage. She let out a low whistle at what the production crews had already accomplished. The headliner's team had arrived the day before, and the large pieces of the puzzle were already assembled. Lighting units were erected, backdrops were ready, and risers had been set for the drummer and steel player. But Austin's guys still had work to do. Production was the first to arrive and the last to leave. They worked hard, and it was manual labor. There was no glitz and glamour to this side of the business. But when the set came together and the show worked to perfection, the crew celebrated. They high-fived each other, shared a celebratory drink, and gave compliments like, "The light show was perfect. Spot-on tonight."

"It takes a village, huh?" Christine said to Matt.

"Yep. If people only knew."

Hours later, with sound check complete and the show not until the next day, Matt checked everyone into the hotel and gave them the night off.

"I'm going to the view tower," Matt said. "It's open until ten. And I hear they have fireworks on Wednesdays. Anyone want to go?"

"I'll go," Christine said. If Matt said he was going to get in a barrel and ride the falls to the bottom, Christine would agree to go along. They might not survive, but she'd go out rolling around with Matt. Didn't sound all that bad.

"Yeah, I'll hitch a ride with ya," Austin said.

Alicia walked up and asked Matt about the exchange rate and how the percentages worked in Canada. "Do you mind if we go over that tomorrow? We're heading out to see the falls from the tower."

"Mind if I go?" Alicia asked.

"Not at all. Come on," Matt said. The four of them grabbed a cab and headed to the top of the tower.

Canada's Horseshoe Falls, one of the three waterfalls that make up Niagara Falls, was aptly named for its horseshoe shape. It exceeded 180 feet in height, and nearly 682,000 gallons of water gushed over it per second. At night, the water was lit with multi-colored lights in red, yellow, and blue. Bright lights from hotels and other buildings were visible on the shore behind it.

"That is one big mother-freaking wall of water," Austin said.

"I've never seen anything like it," Christine said.

"I'm a proud American, but I gotta give credit to the Maple Leaf folks. They win when it comes to Niagara Falls," Matt said.

"Let's take a picture. I brought a selfie stick," Alicia said, pulling it out from her cargo pants. "Squeeze in tight."

Christine had no problem with that part and planted herself between Matt and Austin. Alicia moved to Austin's other side, and they took half a dozen photos before they managed to get one that showed the falls below them.

"Are we good on photos?" Matt asked.

"I'd actually like one with you, Austin. I never take pics with you. You cool with that?" Alicia asked.

"Sure. You're only the best merch girl around."

"Most merch people are guys. Not sure it's a compliment."

"You're only the best merch *person* around. How's that?"

"Better," she said with an uncharacteristic blush.

Christine was impressed by how important Austin could make his staff feel. He'd clearly given Alicia a thrill.

As they posed for the photo, Christine wondered how she could ask for one with just Matt. The moment passed before she could figure it out.

They stayed for the fireworks. Bright lights burst over the falls, raining color down on the already colorful water.

"I didn't think it could get any better," Austin said.

"Yet it did," Christine said. Matt was behind her and she scooted back slightly, bumping into him. He put his hand on her waist. Neither moved away.

THE TOUR'S FIRST SHOW KICKED off with ear-shattering applause. The Canadian audience's appreciation was obvious from the first note. Nobody knew for sure if it was because they loved the music or because they were happy to have a reason to go outside and do something.

Austin convinced Christine to stop looking at social media, and she had done well for two days. But on day three, she couldn't resist. Sure enough, there were pictures of her along with nasty messages. "It's like they try to take bad pictures of me," she said when they were backstage in the dressing room. "These weren't even taken this week. They're posting old ones."

Austin had been playing her some songs and stopped in the middle of one. "Why do you pay attention to that shit?"

Christine shrugged. "I don't know. Why do we look at accidents when we pass them on the road? We all have the macabre in us. Or maybe I'm hoping not to see more mean posts. Or bad pictures. Like it will magically disappear."

"The only person you're hurting is yourself. It's time to tell that sixteen-year-old bully to shut the hell up," Austin said.

"You want me to go find the people who bullied me?"

"No, you're the bully."

"That doesn't make sense."

"It makes perfect sense. Those high school people are long gone, living their lives, working jobs, getting married, making babies, and going to PTA meetings or whatever they're doing. You're the one who continues to bully yourself, convincing yourself these cyberpeople have a right to tear you down. You have to squash that inner bitch and stand up to her."

"What would you know about it?" she said. She wanted to say, *Give me a break. You're the hottie everyone wants.* But she didn't.

Austin grabbed his backpack and pulled out an old, worn photo. "See that short, chubby kid right there? That's me in ninth grade. Seniors threw me in lockers every day. Girls blew me off when I tried to talk to them. I keep that photo to remind myself I'm not that guy anymore. When he rears his head, I squash him."

Christine stared at the photo, not believing her eyes.

"So how did you get past it?"

"I grew four inches in one summer. I started running and lifting weights. Walked into tenth grade a lean, mean, ready-to-fight machine. Bullying over."

"Well, Mr. Adonis-Since-High-School, that never happened to me." She gave him a head shake and an eye roll.

Austin stood up and reached out his hand to Christine. "Stand up."

"What? Why?"

"Just do it," he said. "Please." His eyes turned down like a puppy dog's.

She stood up.

He gently turned her around until her back was to him and they faced a full-length mirror. He let go of her arms. He spoke quietly, tenderly, and she couldn't deny the stirring she felt with his mouth so close to her ear. He reached up and ran his hands through her thick hair.

"You know what I see here? I see long, thick, wavy hair. Women spend thousands of dollars buying extensions to get hair like this. Yours is natural."

"But—"

He shushed her. "I'm not finished. He moved his hands to her hips, and she gasped. He gave a little squeeze. "You know what I see here?"

"Childbearing hips?" Her mom had always teased that the women in their family came with good childbearing hips, and she should be glad because giving birth would be less painful.

"Sexy hips. Hips that would give me an orgasm to last a week."

"Austin!"

"I'm telling it like it is, Chrissy."

"You date girls like Phoebe who have no hips."

"And there's nothing wrong with that. But, Chrissy, God made women in all shapes, and that's the beauty of it."

"Okay, but—"

"I'm not finished." He slowly moved his hands up to her waist. Then around to her tummy. Her stomach wasn't big, but it was soft. She hated sit-ups and crunches. Despised them. She'd never have a six-pack. She flinched when he touched it and tried to pull his hands away.

"Don't touch me there."

"Why?"

"'Cause I'm flabby." He pushed her hands away and reached around her again.

"You are not. And it's nice to touch a woman's stomach and not feel like my fingers might break."

Christine giggled. You could bounce a coin off Phoebe's body.

Christine looked up and saw Alicia pass by. She'd forgotten the door was wide open. Alicia made eye contact before quickly looking away.

"You're a beautiful woman," Austin said. "You can choose to believe what you read on social media, or you can believe me and friends like Julianna. But eventually, you just have to believe in yourself."

In the mirror, she made eye contact with Austin and felt her heart miss a beat at the sensuality of the moment. Then she caught movement in the hall and briefly saw Matt as he looked at them while closing the door.

"No!" she yelled, upset Matt had caught her in a compromising position with Austin. She headed for the door, wanting to explain, but Austin reached out for her arm, pulling her back.

"Yes. Now enough beating yourself up. If my fans, groupies, stalkers, or whatever they are want to bash you, let them. But no more bashing yourself. Okay?"

Christine didn't hear him. She was thinking about what she could say to Matt to fix what he'd just seen.

"Okay?" Austin said again.

"Huh? Yes, Okay."

"I'm not kidding, Chrissy. Tell me that from now on you'll believe in yourself."

She focused on Austin. "From now on, I'll believe in myself."

He nodded. "Bring it in for a hug, girl."

She turned around and hugged Austin. If any other guy had touched her the way Austin just had, she'd have slapped him. But this was Austin. A man who cared about her. And he'd accomplished what no male ever had. The hottest guy in country music had just convinced her she was attractive.

"Thank you," she said.

"You're welcome." He pulled back and looked at her. Then he kissed her cheek. His mouth moved to her neck and started to trail down to her chest.

Her mind ran to Matt and then started its endless circle: *Matt has a girlfriend, and Austin is right here, and I really like*

Austin, and if I can't have Matt, why not have a fling with Austin? But if Matt ends up single, will I have a chance with him if I sleep with Austin? And will sleeping with Austin make it awkward to work together, thus messing up my career? And . . . The same old record was spinning and spinning through her brain. No, this was a bad idea. It could ruin everything.

"You're dating Phoebe."

"We aren't exclusive."

"It's too weird, Austin. She's kind of my friend."

"I'm your friend," he said, still trailing kisses across her face, landing on her ear.

It took every ounce of resolve she had, but Christine knew she couldn't have sex with Austin if she was ever going to have a chance with Matt. Her body was on fire, throbbing, wanting to have sex right that minute. *It had been so long.* She sighed and pulled away.

"We can't. We have to show respect to our friends," she said.

"What friends?"

"Phoebe."

"That's one friend. Singular. And she's probably getting laid as we speak. I told you, we aren't exclusive. What other friend are you talking about?"

Christine needed to think fast. She couldn't say Matt. "Um, Julianna, of course. She and Phoebe are very close, and this would put her in the middle of us. That's not fair."

Austin stopped. "I want you."

"In this moment, I want you, too. But when the moment passes, I think we'll regret it."

"I won't."

"Okay, I think I'll regret it."

Austin stepped back. "Damn you, woman. You are unlike anyone I know."

"Is that good or bad?"

"Usually, it's good. Right now, not so much." He smiled to

show her he wasn't angry. "I'm going to take a cold shower." He hugged her, and she lightly kissed his cheek.

"I'm sorry."

"Don't ever apologize for telling a guy no when you don't want to do something. And if he doesn't listen, kick him in the nuts. Even me." He grabbed a towel and walked into the bathroom.

Christine stood in shock. She'd never told Austin her high school story. His words further validated that she'd done the right thing that night. She liked hearing that Austin had so much respect for women. Further proof that not all guys were like Bryan. Christine left the dressing room wondering what was wrong with her that she'd pass that up. One day, she'd either get a chance with Matt and be glad she'd said no to Austin or she'd forever regret turning him down. She prayed it was the former.

AFTER NIAGARA FALLS, THEY played to a packed house in Toronto and then made their way to Ottawa. Matt and Christine were standing by the buses discussing the day's logistics. Matt now depended on her to be his right hand. As much as she enjoyed song plugging, road life brought a different level of excitement. Christine loved hearing the songs come to life onstage and watching the audience react by singing every word to every song. And the screams of appreciation as each song ended were so loud you could barely hear the next song starting. No wonder artists lived for these moments. It was a high no drug could offer.

Christine wore a parka, knitted cap, scarf, and gloves. She was bundled up from head to toe trying to stay warm.

"How do I know it's you in there?" Matt asked, lightly pulling on her hood.

"I'm not one of those cool chicks who can wear barely any clothes in subzero temperatures and seem fine. I'd rather be warm than cute."

"Stupid chicks, if you ask me. And you are cute," Matt said. He rubbed his hands up and down her arms. She trembled. "Am I making you colder? That was supposed to help warm you up."

"Oh, you definitely warm me up. I mean, warmed me up."

"I'm okay with both."

Christine looked into his eyes. They were having a moment. Or at least she was. Christine usually focused on Matt's mouth, finding eye contact too personal. She was afraid he'd see how much she wanted him. Then again, staring at his mouth made her want to kiss it.

A commotion near the security gate at the top of the driveway brought her attention to two women in skintight clothing with tiny jackets and little scarves.

"See? Tell me they aren't freezing," Christine said, breaking eye contact.

One of the women was gesticulating wildly and flashing a laminate.

"God, what now?" Matt said. "Come on. Let's go see what's up."

Christine followed him halfway up the drive.

"Matt, wait a minute," Christine said, stopping him before the women saw them.

"What?"

"Do they look familiar to you?"

"Um, I don't think so." The two women shifted so they were facing Matt and Christine.

"Tell me I'm not seeing who I think I'm seeing," Matt said.

"You are," Christine said.

"Oh, Lord. Phoebe doesn't surprise me, but Cait? This isn't like her."

Christine's heart bottomed out. Of course he knew what she was and wasn't like. She was his girlfriend.

Phoebe saw them and started pointing and waving.

"Guess we can't run away, can we?" Matt asked.

"Nope."

"Let's go." They walked to the security gate and Phoebe launched into her complaint before Matt could say anything.

"Mr. Canada here won't let me in even though I have an All Access pass," Phoebe said.

Matt reached over and gave Cait a quick hug.

Christine looked away.

"We're using a different laminate on this tour. He didn't acknowledge it 'cause it's not an approved one on his list," Matt said.

"Oh. Well, he could have explained that," Phoebe said.

"I did," the security officer said, folding his arms and widening his stance. "Are you accepting responsibility for them?"

"If I have to," Matt said, causing Phoebe to huff and Cait to blush.

"I'll handle it. Thanks," Matt said to the security guard before turning to the ladies. "What are you doing here?"

"We wanted to surprise our men. Thought we'd come keep you warm," Phoebe said before turning to Christine. "Hello, Christine."

"Phoebe. Hey, Cait."

"Hey, Christine. So sorry to cause a problem," Cait said.

"We aren't causing any problems. Rent-a-cop there is causing the problem. We have every right to be here," Phoebe said.

Matt's cell phone dinged. "I've got to go deal with something. Christine, would you take them to production and get them some laminates?"

"Should we put our suitcases on the bus?" Phoebe asked.

"Suitcases? How long are you staying?" Matt asked.

"The rest of the tour," Phoebe said.

"Where's your car?"

"We don't have a car. We're not going to be some diesel sniffers across Canada. We're the girlfriends, not the fans. We'll ride the bus," Phoebe said.

Cait remained silent.

"Does Austin know about this?"

"It's a surprise," Phoebe said with a smile.

"The bus is pretty tight on space," Matt said.

"I'm sure Austin won't mind sharing his bunk with me, and you and Cait can cozy up in yours. If she can ride the bus, we can." Phoebe pointed directly at Christine.

Christine had a horrible vision of Matt and Cait sharing a bunk.

"Alrighty then. For now, take your luggage to production. Christine will show you where it is. Christine, I need to talk to you first." Matt pulled Christine to the side and spoke quietly. "I don't know what's going on here, but Austin will not be happy about this. I'm going to talk to him. Stall them as long as you can."

"Got it."

They returned to Phoebe and Cait.

"Christine will get you set up with credentials and then take you to catering for a bite to eat."

"Where's Austin? Can you take me to him?" Phoebe asked Matt.

"I don't know where he is at this exact moment. But it's not our tour, and you can't just walk around looking in rooms. Go with Christine, and I'll find him and catch up to you."

"Don't tell him I'm here. I want to surprise him."

"Cait, I'll see you in a bit," Matt said.

Christine suddenly wanted to be back in her apartment in Nashville. As far as she was concerned, this trip was over. She decided to book a flight home. That night, if possible.

"Come on. I'll get your laminates," she said, leading them down the driveway and into production. Then, once their laminates were secured on lanyards around their necks, Christine took them to catering.

"This looks awesome. I'm starved," Phoebe said. Catering had set up Italian cuisine. Bread, salad, and various types of pasta and sauces were arranged on a long table. Phoebe piled her plate high with pasta and meat sauce, pouring on the cheese. Christine watched, mouth agape. She couldn't imagine what Phoebe's workout routine looked like if she could eat like that.

"We didn't stop to eat," Cait said. "We were eager to get here."

"Yeah, we wanted to surprise our men, didn't we, Cait?"

"I hope they're okay with us showing up like this. When Phoebe called, I was reluctant. But she convinced me."

"I'm sure she did," Christine said, knowing how persistent Phoebe could be when she wanted her way.

"Do you need some help? Matt said you were taking on a big role, practically his assistant," Cait said.

Christine could not fathom spending time in a small production room with both Matt and Cait but was grinning on the inside that Matt had told his girlfriend about her.

Christine's phone rang and Matt's name popped up on the screen along with a photo of him she had snagged from Instagram. He was shirtless. She turned away, hoping Cait wouldn't see it.

"Excuse me." She left their table. "Matt. What's up?"

"Can you come to the bus? Austin is seriously PO'd."

"What can I do about that?"

"You have a calming effect on him," Matt said.

"In this situation? Yeah, good luck with that."

"Please," Matt pleaded.

Christine couldn't turn him down. "I'll try."

"I'll be back," she said to Phoebe and Cait.

Phoebe's mouth was full but she managed to get out, "If you see Austin, bring him here but don't tell him why."

Christine looked from Phoebe to Cait. Cait mouthed the words, "I'm sorry."

Christine found Matt outside the bus.

"He is hot! Mad as hell. Austin doesn't like women blind-siding him like this."

"I figured as much. Let's go talk to him."

She followed Matt onto the bus.

"I assume you didn't know about this?" Austin said, looking at Christine.

"How would I know?"

"She's your friend."

"Not really. And she's your girlfriend."

"Not really."

They laughed.

"God, why can't women just enjoy casual sex?" he asked, plopping down on the couch.

"Because we can't," Christine said, sitting beside him.

"Phoebe acts like she can. That's why this pisses me off so much. It's not her MO."

"Maybe she missed you," Christine said. "It's three more shows. Let her stay. It might chill out the people who are angry that I'm here."

Austin put his head in his hands. "It's just so high maintenance having someone out here."

"Suck it up, big boy. You can handle it," Christine said, lightly punching his shoulder.

Matt had been standing back, not saying much.

"What about you, Matt? Now you've got a chick out here, too," Austin said.

Matt looked at Christine. She returned his gaze. Neither said anything. Austin looked from one to the other, his eyes narrowing. "Or maybe you already had a woman out here?"

Christine didn't know if Matt heard Austin and chose to ignore him or if he'd missed the implication. Christine stayed silent.

Matt broke eye contact and turned to Austin. "Cait would never do this on her own. Phoebe convinced her."

"Well, she's here now."

"Yes, she is. We may as well accept it and deal with it. Look, Phoebe wanted it to be a surprise. They're in catering. Why don't you saunter in and act all surprised and happy? Unless you're ready to send her packing for good," Christine said.

"I guess I can act surprised and happy. But damn, this is like taking a paper bag lunch to a restaurant. I may have preferred something off the menu," Austin said.

"That is so crass," Christine said, shaking her head and frowning.

Austin's eyes crinkled as he laughed. "I know. Okay. Here goes nothing." Austin left the bus, leaving Matt and Christine alone.

"I guess it's going to get a bit crowded on here," Matt said.

"Maybe not. I'm going to book a flight out of here tonight or tomorrow."

"What? No. Why would you leave?"

"It's a chick thing. You wouldn't understand." There was no way in hell Christine was going to sit around on the bus watching Matt and Cait together, much less sleep knowing they were cuddling in a nearby bunk.

"I'm not that dense. I get it. Watching Austin and Phoebe hang all over each other can't be easy," Matt said.

Matt had no idea she was talking about seeing him with Cait. She figured that was better. She neither confirmed nor denied, choosing instead to be silent.

"It was good having you here," he said.

"Thanks. I enjoyed it." Matt walked over and hugged her. A nice, long hug. She didn't want to let go. When he left, part of her crumbled. She fell back on the couch and gave herself a moment to grieve her fantasy. Then she stood up, shook it off, grabbed her computer, and searched the travel sites. She found a flight that would get her back to Nashville that night and booked it.

She packed her bags, called a cab, and, without saying a word to anyone, headed for home.

As the flight attendant asked everyone to turn their phones to airplane mode, Austin texted her. *I can't believe you left without telling me.*

She texted back, *It was about to get very crowded on the bus.*

Kinda pissed me off. Not gonna lie.

I'm sorry. But this was about me. Not you.

Austin responded, *I'm the star. It's always about me.*

She laughed. *Thanks for adding levity to the moment.*

See you when I get home?

Of course. Enjoy the rest of Canada. Gotta go. Flight attendant glaring at me.

She switched her phone to airplane mode, glad this wasn't a Wi-Fi flight.

She needed the break.

CHAPTER THIRTEEN

"You just left?" Julianna asked on Monday morning.

"Yep."

"And didn't even say goodbye to him?"

"Austin? Nope."

"Is he pissed?" Julianna asked, sitting on the edge of Christine's desk, swinging her long legs.

"Yup."

"Can you string more than one word together?"

"I don't know what to tell you. They showed up with Phoebe acting all smug and demanding. And as sweet as Cait seems to be, and she really does seem sweet, I couldn't be on the bus with her and Matt in a bunk together. I'm strong, but not that strong."

"Does Matt have any idea how you feel about him?"

"No, and he's not going to."

Julianna raised her eyebrows.

"Julianna, I don't know what you're thinking about doing, but don't do it. I've never agreed with going after a guy who's already spoken for."

"They're just dating. He should know his options."

"If he wanted to go out with me, he'd ask."

"It's not that simple, Christine."

"Why not?"

"To begin with, you have a very odd relationship with his boss. Just because you haven't done the deed doesn't mean there isn't something between you and Austin that is strong. That would have to confuse another guy."

"Austin flirts with everyone, but . . ."

"But what?" Julianna asked.

"You could have a point about Matt being confused."

"What does that mean?"

Christine told Julianna about the moment in the dressing room that Matt witnessed. "But it was nothing," she insisted.

"Matt sees you in a dressing room with Austin, who happens to have his hands on you, and Matt is supposed to assume it's nothing?"

"Austin was just making a point," she insisted.

"The point being he thinks you're hot!"

"He never said that. Although . . ."

"What?"

"He kissed me again. And wanted to do more."

"Wait. What? Did you?"

"No, although I was tempted. He is a hell of a kisser," Christine said, touching her lips.

"Why didn't you, then? God knows you need it."

"'Cause it would close the door on Matt and me."

"You're really choosing an outside chance with Matt over Austin?"

"Sex with Austin would be amazing. But do I see us married with kids? No. And I want that. Having sex with him would screw up a great friendship and working relationship. And Matt doesn't seem like the type of guy to take sloppy seconds after Austin."

"I haven't heard that term since high school," Julianna said.

"So, I'm passing on Mr. Right Now in the hopes of getting Mr. Right."

Julianna stood to leave. "Did you ever think you'd be stuck between two men like Austin and Matt?"

"Not in a million years."

"Just play it smart, Christine. You could end up with neither."

Julianna's words lingered long after she left Christine's office.

CHRISTINE HADN'T HEARD FROM Austin in a week. She knew he was mad, so she gave him his space. When he did call, it was to tell her he was being interviewed on a national radio show.

"You've got to listen, Chrissy."

"You're not mad at me anymore?" she asked.

"I still think it was a lame thing to do, but no, I'm not mad anymore."

"Okay, I'll listen. What time?"

"Tomorrow at six."

"In the morning?" Christine's voice rose. She was not a morning person.

"Yep. Morning shows have the biggest audience. Set your alarm."

Christine set it for exactly five minutes before six, not willing to get up one second before. The morning team consisted of Billy and Carly.

"Welcome to our new studio," Billy said.

"This is nice. You used to kind of be in a . . ." Austin said.

"Dump?" Carly said.

"Ha. Yeah, thanks. I didn't really want to say it. But this is state of the art. Everything is so clean. And there are so many microphones."

"It works well for having guests. Especially when we have a band in here. They used to have to share microphones. How awkward, right?" Billy said.

"Definitely awkward. Nobody enjoys sharing a mic," Austin said.

"You've had three number one hits and just came off a Canadian tour. Then there's the award nominations, TV shows, and you recently won a CMA award. It's been a big couple of years for you," Carly said.

"Yeah, it has. I'm crazy fortunate. But there's a lot left to do."

"Let's talk about the situation surrounding your personal life," Billy said.

"What situation?"

"He's being coy," Billy said.

"Like a fish," Carly said.

"So?" Billy asked.

"I'm not sure what you're asking me," Austin said.

Billy hit a loud buzzer, causing Austin to jump.

"What the—"

"Don't say it!" Carly said.

"What was that noise for?" Austin asked.

"It's a dodge buzzer. You're dodging the question. Every time that happens, we hit the buzzer."

"We had one artist, who will remain nameless, where we had to hit the buzzer so much it got stuck," Carly said.

"Buzzed through the entire interview. Was pretty horrible actually," Billy said.

"Now back to the question," Carly said.

"I haven't really heard a question yet," Austin said.

"Don't you follow social media?" Carly asked.

"Sure I do."

"He's going to make us just ask it outright. Okay. Tell us about Christine," Billy said.

"Ah, Chrissy."

"What is she to you?" Carly asked.

"Chrissy is very special to me. She's a friend, a confidante, and a colleague all wrapped up in one."

"And Phoebe?" Billy asked.

"Phoebe and I hang out from time to time," Austin said.

"Is Phoebe your girlfriend?" Carly asked.

"I don't have time for a girlfriend."

Billy hit the buzzer.

"Geez. It's early, dude. Quit hitting that thing," Austin said.

"Quit dodging questions," Carly said with a singsong voice.

"I'm not. My world doesn't allow for a girlfriend right now. I'm always on the go. The idea of leaving a woman behind isn't appealing. Now isn't the time for personal relationships."

"So, Phoebe isn't your girlfriend?"

"No."

"And Chrissy isn't your girlfriend?"

"Can we talk about my music?" Austin said. Christine could tell he was getting angry. His words were clipped and his voice had lowered.

Someone hit the buzzer again.

"He didn't answer the question," Carly said.

"I noticed," Billy said.

"Seriously?" Austin asked.

Christine was yelling at the radio. "Tell them I'm not your girlfriend. Please, Austin. For the love of God, tell them."

He didn't tell them and the interview continued.

"Okay, okay. About your next album. How do you follow up an album that had three number one singles? Are you worried about the sophomore album curse?" Billy asked.

"No, not really. I have some great friends who are incredible songwriters, and I'm taking them on the road and writing with them. And now that I'm a bit of a proven entity, A-list writers are sending me their best songs. So, I have a lot to choose from. I also have the best song plugger in all of Nashville. I'm excited about taking this album to the next level."

"The best song plugger being Christine?" Billy asked.

"Yes."

The interview went on for another five minutes, all questions about Austin's music and touring. It was over by six fifteen. Christine tried to fall back to sleep but couldn't. Austin had the chance to put an end to it and get rid of her stalker and her cyberbullies. Instead, he egged it on. She got ready and left for work. Listening to music always made her feel better, and after that interview, she definitely needed something to make her feel better.

She arrived at work and was digging into her day when Rick stopped down.

"How's it going with Austin picking a song? Preferably one with our publishing company?"

Christine felt her chest constrict. Her breathing shallowed as the heaviness set in. Classic panic attack.

"I'm working on it. He's narrowed it down to three songs. Two are ours, one is with another publisher."

"We need his next single, Christine." Rick sat back, arms crossed against his chest.

"I know, Rick. I'm doing the best I can. He's an artist. He's going to pick the song that's best for him whether it's mine or not."

"I realize that, Christine. But you can sway him. One song only does so much for us for so long. 'Promises to Me' was big, but we need more of those."

"Right. I'll check with him again tonight. Is that why you stopped down?" Christine was trying to keep her breathing even, not wanting the starting panic attack to escalate into a full-blown one.

"No. We just got information that a big artist is looking for a classic country song. Something that may have been written years ago that he could make relevant to today's sound. Weren't you listening to some of the older songs recently? Going back as far as cassettes?"

"Yes. I took a box of them home one weekend. Would you like me to recommend something?"

"Is the box still at your apartment?"

"It is."

"Hmmm . . ."

"I should have brought it back, but nobody has touched those songs in years, and I don't have a cassette player here. I've been slowly making my way through them in the evenings. I've taken notes on every song. I'll bring them in tomorrow."

"We need them here by this afternoon. I'm going to split them up between you and two other pluggers, and we need to move fast. Superstars don't always come calling, and I want to have something of quality in their hands tonight. Can you run home and get them?" Rick stood up and started for the door.

"Sure. I'll leave right now." Christine grabbed her purse and came around her desk, following him.

"Thank you. And by the way, nice press in Austin's interview this morning. Not sure what's going on with the two of you, but every time he mentions you, it gives our company a boost. We appreciate it."

"Absolutely, sir. Glad to help," Christine said, thinking how the interview might have helped the company but most likely hurt her.

Her cell phone chimed in a text from Phoebe: *Nice. Sounds like he's more into you than he is into me. And we know that's not true 'cause I woke up in his bed this morning. How do you always manage to steal the show?*

Christine felt faint. Hadn't her stalker said the same thing? It couldn't be. She wouldn't. Would she? She stopped her mind from going in that direction and deleted the text.

On the way to her apartment, Austin called. She wished she could just tell him the truth, that she needed him to cut one of her songs to save her job and the publishing company, but she'd never put that kind of pressure on him.

"Hey, Austin. What's up?"

"Chrissy, girl. Did you listen to my interview?"

"I did. I heard you give all my haters plenty of ammunition against me," she said, not feeling in a nice mood.

"What are you talking about?"

"Why didn't you just tell them I'm not your girlfriend?"

She arrived at her apartment, threw the car in park, grabbed her phone off its holder, and walked to her door. She unlocked all three locks and saw a piece of paper flutter to the ground. She bent to pick it up, figuring it was an advertisement until she saw the handwriting. She recognized it. She'd received enough notes from the same person.

Nice interview. You're not very smart to keep this relationship going. I obviously know where you live, what kind of car you drive, and where you are at all times. Just saying . . .

Christine squeezed her eyes shut, crumpled the note, thought better of it, straightened it out, and went into her apartment.

"Chrissy? What's wrong? Are you still there?"

She heard Austin yelling and put the phone on speaker. "Yes, yes, I'm here. Can I talk to you later? I'm a bit busy."

"Whatcha busy doing?"

Her tone took on a hint of frustration. "Austin, I'll call you back. I just got home and have to be back at the office within the hour. I just want to have a cup of tea and relax for a few."

"Yeah, yeah. Sure. Talk later."

She hung up the phone, her chest tightening again. She knew she needed to let go of her stress, but getting angry with Austin wouldn't help. It wasn't his fault. Her relationship with Austin was precious and she didn't want to risk it by telling him about

Rick. She didn't want to upset him by telling him about receiving another note from her hater, either. She slammed her hands on the kitchen counter and yelled at the walls. "Argh! What's wrong? I'll tell you what's wrong. I need you to freaking cut one of my songs so I can keep my job and Rick can stop putting fucking pressure on me to save the company. I need you to stop talking about me on the radio so I don't come home to threatening letters from your stalkers. I need my life to just get back to the way it used to be. Boring but easy. I'm okay being boring. I liiiikke being boring."

She stood for a minute, leaning against the sink, letting her breathing return to normal. As a creature of habit who found solace in her routine, she reached into the cabinet for a mug, grabbed a tea bag, poured some water over it, and popped it in the microwave. Two minutes later, she added some cream and sugar and took it to her living room. She sat on the couch, putting her feet up on the glass coffee table. It had been her grandmother's, and she felt safe when she was touching it. She imagined her grandmother had done the same thing, many times, maybe even when she was happy to be home, relaxing. But Christine couldn't relax. Not with Rick's reminder that the company's success was resting on her shoulders and another note from her stalker. She closed her eyes, sipped her tea, and tried to find her happy place.

A knock on the door startled her. A shriek escaped her lips. Nobody ever showed up to Christine's apartment unannounced. Her stalker?

She walked to the door and looked out the peephole. "Austin?" She had barely cracked the door when he barged in.

"What the fuck, Christine? Why didn't you tell me?" His face was red, his eyes narrow, his lips pursed. She'd never seen him mad at her.

"Tell you what?"

"That you needed me to cut your song to save your fucking job. Seriously?"

"Oh shit. My phone didn't hang up, did it?" She looked at her phone and saw it was still connected. She hit DISCONNECT twice and it hung up.

"Nope. And you got another note from your stalker. What the hell? We were on the phone and you couldn't have just told me all this?"

"Austin, I'd never pressure you to cut a song that wasn't the right one for you. You know me better than that." She sat on the couch and pointed to a nearby chair. He walked over to it and plopped down.

"But you could have told me. I'd do you that favor. Every song you bring me is great."

"But I wanted you to choose it because it's what you wanted to cut. Not because you wanted to help me."

Austin ran his hands through his hair. "I was calling to tell you I'd made a decision. I'm not just cutting one of yours—I'm doing both of them. And they will be my next two singles."

Christine slumped back. Relief mingled with anxiety. How did she know he was telling the truth? He could just be saying that after he'd heard what she said.

"I know that look, Chrissy girl. I can show you an email I sent my producer and record label two hours ago telling them what I was cutting and how I wanted them to be singles."

"Two hours? You waited two hours to tell me?" She sat up and slammed her arms down.

"Damn, woman. Does anything make you happy or are you just pissed at me for anything right now?"

She laughed. And then laughed more. Then she couldn't stop laughing. Then she started crying.

"What the hell is happening right now?" Austin said, walking over to sit down beside her. He put his arm around her and she leaned into him.

"I've been carrying this stress about the company for so long.

I didn't want to tell you, and at the same time, you're the only one who can help me." She looked up at him, knowing her eyes and nose looked red and her face was a wreck. She looked away.

"Chrissy, I need you to trust me. If they weren't the right songs, I'd have been honest with you. We could have figured out another solution together. There are album cuts, digital releases, and other ways to help. But they *are* the best songs." He tilted her head up so she was looking at him. "You need to trust me, okay?"

She nodded. "Okay."

"Now let me see this letter. This shit has got to stop."

"I feel so vulnerable. Whoever it is could get to me at any time."

"Matt mentioned having an idea he wanted to talk to you about. I think it had to do with this whole debacle. I'll have him reach out to you."

Christine's mood lightened. Matt had talked about her. He had an idea for her. She felt tingly and worked to suppress her excitement so Austin wouldn't pick up on any vibes.

"I'm open to any idea, but Austin, the main way for me to stay safe is to distance myself from you," Christine said, her hand reaching out for his arm.

"Uh-uh. No. I don't buy that." Austin backed away, shaking his head.

"We have to. Just for a while. Let's see if this person will back off before it gets any worse. Or more dangerous."

"You're scared." It was a statement, not a question.

"I am."

"I don't want you to be scared," he said, reaching for her. She moved in and hugged him.

"I can't keep living this way."

He backed away from her. "So what exactly does this mean? I cut your songs and you're dropping me?"

"Of course not. I'll still be working with you. I just can't hang out with you or go on the road with you. We need to keep it professional. It worked the last time and is the only thing that has worked."

Her phone alarm went off, reminding her she was supposed to be back at the office.

"Oh, crap. I'm late. I've got to run, but thanks so much for coming by. I'm sorry you heard my rant, but I'm glad we cleared the air. About that and needing some time apart."

"Your rant explained some of your moodiness when we discussed music. I didn't realize that every day I put off making a decision was another day of stress for you. I respect that you didn't want to tell me why, and it means a lot that our friendship means more to you than our business relationship."

"It does."

He held up a finger, shushing her. "But you need to be honest with me. Okay?"

"Okay. You made my day brighter. Heck, my year. I just wish things could be different. That there wasn't this crazy person threatening me."

"Me, too. I've never had anything like this happen. I mean, I have my share of fanatic fans but never someone who wished another person harm. It's insanity."

"Yes, it is. And unfortunately, it's directed at me. Anyway, I've got to get these cassettes to Rick or he really will fire me. But we'll talk. Over the phone, through text, about business. That's the best I can offer for now."

"Then it's what I'll have to accept, for now."

Austin grabbed the box of cassettes and they left her apartment. He put it in Christine's back seat and gave her a quick hug goodbye before going to his car. Christine drove back to work feeling both lighter than she'd felt in a long time and sadder than she'd felt in a long time. This stalker was ruining their friendship yet again. Christine felt a new determination to find out who it was. She called Rick and gave him the good news. He was ecstatic, thanked her, and told her he'd extend his line of credit until the songs paid off, which they would. She'd done it. She'd saved the company.

CHAPTER FOURTEEN

Two days later, Christine texted Matt about the idea Austin had mentioned. Maybe it was something that could help. And it was an excuse to text him.

Hey. Austin mentioned you had an idea to help with my stalker. Care to share? she wrote.

He texted back, *I study tae kwon do and hapkido. Maybe you should take the beginners' course.*

Christine's mind raced at the idea of spending quality time with Matt while learning how to defend herself at the same time. Two birds, one stone.

Sounds interesting. I've never been athletic, she texted.

You don't need to be. At least not in the way you're thinking. Beginner class meets Monday and Thursday evenings. Let me know and I can meet you there.

You wouldn't normally be there?

No, I'm in an advanced class. But I can get you started. I sometimes help teach the beginner class when I'm in town.

How about this Thursday?

I can do that one. I'll share the contact information and meet you there around 6:30.

TY, Matt, she wrote.

You got it.

CHRISTINE MET MATT AT THE *DOJANG*, which she learned meant "training place for Korean martial arts." He was in his white uniform with a brown belt tied around his waist and had no shoes on his bare feet. "Sexy," she said under her breath.

"Huh?" Matt asked.

"Oh, um. Nothing. Just talking to myself. How did I not know you do this?"

"I keep it pretty private. We have some loaner uniforms, always washed and clean, that you can use tonight. I'll help you get the belt tied once you change."

"Okay." She was nervous and took a deep breath before painting a smile on her face.

"It'll be great," Matt said.

"Uh-huh. You'll get to see I have two left feet."

"We all do at first. Anything you're overly concerned about?" Matt asked.

"Kind of. I'm not really allowed to do any contact sports. I only have one kidney. And if I were to get kicked or punched in the other one, it could kill me."

"Oh. Yeah, that is a concern. Were you born with only one? My aunt was."

"No. I gave my left one to my cousin."

"Damn. You're a living organ donor?"

"I am." Christine smiled. She didn't share the information with many people because it was so personal. But she couldn't hide her pride that she'd saved a life.

"You just keep getting more impressive. I'll talk to Master Joe about putting together a program that focuses on you being able to defend yourself more than you being taught to spar."

"Thank you, Matt." Christine's smile took over her whole face. God, she liked him. So much.

Christine stepped into the ladies' room, changed into the uniform, and came back out. She held up the long belt. "What do I do with this?"

"I can show you or I can try to explain how to tie it," Matt said.

"Might be better if you show me," she said, relishing the thought of his hands on her.

Matt told her to turn around. When she did, he wrapped his arms around her, causing her to shiver.

"Are you cold?"

"Just a bit chilled after changing clothes," she lied.

"It'll warm up once we start working out." He stood behind her, explaining how to tie the belt while doing it for her.

She wasn't listening to a word. Instead, she focused on the way his hands moved from her front to her back as he wound the long belt around her before tying it in a square knot at her navel.

"There. You're ready."

Christine looked around the room and realized they weren't alone. She'd been so focused on the physical contact with Matt that she hadn't seen a dozen white and yellow belts come in. Their ages surprised her. She'd expected a bunch of teenagers and twentysomethings. But there were kids as young as seven and some adults with gray hair, clearly in their fifties and sixties. And the women outnumbered the men. Another surprise.

The instructor, a fifth-degree black belt named Master Joe, told them to line up and they instantly created three rows of four. Matt led Christine to the back of the room, and she took her place at the end of the last line. First, they all bowed in. Then they did a warm-up that was rather simple, with some twists and stretches.

Christine wasn't overly limber, but she didn't struggle to do what she was told, either. She was the only new student, and when they broke up into groups, Joe asked Matt to work with her on the basics. When he explained how she should hold her fist to avoid breaking her fingers when she punched, he stood behind her and wrapped his right arm around her right side, closing his hand over her fist. She melted back into him. For a few seconds, neither of them moved. She forgot anyone else was in the room. His breath was near her ear, and she closed her eyes. Her hand unrolled and she interlocked her fingers with his.

"Um, Christine . . ."

"Oh, God. I'm so sorry." Her face turned pink and she tried to pull away from him, but he held her steady.

"If only there wasn't a room full of people, huh?" he said. "Now make that fist again."

She did, and he explained how to punch without hurting herself. She wanted to ask what he meant about the room full of people, but he moved on to showing her a kick.

"It's called a front snap kick, and the power comes when you snap out from your knee. But you need to strike with the ball of the foot so you don't break your toes."

"So far, it sounds like the only person I may hurt is myself," Christine said, giving a little huff.

"I never thought of it that way. But yeah, if you do it wrong, you can seriously hurt yourself."

He put her hand on his shoulder while he held her leg up, gently grabbing her under her thigh so she could practice snapping her leg in a kick. She imagined his hand sliding up and over a few inches. The delicious thought caused her to stop kicking. Her mind wasn't on self-defense.

"Is your leg tired? We can take a break," Matt said.

"Huh? Oh, no. I, um, just wanted to make sure I was doing it right."

"You're doing great."

She tried to concentrate on everything he was teaching her, but her focus was on how he touched her. At this rate, she'd remember so little it would take years to get past the white belt.

Christine didn't ever want this lesson to stop. Who knew martial arts could be so intimate?

When the instructor called for the class to line up again, they did a short cooldown before bowing out. Christine felt breathless, and it wasn't from the workout.

Matt was staying for the advanced class. Christine thought about watching but wasn't sure she was supposed to, so she made her exit.

"Thank you so much. This will be helpful."

"Think about joining the class for a three-month trial period. If you like it, you can keep going. If not, you haven't committed for too long. And anytime you need extra help, let me know. I'll be happy to do some instruction on the side."

Christine's body tingled.

"I will." She gave him a quick hug goodbye, and when she pulled away, he pulled her back for a longer hug.

"Please be careful, Christine." He kissed the side of her head and went to line up for his class.

Over a much-needed spaghetti dinner with Julianna, Christine filled her in. "When he wrapped his arms around me to tie my belt, I thought I'd faint. And when he showed me how to punch and kick, he touched me from my shoulder to my thigh. His hand was so close to being, you know, right there. And I wanted it to be. In the middle of a damn gym, I was practically having sex with him in my mind."

"Austin makes out with you, and you can still say no. Matt touches you and you're Jell-O."

"The heart wants what the heart wants."

"So true. Why don't you just go for it? He's clearly flirting."

"Everyone in our industry flirts with everyone. We're a business based on making people feel something. We live our lives on emotion. Music makes people feel good, or sad, which sometimes feels good. How many times have we heard someone say, 'He flirts with me so I thought he was interested. How embarrassing when he put me in the friend zone after I tried for more'?"

"Good point. We've all been on one side of that or the other. I guess you just go for it and see."

"Too risky until I get a better feel for it. But I can't wait until my next class. I want to make him proud." Christine took a bite of her garlic bread and gave Julianna a thumbs-up. It was that good.

"I'm sure you will. You seem to be feeling better in general," Julianna said.

"I am. Social media has been quiet, and I've been staying away from Austin, so I'm not giving them ammo. But it leads me to believe the person who left the notes is probably behind most of the harassment. Who knows? Maybe she has a dozen screen names and makes it seem like everyone hates me when it's just her. The cops have no clues to go on. I called again today, but they just said they're working on it and to keep updating them."

"People open multiple accounts all the time," Julianna said. "You're one strong woman for putting up with this. And now learning how to defend yourself in case it gets worse. Damn."

Christine thought about how anger was making her stronger. When she felt sad and defeated, she was weak. She'd gotten mad the night she was assaulted in high school, and as scared as she was then, her anger was stronger. She'd struck out instead of cowering. That feeling was coming back. The more this unknown person attacked her, the madder she got. The madder she got, the stronger she felt. Nobody had a right to come into her home and make her scared in the one place where she should feel safe.

In general, she wasn't a fan of anger; she felt it was better to talk things through and let calm prevail. But in this case, she'd been pushed to her limits.

"You never know until it happens to you."

CLASS AFTER CLASS AFTER CLASS, Matt and Master Joe worked with Christine on self-defense. She had not only signed up for the three-month course and taken every class available to a beginner but also paid for private instruction. She needed to fast-track her progress. Her private classes with Joe and Matt were her favorites. Tonight, they were doing their best to challenge her.

Master Joe grabbed her from behind in a choke hold. While he wasn't really choking her, his grip wasn't light either. Her stomach tightened as a slight panic took over.

"Come on, Christine. You know what to do," Matt said. He was standing beside her, watching each move she made.

She raised her right arm, spun her body toward Master Joe, and brought her arm under both of Joe's arms, pinning them in the crook of her elbow. She raised her knee to his groin without touching him. Joe faked like he'd been hit and bent forward. She raised her knee to his face.

"Perfect," Matt said. He patted her on the back, and she beamed.

"But you can't hesitate. You must move fast. If an attacker gets any indication you're going to fight back, they'll tighten their grip. The element of surprise is your advantage," Joe said.

Christine nodded. She had hesitated. Mere seconds could be the difference between life and death.

"Let's try another one," Matt said. He put her in a mugger's hold. He held her tightly from behind with one hand over her mouth, the other arm across her torso. She couldn't move backward or forward. But she could move side to side, which is what she'd been taught to do.

She stepped to the left, forcing him to loosen his grasp, and swung her right fist back into his groin. She didn't mean to make contact, but she was still a beginner and hadn't learned complete control of her movements. Matt dropped to his knees, cupping his groin.

Master Joe roared. "Now you know it works. And Matt knows not to forget his athletic cup."

Matt rolled on the floor, groaning. Christine dropped down next to him and put her hand over his. Now her hand was one hand away from holding his groin.

"Need me to leave you two alone for a minute?" Joe said, his eyes twinkling.

Christine pulled her hand back.

Matt moaned. "I couldn't do anything sexual if I tried right now."

"I'm so sorry, Matt," Christine said.

"Nope. Don't apologize. I will remember to wear a cup next time. Great execution there, Christine." He sat up and took some deep breaths. "I think I'll call it a night for this lesson."

Christine felt horrible. She still felt bad when she got home and texted him an apology: *I'm sorry for not having better control.*

Matt texted back. *All good. But the next time you touch me there, be gentle.* He included a laughing emoji.

Christine's eyes flew open. She read the text and reread it. Was he teasing? Or was he giving her a hint? And how could she know the difference? The laughing emoji made her think he was just joking with her.

She sent back a winky face and texted, *No guarantees!*

If he could be fun, so could she.

THE BOX OF OLD CASSETTES HAD proved to have some real gems. Not only had she sent some to Austin, but she had also discovered a song that would be great for Lynda. She'd had to convince her to try it.

"It's very Loretta Lynn," Lynda had argued.

"Speed it up, add your electric guitar, and make it yours. See if you don't hear it like I am," Christine said.

Lynda took her advice and performed it at a few shows around town. She hadn't recorded it yet, but there was already a buzz on it running through the Nashville community. Getting a nod from your creative peers meant everything to an artist. Whenever she performed the song, Lynda credited Christine for finding it and convincing her to play it. It wasn't often the non-creative team got recognition, but it was a gift when they did.

WHEN AUSTIN'S NEW TOUR STARTED, he called Christine and asked her to go back on the road with him.

"Austin, how can you ask me that?"

"How can I not?"

"Does my safety mean nothing to you?"

"It means everything to me. I've thought a lot about it, and I don't want to leave you behind in Nashville. You'll be safer moving around the country with me than staying home."

"I doubt that," Christine said, giving a huff.

"Whoever it is clearly lives in Nashville. Nobody will touch you out on tour. I'll make sure of it. I have security around me at all times at the venues." Austin's tone had become pleading.

"Nothing has happened since the note weeks ago. If I stay away from you, I'm safe. Going out on the road doesn't feel like the right decision."

"Just one run. The first week. We can listen to new songs,

and you can pitch me anything you want. Maybe I'll cut three of yours," Austin said, a teasing lilt to his voice.

"Now you're playing dirty. You know too much."

"Yep, and I will use it to my advantage," Austin said.

He had a point about her stalker being in Nashville. She'd never received one note or threat anywhere outside of Nashville. She probably was safer on tour.

"I CAN'T BELIEVE YOU'RE CONSIDERING IT," Julianna said later that afternoon, kicking back in Christine's office.

"I'm nuts, right?"

"Pretty much. You know the crazies will cyberbully you again. You'll be trending. Again."

"I know. But I feel like flipping the bird to the haters. I'm tired of living in fear. Hell, I haven't even gone back to the Bluebird in months. And I love songwriters' nights. Maybe if I show strength, they'll back off."

"You believe that?" Julianna asked.

"I have to. Otherwise, I would never leave my apartment. I can't become agoraphobic over this. I have to hold on to something, and I'm trusting that this person isn't out to harm me but just harass me."

"God, I hope you're right."

"Me, too, Julianna. Me, too."

Christine berated herself the entire time she packed her bags, questioning her sanity for going on the road. But the minute she climbed onto the bus, she felt like she was right where she belonged. The guys were watching *Vikings*. She smiled. These were her people, and she'd missed them. She couldn't go back to life before she knew them, and she didn't want to. She dropped her bags and squeezed between Cat and Kennedy, her eyes not leaving the TV.

"You watch *Vikings*?" Kennedy asked.

"I watch Bjørn Ironside," Christine said. "Hot-tie!"

Austin walked up from the back of the bus and saw her. "Chrissy!"

She stood, a little reluctant to be pulled away from the show. Austin grabbed her in a bear hug. "I've missed you."

"I've missed you, too," she said, noticing that Matt was standing behind Austin. "All of you."

"Give someone else a chance, Austin," Matt said, hugging Christine and sending chills down her back . . . and her front.

"We've all missed you," Cat said.

"Thanks, guys. I can't let fear rule my life."

"We'll keep you safe," Kennedy said. "We all have your back."

"As long as none of you jokers have her front. Or you'll have me to answer to," Austin said.

"Party pooper," Cat said.

Matt helped Christine put her bags in her bunk.

"Are you sure you're okay in the upper bunk? You can have mine," Matt said, pointing to his lower bunk.

Christine felt daring. What was some harmless flirting? "Will you be in it?"

Matt looked behind him. "Austin would kill me," he said.

"Kill you for what?" Austin asked, walking up beside them.

"Shacking up with your song plugger," Matt said.

"Yep. I'd probably cause you bodily harm," Austin said.

"Am I never going to get laid?" Christine said.

"Not on this bus, you're not," Austin said.

Christine rolled her eyes and Matt snickered.

"We'll let you get settled in," Austin said, heading to the back lounge while Matt went to the front. Christine stored her luggage and put her purse where she could easily reach it. She tried to keep all her stuff in her bunk, reasoning that if everyone kept their personal items sitting out, nobody would be able to move. There was only so much open space on a tour bus.

She heard music coming from the back lounge and saw the door was cracked. She peered in. Austin and another guy were sitting on the couches, playing their guitars. Austin looked up and motioned her in.

"Do you two know each other?" he asked. "Christine Matthews, this is Ryan Geoffries."

"I certainly know *of* you," Christine said, extending her hand. "I love your writing. Your lyrics have depth, and your syncopated backbeats are unique."

"Thank you. I've been very lucky. And Austin tells me great things about you. Our songs only go so far without someone out there playing them for the artists."

Christine blushed.

"Sit in for a few minutes and watch the process," Austin said.

Christine sat down, eyes wide and ears tuned in as she listened to Austin and Ryan work through guitar riffs, tempos, and chord structures before settling on a melody. Then they started putting their thoughts into phrases and matching them to the notes. She was witnessing a song come to life. She thought of a seed and how, once planted and watered, it would grow into a flower. Writing a song was a similar process.

Her phone chimed and she silenced it. She felt it vibrate and ignored it. Then she saw Julianna's photo show up on the screen. Being a part of the texting generation, she knew Julianna would only call if it was serious.

Christine stood and backed out of the room, making as little noise as possible. Austin and Ryan were deep into their collaboration and didn't look up.

"Hey, Julianna. What's up?"

"Get off that bus now," Julianna said, her voice tight and urgent.

"Why?"

"There are some massive threats all over Austin's socials. You're in danger. And it won't matter if you're on the road or in Nashville. Get off that bus and go home."

Christine felt the bus engines roar to life. She had mere minutes before it started rolling. She grabbed her stuff from her bunk and headed toward the door.

"Christine? Where are you going? We're about to leave," Matt said.

She looked around the bus. Multiple sets of eyes were on her, wide and inquisitive.

"Sorry, everyone. I've been alerted to a potential threat with me being here. I can't put myself, or you, at risk. I've got to get off the bus."

She didn't give anyone a chance to respond as she stepped off the bus. Matt was right behind her. She heard him address the bus driver.

"Earl, give us a few minutes."

Matt grabbed her luggage and carried it to her car.

"Are you sure you want to stay here?" Matt said. "I feel you're safer out with us."

"I won't be when I get back. I have to stay."

"So, this person wins?" Matt asks.

"If I'm safe, I win," Christine said, opening her trunk so Matt could put her suitcase in.

"Anything I can do?" Matt asked.

"No. Have a great run. Maybe I'll see you at tae kwon do when you get back."

Matt nodded. "Count on it." He reached out and Christine went in for a hug. His arms felt strong, reassuring, and safe. He kissed the side of her head.

Christine released him and rushed around to the driver's side. She didn't want to get emotional, and she felt it coming on.

She adjusted her rearview mirror and saw Matt watching her before turning around and climbing back on the bus.

She texted Julianna. *I'm off the bus. Heading home. Thank you. You may have just saved my life.*

She drove home, checked her surroundings, grabbed her purse and suitcase, and carried them up to her apartment. Once inside, she locked all three bolts. Her phone rang and she saw it was Austin.

"What the hell, Chrissy? I come out from writing a song to get your opinion and you're gone."

"Didn't Matt explain?" she said.

"He did, but you know you'd have been safe. You're in more danger there, alone, without a security team."

"No, I'm in more danger if I'm seen out with you. I'm safe as long as I stay home."

"This is crazy."

"You're right. It is. And I'm way too sane to keep going like this. I shouldn't have gone anywhere near your bus. Lesson learned. Have a good run, and we'll talk when you get back."

"Promise?" he asked.

"Promise."

Christine went into the bedroom, unpacked her bags, put on her pajamas, and started binge-watching *The Queen's Gambit*. She'd heard a lot about it but couldn't imagine a show about chess being fascinating. She was wrong. She didn't shower or get out of her pajamas for the whole weekend. She turned down Julianna's offer for dinner and skipped a guitar pull even though some of her favorite songwriters were performing. It took all her energy to go to work on Monday morning. The only thing she looked forward to was walking into the dojang and hoping to see Matt.

AFTER WORK, CHRISTINE LEFT FOR her tae kwon do class. She parked as close to the building as she could and then got out of the car, looking in every direction before fast-walking to the door. She felt like a fool being afraid of every shadow. When and how would this ever end?

"Christine?"

Her body gave an involuntary shiver, and a smile appeared on her lips when she heard Matt's voice. She turned.

"Matt. So good to see you."

"It's good to see you, too. We missed you this weekend. Did you get time to relax?" he asked.

"As much as I relax anymore," she said, shrugging her shoulders.

"I can't imagine living the way you are right now. We have to find this person. It's got to be someone close to us. Maybe someone one of us works with?" he said.

"What would make you say that?" She turned toward him, intrigued by this thought.

"Austin and I were talking about it. They know too much. And they know it too fast. It's got to be someone who interacts with us regularly. I didn't say anything to Austin, but my first thought was Phoebe."

"Yeah, I've gone there a few times, but Julianna swears it's not her style," Christine said, scrunching her face.

"You don't believe her?"

"I think Julianna is too close to Phoebe to see her true colors," Christine said.

"Maybe. It's worth keeping an eye on her."

"Did you mention her to Austin?"

"No, but he's said some things that make me think he might wonder, too," Matt said.

"Then why still date her?"

"What do they say? Keep your friends close and your

enemies closer? Plus, I think he enjoys the casual nature of their relationship."

"Sex without commitment?" Christine said.

"Something like that. Austin and I tossed around a bunch of ideas to keep you safe and find this person. He'll probably call you this week."

"Anything I'll like?" Christine asked.

"Probably not," Matt said, chuckling. "But try to keep an open mind."

"Awesome."

"I think your class is lining up. We'll chat soon, okay?"

"Absolutely. Thanks, Matt."

He gave her a hug and she held on. If she could just start dating him, she'd be perfectly safe. And happy. Being in Matt's arms felt natural. They fit together, in personality as well as physicality. She'd have held on forever but the class was about to start. As his hands slid from her shoulders, she felt her sense of security slip, too.

MATT WAS RIGHT. She didn't like Austin's idea.

"I don't want you to live here anymore. I want you to live in Julianna's complex," Austin said, sitting on her couch, facing her.

"Julianna already offered, but I can't impose on her. Two grown women living together can get too close."

"I want you to live in her building, but in your own apartment."

"Oh. Did I win the lottery? Funny, 'cause I don't even play. Look, Austin, I want to drive a Mercedes, but I have an old Toyota. I don't have family money like Julianna, and I'm not a rich and famous singer. I'm a lowly song plugger. One of Nashville's musical matchmakers. I live in an apartment I can afford."

"Not anymore." Austin had a tentative smile on his lips, like he was proud of something and nervous about it at the same time.

"What did you do?" Christine put her hands on her hips.

"I bought you out of your lease. Paid off your last few months and ended your contract."

"How dare you!" Her face turned red, and her eyes narrowed.

"I dare to try and keep you safe. I'm the cause of all this, and I have to fix it."

"You can't fix it."

"I can try." Austin jumped to his feet and started pacing. "Just listen to me. I fixed it so your rent there is the same as it was here."

"That's not possible."

"It is possible."

"If you're paying the extra money for it, then no. I won't be your charity case." Christine folded her arms across her chest and shook her head.

"You aren't my charity case. Banks are willing to work with people who have money. I have money. I worked out a deal. You can move in to the condo right next to Julianna."

"Did you pay off the tenants to move?" Christine asked, her words clipped.

"I made it work. That's all I'm going to say. You'll have password-protected parking, a lobby entrance, and a guard posted downstairs at all times." He took her hand in his. "You'll be safe."

"I can't let you do this."

"You don't have a choice. I've already done it. I hired movers to come here tomorrow and take everything there."

"Tomorrow? How?" Christine asked.

"I've been working on this for a few weeks. I didn't want to mention it until I knew I could pull it off. And if I gave you too much time to think about it, you'd say no."

"I am saying no. Austin, you have way overstepped your bounds."

"I know. Please, Chrissy. Do this for me." He put his hands in a prayer position.

She looked away from him and said nothing.

"I know you're angry," he said.

"I'm freaking pissed." She stared at the wall.

"Let me do this for you. Please."

She stood up. "I'll be back." She walked into her bedroom and shut the door, leaning against it. She was a rational person and knew this situation was not her fault. She had done nothing wrong, nothing to incite this vile person who was determined to destroy her. Yet she was also in potential danger. And she did feel safer in Julianna's complex, where tenants could park their cars in a locked garage and have access to a secure elevator. At her apartment, she had to leave her car, walk up two flights of stairs, and stand outside in an open foyer to unlock her apartment door. Even though the community was gated, the gate was only secure against cars. Anyone could walk right in. That wasn't the case at Julianna's. She thought of the saying "Pride cometh before a fall." It was her pride telling her to say no. Her brain knew this was the best thing for her. How could she reconcile the two of them?

A light knock on her door brought her out of her thoughts.

"Christine?" Austin asked. "Do you want me to leave?"

"No. Give me a minute and I'll be out."

Christine took a deep breath and prepared to answer. She walked up to Austin and he stood. "Okay. I'll do it. For my safety. Although it won't take a genius to figure out I'm living there. Before long, my stalker will know."

"But there, they can't get to you. There are cameras all over the place. If she tried to follow you in, she'd get nailed immediately. Shy of you going into complete hiding, this is the best we can do."

"Then let's do it."

Austin gently pulled her into his arms. "Thank you, Chrissy."

MOVERS CAME THE NEXT DAY, EMPTIED her apartment, and set everything up in the new condo. It was slightly smaller than Julianna's place but much bigger than her old one. She couldn't help but make plans for the spare bedroom that included setting up a comfortable space for listening to music. It would be her zen-style room. She'd need more furniture. She was excited at the thought of a new beginning.

Austin had left first thing that morning for his tour. This one was in Texas, and he'd be gone for two weeks. She had wished him luck, sad that she wasn't able to go. She thought of helping Matt with the paperwork, working side by side with him, getting to see him every day, and watching Austin win over a new audience. She put the thought out of her head. *That would have been a big mistake, Christine.*

CHRISTINE LOVED RETURNING home to her new condo. As the weeks went by, she felt more and more at home. And much safer. A decade ago, downtown Nashville had been made up of quaint houses and shops intermingled with record labels and recording studios. Now it was skyscrapers and condo buildings. She'd often looked on with envy, wondering who could afford to live in such places. Then she met Julianna and knew one person who could. Now, thanks to Austin, she was also living there.

Christine worried that Julianna would feel she was invading her space. They already worked together, and now she lived next door. Surprisingly, they sometimes went days without seeing one another outside the office. While neither of them said anything, Christine felt it was natural they gave each other space. And Christine felt a sense of peace knowing she had a friend so close.

NOT BEING ON THE ROAD WITH MATT meant her only chance of seeing him was at tae kwon do class. She always stayed in the back of the class and tried to concentrate on what the instructor was saying while just wanting to see Matt.

She glanced back every time the door opened, not knowing if Matt would be coming in. She hadn't followed Austin's travel schedule since he'd left for Texas, but she knew that tour was over. She'd avoided looking at social media. She didn't want to know where he was, what he was doing, or what people were saying about her. She had purposely taken on a new male client. He had just signed a deal with BMG, and Christine was immersing herself in his first album. The more she could distance herself from Austin, even professionally, the better. A new apartment, a new client, a new lease on life.

After class, she changed into her street clothes. When she emerged from the ladies' room, she saw Matt. Her quick intake of breath sounded so loud in her head that she was surprised he didn't hear it. She stared at him, taking in the new haircut that accentuated his cheekbones and the fitted T-shirt that showed off his strong arms. She glanced away when she saw him turning in her direction.

"Christine?"

"Oh, hey, Matt. How are you?"

He walked straight up to her and wrapped his arms around her in a warm embrace.

"It's good to see you. We miss you. I think the whole crew is tired of hearing Austin and me talk about you. Every time I screw up the tickets and put them in the wrong envelope, I tell people if you were with me, it would be perfect. Austin just mopes."

"It's good to be missed. I miss you guys, too." Christine knew she should let go, but she didn't want to. Moments with Matt were a rarity now, stolen during these classes.

"Line up," Master Joe yelled.

The moment was broken.

"I better go change," Matt said, his hand still on her side.

"Might be a good idea." Her voice came out a whisper.

They moved in to hug each other, but instead of turning their faces to the opposite side, they met in the middle. A kiss on the cheek became a kiss on the lips. Christine knew she should pull away, but she leaned in, loving the feel of his lips on hers. The sound of other people in the room made her pull back.

Christine was mortified. She was sure that hadn't been his intent, and she didn't want him to think it was hers. "Oh, I'm sorry, Matt."

"Why? I'm not. Where'd you park? I'll walk you to your car."

She had a flash of him walking her to her car in the dark parking lot, pulling her in for a hug, and then telling her he could no longer stop himself and had to kiss her. A real kiss. The visual ended when she pointed out the window to her car. Matt and everyone else could see it from the window. It was parked in front of the dojang. There would be no kiss.

Matt nodded. "Nice and safe. I've got to go change. See you soon." He squeezed her upper arm ever so gently and went into the men's room.

She wanted to stay and let him continue touching her, but they could hardly do that in a crowded room. She bolted out the door, opting to leave well enough alone. Even though everyone in the class could see her car, she rushed to unlock it, jumped in, and immediately locked the doors.

She arrived at her condo just as Julianna walked off the elevator carrying four plastic bags from the grocery store.

"Hey, how'd your class go?"

"Good. Very good."

"Did you see Matt?" Julianna asked.

Christine grabbed two of Julianna's bags and followed her.

"We kinda kissed but not really," Christine said, dropping her head down while looking up at Julianna.

"Eeeek! Come in. Gotta hear this. Cup of tea?" Julianna asked.

"Always."

"Earl Grey or French vanilla?"

"French vanilla. Decaf if you have it."

"Just bought some. I think it's in the bag you have," Julianna said, pointing.

Christine dug through the bag and pulled it out.

Julianna was putting away groceries and Christine felt comfortable enough helping herself in the kitchen.

"Do you want some tea?" Christine asked.

"Sure. Thank you."

They finished their tasks and moved to the couch, propping their feet on the coffee table, which Christine was sure had cost at least three thousand dollars.

"So?"

"You know how sometimes you go to hug someone, and you both move your face to the same side and you almost kiss?"

"Yeah."

"We did that, but then we kept going and had a brief kiss. Well, not too brief, 'cause I leaned into it and paused," Christine said, then took a sip of her tea and watched her friend over the rim of the cup.

Julianna's eyes widened. "Nobody accidentally kisses when that happens. Everyone pulls away and then feels awkward."

"I know."

"What else?" Julianna moved forward on the couch and clapped her hands.

"I apologized 'cause I was trying to figure out if I had leaned in and made it happen. I knew I wanted it, but I didn't know if he did."

"And?"

"When I said I was sorry, he said he wasn't and winked at me."

"Oooh! Christine. He likes you." Julianna's eyes sparkled.

"Maybe. But how can I be sure?" Christine shrugged. "For now, I still have hope. If he puts me in the friend zone, it's over. I will forever feel awkward around him."

"Is he still seeing Cait?"

"I don't know. We never talk about her. And I'm not sure how to ask. I refuse to play the role of the other woman."

"Never a good role. So, your first kiss with Matt."

"Um, wasn't my first," Christine said with a coy grin.

Julianna sat up straight.

"What? You've been holding out on me? Spill it, girl."

"It was kind of our third."

"Third? And you never said a word?"

"One was just a quick peck, so not a big deal to anyone but me. But there was one night that I've been embarrassed to tell anyone about." Christine's hands flew to her eyes, hiding her humiliation.

"You can tell me." Julianna's voice was gentle, trusting.

"Oh, Julianna. It was one of the most humiliating nights of my life. I drank Fireball and then this girl offered me a weed cookie."

"I didn't know you liked weed," Julianna said, her eyes widening and her grin ever present.

"That's just it. I don't. I thought she said wheat cookie."

"Who carries wheat cookies to a party?" Julianna asked, giggling.

"I don't know. I'd had two shots of Fireball. Then, I was both drunk and stoned while I danced on a coffee table at an after-party."

"Oh, shit."

"Matt rescued me and took me to the bus, but there was no way he was getting my drunk ass into the third-tier bunk, so he took me to the back room."

"We all know what the back room means." Julianna wiggled her eyebrows.

"And that's what I said. I practically assaulted him. He fought off my advances quite valiantly, until having a momentary oh-what-the-hell moment and kissing me back."

"And?"

"From what I can remember, it was amazing. But then he stopped and said he couldn't do it. In hindsight, I'm guessing it's because of Cait. He left the room to get my pillow and blanket. And that was it. Although he did stay with me all night. I kind of passed out."

"How did you handle it the next day?"

"I immediately apologized for my drunken behavior and told him how embarrassed I was, and that I hoped he realized I'd have never done that sober."

"Let me get this straight. You basically told the guy you have a crush on that the only reason you came on to him was because you were drunk and high."

"Huh?"

"Christine. Think about how that sounded to him."

"I didn't want him to think I was a slut."

"But is that what he heard? Or did he hear, 'I'm only worth making out with if she's not in her right mind'?" Julianna said.

Christine slumped back on the sofa. She replayed all the things she had said that stated just that. "I never thought of it that way. I told him I just wanted to forget the whole thing and pretend it never happened."

"Just what every man wants to hear a woman say after they've had an encounter."

"Shit."

"Yep."

"I wonder if I can ever make it right," Christine said as much to herself as to her friend.

"I'm sure you can. One day, the opportunity will present itself. Don't let it pass."

"I won't."

Christine lay awake in bed, thinking about everything she'd said to Matt. It all pointed to exactly what Julianna had said. She beat herself up so long into the night she was amazed not to wake up and find herself bruised and battered.

CHAPTER FIFTEEN

B y early summer, Christine's career was on fire. Lynda recorded two of the songs Christine had pitched her. One had been released as a radio single and rose to the top five on the charts. She had also met with two mid-level artists who had each cut a song from her publishing company. Rumor had it that one of those was being considered for a radio release as well.

The only time she had seen Austin in recent months was during pitch meetings when they were in a room with his producer and label A&R rep. Otherwise, she pitched him songs via email, and he sent some for her to hear. But that was it. No more Austin meant no more cyberbullies. Most importantly, her stalker had gone away.

She missed being on the road with Matt but saw him from time to time at the dojang and decided that would have to suffice. They hadn't kissed again, but she always hoped it would happen. It gave her something to look forward to.

"Life is about balance, Julianna. You have to weigh the good and the bad. The good of Austin was great. But the bad was getting too bad."

"I get it. Sure do miss riding the coattails of your life with him, though. We'll be talking about those stories when we're eighty," Julianna said.

"Now I have a chance to live that long."

Later that night, Christine was scrolling through email in her condo and stopped when she saw an odd Facebook alert. And then another. And another. Numerous high school classmates were talking about her on a group thread. Someone had tagged her, so she logged in to Facebook and read from the beginning.

Austin Garrett is coming to our hometown. Think Christine will be with him?

Probably. Aren't they best buds now or something?

Think she can get us backstage to meet him?

If she's as close to him as we think she is. I'm going to private message her and ask.

Christine opened the inbox for her Facebook messages. The requests for meet-and-greet passes topped fourteen. She had a vision of herself hosting a group of former high school acquaintances as they all swooned over Austin Garrett, vindicating her geeky high school years. She wondered, *Do the teen years ever disappear, or do they live on in some time warp to forever circle back and haunt you?*

Christine had avoided looking at Austin's schedule so she wouldn't be tempted to go to a show, but now she googled it, and sure enough, he was due to play in central Pennsylvania. He was headlining a tour and was booked at a downtown theatre. *Her* downtown theatre, where she had gone to concerts as a teen, dreaming that one day she'd be a part of country music. She loved that old theatre with the red velvet curtains and box balcony seating. She would close her eyes and envision men in top hats and coattails and women in long fancy dresses. She could only imagine the number of performances, concerts, and plays the old theatre had seen. And now, she could be a part of one. Her life had come full circle and she couldn't imagine missing this. Had enough time passed that her stalker believed she was no longer involved with Austin?

She called Julianna. "I have a dilemma."

"Lay it on me."

"Austin's tour is going to central Pennsylvania," Christine said, hearing the fear in her own voice.

"Ah, home sweet home."

"What do I do?"

"Well, I know you'd like to be in your hometown flaunting your relationship with one of the hottest male acts in country music."

"I don't want to flaunt . . ."

"Sure you do. Who wouldn't? Even popular people had haters in high school. We all want to prove we made something of ourselves. It's human nature."

"I already have fourteen requests for meet-and-greet passes. I'll be lucky to get four."

"Bullshit. Austin would do anything for you. He'll meet anyone you ask him to," Julianna said, and Christine knew it was true.

"Ugh. What a terrible position to be in. Do I risk my stalker coming after me if I'm seen out with him again, or do I pass up a lifelong dream come true—returning to my hometown theatre with the headliner?"

"My first inclination is to say don't go anywhere near Austin," Julianna said.

"That's my first thought, too. It's my second thought of really wanting to be there that is messing with my mind." Christine let out a low sigh.

"Let me think about it for a few days. We'll come up with a plan."

"Thank you."

"OKAY, I'VE GOT IT," JULIANNA announced, breezing into Christine's office.

Christine set aside her paperwork and looked at her friend. "You've got what?"

"We can fly to Harrisburg. You don't get on the bus or go into the dressing rooms. You stay low-key and keep your distance from Austin, except during the meet and greet. At no time do you allow the public or audience to see you. Wear a hoodie and big sunglasses or something. Do not stand on the stage. We make sure someone is always with you. We duck out before the show is over and make our way back out of town."

Christine sat back and thought about it. "And we're never without our cell phones. We stay connected at all times," Christine said.

"This will work," Julianna said.

Christine paused. She had a flashback to the last time she thought it was okay to go on the road. It hadn't been. She hadn't made it out of the parking lot before returning home, fearing for her life.

"I don't know. I'm being stupid again. They might come after me when I return home. Maybe I'll see if I can work from my parents' house for a couple of weeks after the show. That way, if somehow someone does see me, I'm not in Nashville and can give it time to die down. I've never been threatened on the road."

"Exactly. Oddly enough, being with Austin has seemed to be the safest place for you."

"I used to love irony. Now, not so much."

Christine was hesitant. All afternoon, she'd debated about whether she should go. She was listening to a new song by one of her favorite female singers, Lainey Wilson, when her Facebook messages chimed. It was Jim, the high school quarterback, asking for tickets. She laughed. He'd never even said "hi" to her in school. Austin was right. It was time to exorcise her high school ghosts.

She sent Austin a text: *Hey. When you play Pennsylvania, is there any chance I can do a fourteen-person M&G with people from my high school?*

Are you going to be there? he texted back.

Yes.

Then you can do anything you want. Should we save you a bunk?

She typed out her message. *No. Flying in with Julianna.*

Okay. Just glad you're coming.

Please don't tell anyone other than Matt!!!

I won't.

She texted back. *I mean anyone.*

I won't tell Phoebe.

She walked down to Julianna's office. "Do you really think we can keep me safe?"

"I won't lie. I'm not comfortable with it. But if you insist on going, I'm with you. What cinched your decision?" Julianna said.

"The high school quarterback asked me for tickets and meet and greets."

"Oooh, that's a big one." Julianna spread her arms wide.

"Yep. I need a favor."

"What's that?"

"Don't tell anyone we're going," Christine said.

"Who would I tell?"

Christine raised her eyebrows. "Oh, no, I won't even tell her," Julianna said. "But Austin probably will."

"He said he wouldn't."

"It's not her, Christine."

"Okay."

Julianna stared hard at her. "It's not."

"I said okay," Christine said.

CHRISTINE SET TO WORK ANSWERING all the private messages. She didn't want to say no to anyone, but after going back to Austin two more times to ask if she could include more people, she cut it off at twenty. Even her high school English teacher wanted to come.

Austin texted, *As many as you want, Chrissy.*

Thanks. But I think twenty is enough.

She texted Matt just to make sure he knew. She wasn't sure Austin had thought about how much work this would be for Matt.

Matt texted, *Are you kidding? Austin's so excited. Happy to host your friends and glad you're coming to the show.*

More like acquaintances, but thank you.

Christine felt okay about this. They'd made a plan. They'd stick to it. She would stay in the background, unseen. Nobody in the audience would know she was there. Her parents were out of town, vacationing in Carmel, but she felt that was better. They were savvy enough to follow socials and knew some of what was happening. She'd stopped telling them about the notes and let them believe those had ended. They had finally calmed down and stopped asking her to move home. Christine hated worrying them, and knowing she was going to one of Austin's concerts would upset them.

ON THE DAY OF THE CONCERT, Julianna and Christine drove together to the airport. They arrived plenty early so they wouldn't add any stress to an already stressful day. They were in line at Starbucks when Christine gasped.

"Are you okay?" Julianna said, suddenly on high alert.

Christine pointed.

Phoebe was walking down the hall toward them. She wore thigh-high black boots over tight blue jeans and a low-cut royal blue shirt that showed off her amazing cleavage. With her confident and lengthy stride, she looked like she was walking down a runway at a Milan fashion show.

"What is she doing here?" Julianna asked.

"I'm afraid to ask. And I do mean afraid."

"Well, this is a surprise. Where are you headed?" Phoebe asked. Christine froze.

"Austin's show," Julianna said.

"Cool. Me, too. What flight are you on?" Phoebe asked.

"American into Harrisburg," Julianna said.

"Same. Let's go check if we can get seats together," Phoebe said, grabbing Julianna's hand and pulling her to the gate agent.

Christine stared at Phoebe's back. Was that really all it was? Her wanting to see her boyfriend? Or was there more to it? Christine shook her head to clear her thoughts. Phoebe may not be nice to her, but she was not her stalker. She couldn't be. But the lingering doubt sat heavy in Christine's stomach.

They boarded the plane and Christine took the window seat, Julianna the center, and Phoebe the aisle. Phoebe immediately put on her headphones and opened a magazine. Christine watched people board the plane, not sure what she was looking for but wary of the fact that she was opening herself up to more danger by going to the concert. She didn't see anyone who made her feel suspicious.

She put on headphones, scrunched down in her seat, and listened to music. Sometimes it was best to sink into your own world on planes.

They landed in Harrisburg, grabbed their luggage, and stepped outside to meet their Uber driver.

Christine was their tour guide along the way. "If you take that exit and turn down two streets, you're at my high school," she said as they passed her hometown exit.

They also saw signs for Hershey. "Craving chocolate, anyone?" Phoebe laughed.

"Always," Julianna said.

"They have an amazing arena there. I went to so many concerts when I was younger. Plus, we had the York Fair. I remember seeing Alabama for the first time. I feel like I'm stepping back in time," Christine said.

"You kind of are," Julianna said.

"For better or worse, we all have to do it at some point. Weddings, class reunions, funerals—there's always something to return us to that time," Phoebe said.

"It's like quantum mechanics. We live multiple lives at the same time, if only in our minds," Christine said, the weight of the past heavy on her.

When they arrived at the venue, a huge sign said AUSTIN GARRETT TONIGHT! in bold red letters.

"It's always been a big deal to have your name in lights at this theatre. At least in our little town, it means you've made it," Christine said.

She directed their driver around to the back. "Home sweet home," she said.

"You came to a lot of concerts here, huh?" Julianna asked.

"I did. This was my haunt."

"And now you're here, besties with the headliner. His number one song plugger. Mi vida loca," Julianna said.

"My crazy life."

They hung their All-Access laminates around their necks and headed in. Christine was nervous about seeing Matt. She'd changed clothes at least three times before leaving Nashville and settled on her favorite blue jeans, black heels, and a white top, reasoning that it was best to go classic when in doubt. They weren't high heels but had a fancy mesh on the top that looked pretty. She liked how they played peekaboo below her jeans when she walked. Her sexiest black leather jacket completed the look.

They followed signs through the back, up the stairs, down a narrow hall, and straight to the production room. Christine knocked on the door while opening it.

"You made it," Matt said, looking sexy in blue jeans and a fitted black T-shirt. He stood and reached out to her, pulling her into his strong arms for a hug. Christine closed her eyes, savoring the moment. He didn't usually smell of cologne, but today he did. And his hair was damp and smelled shampoo-fresh. Was it too much to hope it was all for her?

He let go and greeted Julianna and Phoebe with much quicker hugs.

"Good to have you here. Make sure you text Austin. He's been driving me crazy asking when you'd arrive," Matt said.

"Are you talking to me or Christine?" Phoebe asked.

"Oh, uh, he just said all of you in general," Matt said with a stutter.

"I already texted him," Phoebe said.

Minutes later, Austin came bursting through the door.

"Chrissy!" he yelled, picking her up and twirling her around.

Phoebe's mouth dropped open and Christine saw Julianna reach for her hand.

Only when Austin put her down did he seem to realize his girlfriend was standing in the room. Phoebe's arms were crossed over her chest and she wore a scowl.

"Hey, beautiful," Austin said, reaching out to hug her. She kissed him on the lips.

"Hello, Julianna. Thanks for coming to help keep Chrissy safe." He reached out to give her a hug.

"Glad to do it."

"Here's the plan," Matt said. They all paid attention as he explained the night's agenda.

"Perfect," Christine said when he'd finished. "And thank you guys for being so accommodating."

"Anything for you," Austin said. Phoebe gave an eye roll but kept quiet.

They had two hours before Christine's meet and greet.

"Let's check out the new merchandise," Julianna said.

"They usually set up at the main entrance. I don't want anyone seeing me, remember?" Christine said, shaking her head.

"The public won't be let in for another half hour. There's just a couple of local theatre workers out there and some security," Matt said.

"Okay. I guess that'll be all right." Christine nodded.

Phoebe looked reluctant to leave Austin until Matt grabbed him for a radio interview.

"Austin said they got some killer sweatshirts. They're dark gray with a metallic blue emblem. He's trying out some new things," Phoebe said.

"Then can we hit catering?" Julianna asked. "I'm starved."

They headed out to the main merchandise stand. The audience wasn't allowed in yet, but the workers had already shown up. Christine always felt that a venue was a living, breathing thing. It was as if ghosts of concerts past had left their energy behind. You could almost feel the excitement rising from the seats even though they were empty. Vendors were preparing for the rush. The pizza stand was up and running, and the sweet smell of crust and mozzarella wafted past them.

"There's something about the smell of pizza at a venue," Christine said. Julianna and Phoebe nodded their agreement.

Security guards held a meeting in the main hallway. From what Christine could hear, they were figuring out how best to protect everyone against the fans who got too drunk and rowdy. Police officers were posted at each entrance. Security guards could only do so much if serious trouble broke out. Outside the main door, an ambulance was already on-site. You couldn't be too safe when a few thousand people were going to be in a confined space.

"Hey, Alicia," Christine said, her focus returning to the merch table.

"Hey. Long time no see, huh?" Alicia's ponytail was pulled back behind a ball cap that sported one word: SPRINGSTEEN.

"I've been trying to keep a low profile."

"I hear you have quite a posse coming tonight." She took a stack of T-shirts out of a box and started folding them.

"A bunch of people from my high school are going to be here."

"I told Matt I'd help escort them out so he could bring in the regular meet-and-greet folks. Thought it would look better for someone other than you to do it. Let you take the high road out."

"Thank you. That's really nice," Christine said.

"All good. I've been there. Nothing worse than hometown shows to bring people out of the woodwork, huh?" Alicia said.

"Exactly. And some of these people didn't treat me too well back then. The whole thing has my stomach twisted in knots."

"Then why do this?"

"It's closure on old wounds."

"We've all needed closure on something in our lives. I get it," Alicia said.

"Thanks. It helps to have people who understand," Christine said, giving her a smile.

"Whatcha looking for, ladies? The new sweatshirt is amazeballs. That metallic blue on the dark gray. Crazy cool," Alicia said, reaching into a box to show them.

"Austin's been raving about them but keeps forgetting to bring me one," Phoebe said.

Alicia pulled one out of the box and put it on the counter. "And check out that logo. It pops. Practically 3D."

"You've convinced me," Christine said, opening her purse and pulling out her wallet.

"Nope. You're one of us. They're on the house."

"No, I insist on paying," Christine said.

"Me, too," Julianna said.

"You're family. Austin would want it this way. If he found out I made you pay, he'd make me pay," Alicia said, laughing.

"Thanks, Alicia. That's very nice," Christine said.

They looked over some of the other merchandise, but Alicia was still setting up and they didn't want to get in her way.

They returned backstage and found catering. It wasn't as fancy as on the big tours, but they were serving Mexican food with make-your-own tacos.

"This will definitely work," Julianna said.

They spent the next forty-five minutes devouring their meal and relaxing in the catering area. Christine was unnerved and pushed her food around her plate.

"This is really getting to you, isn't it? You barely ate," Julianna said.

"Twenty people from high school? And a stalker. Uh, yeah. I wish I hadn't eaten at all. I know it sounds foolish. I'm an adult. A successful one at that. But I'm pretty nervous."

Her texts had already blown up four times with people confused about how to get their tickets from will call. She had repeated the instructions over and over until everyone had what they needed.

After eating, Phoebe headed in the direction of Austin's bus and Christine assumed they wanted some private time. Christine felt a little pang. When she was on the road with Austin, he spent a lot of time with her, always wanting her close. Giving deference to the girlfriend felt odd.

Julianna watched her watching Phoebe. "You okay?"

"Huh? Yeah. I just don't usually have Phoebe here, and it's kind of weird. I mean, I know they're dating, but I don't usually witness it."

"Jealous?"

"Not in the way you're implying."

CHRISTINE AND JULIANNA were hanging in the production office, scanning their phones and watching the minutes tick by, when five thirty hit. Time for the doors to open and let the throng of fans in.

"It's showtime," Matt said, walking into the room.

"Thirty minutes," Christine said, looking at her watch.

"Stop fidgeting. It's going to be great." Matt moved behind her and started to rub her shoulders. "You need to relax."

Christine let her head droop forward. She closed her eyes and sighed. "Keep doing that, and I'll be asleep."

"Good."

Matt kissed the top of her head and turned back to his computer.

Julianna imitated Matt massaging her shoulders and gave Christine a thumbs-up.

Christine waved her off and whispered, "He was being nice."

Julianna rolled her eyes.

"Why don't you go into the meet-and-greet room and get ready? I'll bring everyone back at six and then get Austin," Matt said, facing Christine again.

"Just a thought here, but why don't you let Christine bring Austin in?" Julianna said.

"Hmm. That'll make an impression. Sure. I'll let him know," Matt said.

"You two are the best. Thank you," Christine said, reaching for Julianna's hand.

"That's what friends are for," Julianna said.

Matt left to get Christine's guests while Christine went to get Austin. She walked onto the bus as he was tugging on his jeans.

"Oh, sorry," she said.

"No worries, Chrissy. Not like you haven't seen it," Austin said.

"Oh, please," Phoebe protested.

"Are you ready for this?" Austin asked.

"No."

"It's going to be awesome. Let's go," Austin said, grabbing Christine by the hand and leading her out. Phoebe followed behind and Christine thought she looked awkward being a step behind them. As the girlfriend, she should be holding Austin's hand.

The door to the meet-and-greet room was closed and Christine took a deep breath. Then she turned to Austin and grabbed his arm.

"I have one huge favor. Please, please do not call me Chrissy. It was a not-so-nice nickname for me back in high school. I need to be Christine tonight."

Austin nodded.

Christine opened the door, immediately clenching her fists and closing her eyes. She expected to see a group of people as they'd looked in high school. But when she looked up, that wasn't what she saw. Like her, they were older. They weren't the cute young kids they used to be—they were adults. Christine thought about Austin saying how they had gone on with their lives, attending PTA meetings, going to work, and not giving her a second thought. The class beauty was no longer stick thin. She was still very pretty, but she had a woman's figure now—she was a little fuller through the thighs and didn't have a twenty-one-inch waist. The baby-faced football player now sported a mustache and a goatee. Austin was right. They weren't here to berate her. They just wanted a glimpse of Austin.

She gasped. Her body stiffened. The big guy in the back? It couldn't be. There was no way Bryan had snuck in. Her body felt warm, and she knew she was about to break into a sweat. But when he stepped to the left, she realized it wasn't him. She exhaled.

She hadn't realized her hands were clenched until she opened her fingers, relaxing them. Austin leaned down and whispered, "Say something. Introduce me."

"Um, hello, everyone. They say you can't go home again, huh? Well, here I am. Home sweet home."

There was some uncomfortable laughter.

"Anyway, you aren't here to see me. You're here to meet the star of tonight's show, so here he is. Austin Garrett." The people clapped, and a few gave a *whoop whoop* or cheer.

Austin gave her a big hug and a kiss on the cheek. "I appreciate you coming to the show tonight. I'm not sure all of you are here to see me," Austin said, pointing to Christine like they were there to see her.

She pursed her lips and crinkled her forehead. She wanted to get attention off her as fast as possible. "Are there any questions for Austin?" Christine asked.

"I have one," said Tammy. She used to be Christine's neighbor. "I love the song 'Promises to Me.' Did you write it?"

"I didn't. This lovely lady standing next to me found it and played it for me. Christine thought it would be perfect for me. At the time, I was known for my party songs so it was a bit of a gamble. But she was right. The payoff was huge."

"Wow. Way to go, neighbor," Tammy said.

Another hand went up and Christine saw it was Tom, a former high school soccer player. "Dude, I've seen you linked to women all over the country. What's it like fending off gorgeous women every night? And feel free to send some our way tonight." He high-fived another guy, who Christine didn't know.

"It's pretty damn great. Every guy's dream, right? Although if I'm being honest and you won't make me turn in my man card, it's also getting a little old."

"I don't think it would ever get old for me," Tom said.

"Anything too easy gets boring, though, right?" Austin said, and Christine thought he made a good point.

When they were ten minutes into their fifteen-minute window, Matt took the lead.

"Let's take some photos. We can start over here to the right. I hate to say 'form a line' like you really are back in high school, but it would be easier if you could," Matt said.

The guests made a line of sorts and Austin started at the front. The guys shook Austin's hand and did the awkward how-do-I-pose-with-a-dude pose. The couples stood with one of them on either side of Austin, the female leaning in toward him. And the single ladies, well, the flirtation meter was off the charts.

"I promise you wouldn't get bored with me," Allison said, and Christine tried to remember who she was. Maybe she was a friend of someone from high school. Everyone had brought a guest, so half the people in the room were strangers to Christine. That unnerved her until she remembered her stalker most likely lived in Nashville.

Christine waited for one of them to say, "Why in the world are you friends with Chrissy the Sissy?" It didn't happen. They were kind, appreciative. She wished her sixteen-year-old self could have seen into the future and known a moment like this was coming.

Matt suggested they pose for a group shot, and Christine realized it was almost over. She'd made it through this reunion without anyone giving a blow to her ego. Matt lined everyone up with Austin and Christine in the middle. It was one of those odd life moments when she felt like she'd actually made it. Her. Christine Matthews was here with the headlining act, and she was partially responsible for his success. She smiled big.

Matt snapped a few photos and gave his usual exit speech. "Thank you all for coming. I know it meant a lot to Christine." He reached out and patted her back.

She melted.

"Alicia in the back will escort you to the seating area. You can find your photos on Austin's website under meet-and-greet photos. Give me a day to get them uploaded."

"Thanks, everyone. I hope you enjoy the show," Austin said. A few people hugged Christine, and they all thanked her as they made their way out of the room.

Matt followed them to get the regular meet-and-greet crowd.

"That wasn't so bad, was it?" Austin asked.

"It wasn't. But I'm exhausted. I didn't sleep at all last night. Thanks so much for doing this."

"Anything for you, Chrissy girl."

"And thank you for not calling me Chrissy in front of them."

"You're welcome."

Matt brought in the next group of people, and Christine excused herself to join Julianna, who had been waiting in the hall.

"Well?"

"You could have stayed in the room," Christine said.

"It was crowded in there. How'd it go?"

"Good. Better than good."

"I knew it would go well." Julianna looked at her phone. "My parents are blowing up my phone. My grandmother isn't doing well. Mind if I step out and make a call? With the crew moving boxes around and the DJ already playing music, I won't be able to hear them. I know I promised not to leave you."

"I'm safe back here. There's too much security to be concerned. Go make your phone call," Christine said.

"You're sure?"

"Positive. Go."

Julianna left with a promise to be right back.

CHAPTER SIXTEEN

hristine leaned back against the wall. She felt safe with Austin and Matt a mere twenty feet away, even if the door was closed. She shut her eyes, thinking she could fall asleep standing up. She marveled at what stress could do to the body and took a moment to gather herself. Seeing people from her high school had given her some much-needed closure, but it had also reopened some wounds. If she'd had a crystal ball and seen her future, she could have let a lot of the insults roll off her back then. But she didn't. High school had seemed like the be-all and end-all when she was living it. It had felt like if she didn't become someone then, she never would. What a ridiculous notion that she should have peaked in life at eighteen. If only teenagers realized they have their whole lives in front of them.

Christine's phone chimed with a social media update. She wasn't going to look but figured it had to be something good. She'd just treated twenty people to a fun encounter with a star. How could it not be good? She beamed, envisioning her classmates mentioning that she had planned the meet and greet, saying that Austin had spent time with them, and remarking that he was obviously her friend. Did she want validation? Of course she did. Doesn't everyone?

She pulled up the post and froze. Her hand went to her mouth and she felt the blood drain out of her face. She fell back against the wall. Her legs were wobbly and she started to shake. There was a video of her with the high school group, Austin in the middle, but someone had dubbed a guy's voice over it.

"Yeah, she's a pretty cool big deal now. But back in high school, she was just Chrissy the Sissy. It was some dumb chant we used to do: 'Chrissy is a sissy; Chrissy is a sissy.' Cruel shit kids do to other kids that you wish now you could take back. It had something to do with a night when a bunch of guys were harassing her. They came up with it, but then we all played along. Why are teenagers so mean to each other? Hey, you're not recording this, are you?" Then it stopped.

The video had been posted on multiple social media platforms with a dozen hashtags, including the venue name, the tour, Hit Songs Publishing, Austin, and various country music sites. Even her high school was hashtagged, along with the year Christine graduated. Who? Who could've done it? Who had said those things?

She sank to the floor as tears flowed down her face. She covered her face with her hands and let her emotions pour. "No. No, no, no," she cried.

"Christine? Christine? What's wrong?"

From somewhere in her brain, she heard Julianna calling for her.

"Austin, help me get her up," Julianna said, but Christine wouldn't move. She couldn't move. She never wanted to move again.

"Chrissy, what's wrong?" Austin was on the floor beside her, hugging her. "Honey, tell me what's wrong. Did someone do something?"

Christine shook her head. She handed Julianna her phone, the social feed still showing.

Julianna played the video. "Oh, sweetie. I am so, so sorry."

"What am I missing?" Austin asked. "What the hell does this mean?"

"Does he know what this means, Christine?" Julianna asked. Christine shook her head.

"Somebody tell me what the hell is going on," Austin said.

"Christine?" Julianna said.

"I can't. You tell him," Christine said, refusing to look up.

Julianna gave Austin the quick version of what had happened all those years ago.

"Jesus, Christine. Why didn't you tell me that's why you didn't want me calling you that?" Austin said, rubbing her back.

Loud footsteps came stomping down the hall. Christine didn't have to look to know who it was.

"Oh, for God's sake. What's wrong with Christine now?" Phoebe said, causing Christine to cry harder. She couldn't handle one more person being mean to her.

"Not now, Phoebe," Austin said.

"Nice attitude, Austin. She sits there crying like a damn sissy and you get pissed at me?" Phoebe said.

Christine's head snapped up. She couldn't form words, but she pointed at Phoebe, moaning.

"It *is* you," Austin said, standing up and walking toward her. "All along it's been you." He was pointing at Phoebe.

"What the hell are you talking about?" Phoebe said.

"Maybe you're misreading it, Austin," Julianna said.

"I'm not misreading shit. You're Christine's stalker," he said.

"Me? Are you out of your fucking mind?" Phoebe said. "Why would I stalk Christine?"

"You're jealous. You're jealous because of me, and you've been harassing her all along," he said, pointing his finger at Phoebe but not touching her.

"I'll break that damn finger if you don't put it down right

now. You are freaking losing it, Austin. You're not so great that I'd stalk anyone over you," Phoebe said.

"You just called her a sissy right after this hit socials," he said, showing Phoebe the video.

She grabbed the phone. "You think I posted that?" Phoebe said.

"Well, someone did, and it's damned ironic you'd use that same word mere minutes after this posted," he said.

"Christine, look at me," Phoebe said.

Christine shook her head no.

"Christine. Please, look at me," Phoebe said again. She stooped down and put her hand on Christine's shoulder. Christine shrugged it off. "Christine. Please."

Christine looked up, barely able to see through the tears.

"I did not post that. I have not been stalking you. I would never do this to you," Phoebe said.

Christine nodded, not because she believed her but because she was afraid not to.

Suddenly, Matt's voice erupted from behind the closed production room door. "You freaking bitch. It's you!"

"Matt's never called anyone a bitch as long as I've known him," Austin said.

Austin offered Christine his hand, and she accepted. He pulled her up. The four of them moved closer to the door.

"I don't know what you're talking about," a female voice said.

"I think that's Alicia," Austin said.

"You know damn well what I'm talking about. I just watched you type that, and so help me God, if you post it, I won't be responsible for my actions." Matt's voice was strained, carrying a harsh edge.

"It's not me," the female said, her voice quivering.

"Yeah, it *is* you. Has it been you all along? It makes sense. You always knew where we were. You know where Christine lives, what she drives, when she's on the road with us, and when she's not. My only question is why?" Matt yelled the last sentence.

"Why? You want to know why? Because she fucking got between Austin and me. Yeah, that's right. Look surprised. We were starting a relationship. He flirted with me. He'd always seek me out, tell me jokes, check in on me when we were on the road. And the touching. He hugged me a lot, and he even kissed me a couple of times. And then, he just stops. Right after he met Christine. And it's never been the same. I just needed her to go away and give me time to get him back," she said, her voice catching, choking up.

"Why Christine when he's dating Phoebe? This whole thing has made absolutely no sense."

"He doesn't love Phoebe. She's a plant or something to get attention off Christine. You can see the difference in how he looks at them. It's Christine he wants. Not Phoebe. I had to get Christine out of the way," Alicia said, her voice rising, pushing her theory.

"And that's how you chose to do it? You didn't talk to her, explain it to her, or talk to him—or even me? What the hell is wrong with you? You've spent the last year abusing the most wonderful, kind person on the planet. Someone who would have bent over backwards if you'd needed her help. Christine is the best of the best. How could you be so cruel?" Matt said.

"Sounds like Austin isn't the only one in love with her," Alicia said, a biting tone to her voice.

"I don't know about Austin. But I know I'm in love with her. And you're done. Fired. Pack your bags and get the hell out of here," Matt said.

"You can't fire me. You didn't hire me. Only Austin can fire me," Alicia said.

Austin opened the door to the production room and stormed in. "You're fired. Get the hell off this property now.

You've broken multiple laws, and I will press charges if any of us ever hear from you again."

"Austin, you can't mean that," Alicia said, looking up at him, her eyes pleading.

"I sure as hell do mean it," he said. "She never did anything to you, and you have been determined to destroy her. Just get out, Alicia. Leave. Now."

Alicia looked at all of them, started to say something, and then stopped. She walked out, coming face-to-face with Christine.

"You know you want him. It's all you've wanted since you met him. And you came between us. You should be ashamed that I'm the one getting fired," Alicia said.

Christine looked at Alicia and then at Matt. "You're right. I do want him. And I have wanted him since I met him." She looked back at Alicia. "You just got the guy wrong."

Alicia looked from Christine to Matt and back to Christine. Then she looked at Phoebe.

"You're not a plant? You're really dating him?" Alicia said.

"Yep. And just try coming after me. I will destroy you," Phoebe said, taking a step toward Alicia, her eyes boring daggers into Alicia's.

Alicia took two steps back. "Well, fuck me," she said.

"Don't need to," Christine said. "You did that all to yourself. But tell me this. How did you do it? How did you get someone to relive the worst experience of my life?"

"I asked. I figured if I escorted them out, I could get some kind of dirt on you. Maybe enough to finally get you to back off. I asked about you in high school. He told. It was that simple. 'Chrissy is a sissy' seemed to be a favorite high school chant. Then I uploaded it to a post trending on Austin's account and it took off. Exactly what happened with those boys the night 'Chrissy is a sissy' became a thing?" Alicia said, a taunting lilt in her tone.

Matt and Austin came forward, eyes wide. Christine stopped them.

She still felt the sting of that chant, but she wasn't going to let Alicia know. "Unlike when I was a teenager, I really don't care what you think of me. Bye, Alicia," Christine said, walking past her and toward Matt.

"On top of that, Alicia, did you read the comments?" Matt said. "They're all in support of Christine. Nobody thinks that high school pain is fair game. Now they're on Christine's side, and you've got the haters. Have fun with that. Now leave before I have you thrown out."

Alicia turned and walked down the hall. Matt called out to their security guy, told him to follow Alicia, and instructed him to escort her off the premises.

When she was gone, Christine exhaled a shaky breath. "How did you catch her?" she asked.

"I walked in here through the side door and she didn't hear me. She was pretty intent on what she was typing on her phone. I walked up behind her to ask a merch question and happened to glance at what she was writing. She was adding a comment to her post. As soon as I saw it, I freaked," Matt said.

"I'm so glad you caught her," Julianna said.

"Me, too. We owe you one," Austin said, putting his hand on Matt's shoulder and grabbing his hand to shake it.

"Uh, hello?" Phoebe said, her voice rising in pitch and volume. "Are we all just going to ignore the fact that you blamed me for this shit about five seconds before Alicia got caught?"

Austin turned and reached for her. She stepped back.

"Phoebe, I'm so sorry. When you said the word 'sissy,' I just reacted. It was a hair-trigger response," Austin said.

"Well, this isn't. Consider us done. If you thought I could do something like that and would hurt somebody so viciously over you, then you need to get the fuck over yourself," Phoebe said.

"I'm a total dick," Austin said.

"No argument here," Phoebe said. "Have a good concert. I'm out."

"Phoebe, don't leave," Julianna said, walking up to her.

Phoebe put her hand up. "Not now. Christine, I'm glad they caught her. Nobody should have to go through what you did. I'm sure there were times you thought it was me, too. But at least you weren't sleeping with me. I've got better things to do than stick around here. See you back at home, Julianna."

Phoebe turned and, with her head held high, walked down the hall and out the door. The four of them stared at the door long after it had closed.

"Think sending her flowers would help?" Austin finally said.

"Yeah, no. I don't think there's any hope for you there," Matt said.

Austin nodded. "Well, shit. How many women can I screw up?"

"You don't really want me to answer that, right?" Matt asked, adding some levity to the moment.

"Rhetorical question," Austin said, clapping his hands. "And for the record, those kisses Alicia referred to? Chaste. I kissed her on the cheek a couple of times and maybe gave one lip kiss but no tongue. It's not like I made out with her. Hell, I've kissed Matt with that much passion."

All eyes went to Matt.

"True story. He's not very discerning when he drinks. And you do have soft lips, Austin. I can see why Alicia got confused," Matt said, a sly smirk on his face.

"Am I the only one who hasn't been kissed by Austin?" Julianna said, looking at each of them.

Austin gave her a wink. "Well, how you doin'?" he said.

"Seriously? After everything that just happened, you're pulling a Joey Tribbiani?" Julianna said.

"Too soon?" he asked, a sheepish grin on his face.

"Way too soon," Christine and Julianna said in unison.

"Okay, okay. I get it. Inappropriate of me. It's been a weird day. I'm a little fucked up right now. We'll talk in about six . . ."

"Months at minimum," Julianna said.

"And she didn't say no," Austin said, his boyish grin taking over his face.

"You're incorrigible," Christine said, giving him a side hug.

"Welp, I've got a show to do," Austin said.

"Yeah, you do. You're due onstage in thirty," Matt said.

"Seriously, are we not going to discuss any of this?" Julianna said, hands up, eyes wide.

"What's there to say?" Christine asked. "Hopefully it's over. I *am* sorry about Phoebe, though, Austin."

"That's on me," he said. "I should never have accused her. But it says something about her and me as a couple that I did. Guess that relationship wasn't meant to be."

"Sorry, dude," Matt said.

"Yeah. Me, too. She was fun. But not the one, I guess. I do see us hanging out as friends in the future."

"The way future, maybe," Matt said.

"It'll take some time, but I'll mend that one. We'll be friends," Austin said.

"Good. She's worth it," Julianna said.

"Yes, she is," Christine agreed, causing Julianna's eyebrows to go up.

Christine looked at her friends and smiled at how they supported each other. She thought about everything that had happened in the last year, the last few months, and the last half hour. Would she do it all again? Would she go through so much pain to be sitting here in this moment with these three people? Yeah, she would. Great gains often come at great expense. It was hell, but these were her people, and she loved them. Even Phoebe.

And hearing Matt say he was in love with her had made it worth it a thousand times over.

"I'm off to the bus to get ready. Matt? You coming?"

"In a minute," Matt said, looking at Christine.

Julianna's eyes moved between Matt and Christine. "Uh, yeah. I need to . . . um . . . do something. I'll be back." She turned and followed Austin.

Once Christine was alone with Matt, her heart rate quickened. Was there a chance he had said that part about being in love with her just to steer Alicia in another direction, away from what she perceived Austin's feelings to be? She held her breath, afraid to speak first.

"I guess you heard what I said?" Matt asked, reaching for Christine's hand. She laced her fingers through his.

"I did. Did you mean it?" She peered up at him from under her lashes.

"Every word," he said, looking into her eyes and pushing a stray curl off her forehead.

"What about Cait?" she asked.

"Oh, we broke it off a while back. It wasn't going anywhere. Hard to move forward when you've got feelings for someone else," he said. "Did you mean what you said?"

"Since the night I met you." She tightened her grip on his hand.

"Why didn't I know that?" he asked.

"I thought you had a girlfriend. Why didn't you tell me how you felt?" she asked, her eyes boring into his.

"I thought you and Austin had a thing."

"How could you think—" She stopped and thought about all the times Matt had come across them. When she'd spent the night at Austin's house and he found her there in the morning. When he saw her in the dressing room with Austin's hands all over her. The many times Austin had laid claim to her. "But he was with Phoebe."

"And he's never been a one-woman man. Women seem to accept that crap when it's a famous singer. I wasn't going to put myself out there and risk the discomfort all of that would have brought. I had visions that I'd tell you how I feel, you'd friend-zone me and tell me you're holding out for Austin, and I'd have to quit my job due to extreme embarrassment. Not a good visual."

"But you did today," she said. "Why?"

"So Alicia would know that you're worthy of love. Not just Austin's, but mine, too."

"Austin doesn't love me," Christine said, snorting. She found the idea hilarious.

"I wouldn't be so sure." He paused. "We need to talk more, but I've got to get him to the stage. I'd really like to spend time with you after the show."

"Julianna and I are staying nearby at a hotel, but you're heading out on the bus tonight, right?"

"Hmmmm. Maybe I don't have to." He put his hands on either side of her face and drew her in for a kiss. "I'm sure Austin will understand."

The kiss wasn't long, but it was thorough. Christine's entire body tingled. She leaned in, wanting more.

His walkie-talkie crackled with the countdown to the show. "You have to go," she said, pulling back.

"I do. See you side stage?"

"I wouldn't want to be anywhere else," she said.

He left the room and Julianna walked in.

"So . . ." she said.

"Yeah. So." The smile on Christine's face was so big she couldn't see past her cheeks.

THE SHOW WAS THE BEST CHRISTINE had ever seen. The stress of the past year had lifted off all of them. Austin was electric, connecting with the audience even more than usual. He was at ease, natural, laughing when he forgot lyrics and encouraging fans to post his bloopers. They loved it. The people in the pit rushed the stage, singing along with him. They reached out to touch him, and he reached back.

Christine stood beside Matt, her love, and Julianna, her best friend, the three of them watching the person who personified their crazy lives. A star, an artist, someone whom millions adored. In some way, they all depended on him—but it was more than that. They loved him. Not because he was famous but because he was their friend, and they liked him for who he was. Now, Christine could openly express her affection without it being a source of fear and pain. The future was looking bright.

CHAPTER SEVENTEEN

M att and Christine arrived at the hotel. Julianna had offered to take his bunk and ride the bus back. Austin assured Matt he'd be fine on his own for the trip home. He also told Matt to stay with Christine and fly back to Nashville with her.

"You're in rooms 223 and 225. Adjoining, as requested," the clerk said.

Christine raised her eyebrows at Matt. He raised his back.

Matt grabbed their bags. They rode the elevator and walked to their rooms.

Christine felt nervous and didn't know what to say.

"I think we could both use a few minutes to get ourselves together. I need a shower for sure. How about I check on you in thirty?" Matt said.

"A shower sounds divine. Thirty should be great. Thank you."

Christine stood under the water, which was slightly hotter than she normally tolerated, and allowed it to wash away the events of the day. She wanted to block certain parts out and pretend they'd never happened. Alicia had caused her so much pain, all over a perceived relationship that didn't even exist. It would take a while to come to terms with what had happened and truly feel safe again.

Christine dressed in her Victoria's Secret sweats, which Julianna had convinced her to buy, and a black tank top. She hoped Matt would find it sexy.

When he knocked, she jumped up, unlocked the adjoining door, and opened it.

His gaze traveled over her tank top.

She went back to the bed, where she sat leaning against the pillows on the headboard with her legs pulled up tight.

Matt sat at her feet and put his arm over her knees. "How are you?"

"I don't really know. On the one hand, it's over. On the other hand, it's freaky realizing the danger was that close and none of us knew it."

"I know. It was right in front of us, and we had no idea. Austin didn't think some minor flirtation would go to Alicia's head. He thought he was being nice—friendly. But when you have Austin's charm and star quality, women sometimes perceive it as more. He may have led her on in a way he never meant to. He feels bad about that, but he feels horrible about how it affected you."

"He shouldn't. I chose to keep hanging out with him long after the threats. It was my decision. But . . ."

"Yes?"

"Do you mind if we don't talk about this?"

"Of course not. What would you like to do?"

Christine froze. Would it be too much for her to say she'd like to do him? She stalled, a minute too long.

"If you'd like me to leave and give you some time, I get it. Just say so."

Christine was losing the moment. It was time to take control. She had to do this. "What I'd really like to do, Matt . . ."

"Yes?"

"Is you. I'd like to do you."

Matt reached over and tucked a strand of Christine's hair behind her ear. His touch felt safe, like coming home.

"Christine," he said. He pulled her to him and kissed her ear, then the side of her head. He used his hand to hold her chin and turn her face toward him. "Kiss me, Christine."

She kissed him with the passion of a woman who was ready to be with the man she loved. She lay down, pulling him with her.

He reached under her shirt, cupping her breast and teasing her nipple. It hardened with his touch. She could hear his breathing speed up. He lifted her shirt and she leaned up, allowing him to take it off.

"Beautiful," he said in a soft voice.

She shook her head.

"Yes. Beautiful," he repeated, staring directly into her eyes.

He took off his shirt and pulled her to him, bare chest to bare chest. Skin against skin. She melted into him. They shimmied out of their pants, and she brought the sheet up over her body.

Matt pulled it back down.

She started to protest but stopped. He was looking at her, all of her, and he wanted to see her.

"I'm not on birth control," she said.

"It's okay. I've got it covered."

She smiled, liking the fact that he had come to her room wanting her. This wasn't mercy sex or mere consolation. He desired her, too.

"Are you sure?" he asked.

"I've never been surer," she said.

She had dreamt of this moment, lived it in her fantasies, and built it up to the point where it would be impossible for anyone to compete with her imagination. He didn't just compete. He won. In a world surrounded by awards, Matt won the gold medal, the platinum album, the Emmy, and the Oscar.

THE NEXT MORNING, CHRISTINE and Matt cuddled in bed, her body wrapped around his. Matt rubbed her back.

She rolled onto her stomach and moaned. "That feels so good."

He pushed the sheet down farther, exposing her back. She felt him trace the tattoo on her lower left side.

"What's this? It looks like a kidney bean. And it says, 'Was here.'"

"My left kidney was there until July of 2018."

"The one you donated. Of course. To your cousin, right?"

Christine nodded.

"Must have made your cousin feel special."

"Talk about feeling special. You brought your A game last night," Christine said, rolling over and planting a light kiss on his lips.

"That's just my normal game, hon," Matt said, looking serious until he burst out laughing. "I can't get away with a comment like that, can I?"

"Nope. But if that's your normal game, I can't wait for overtime."

"Flight's not until two o'clock. Game on." He pulled her on top of him, and Christine couldn't remember a time when she'd been happier.

CHRISTINE AND MATT MET IN the lobby after showering and dressing. He handed her a tea, made just the way she liked it.

"How did you know?" she asked.

"I know," he said, kissing her cheek. "I called an Uber. It'll be here in five minutes."

"Thanks."

Matt checked out at the front desk, grabbed the receipts, and took their luggage outside, where the Uber driver waited.

Last night and this morning had been wonderful, but now that she was in the car, riding along with time to think, Christine's head was spinning. There was so much Matt didn't know about her, and she had issues to work through. The last year had brought things to the surface that she'd tried to bury. Last night had been traumatizing, seeing someone remember her high school shame and having it posted for all to see. Her time with Matt had been everything she'd dreamed of, but until she worked on herself, she knew she couldn't be the person he needed.

She stared out the window, not wanting to look at him. "There are things you don't know about me, Matt."

"Then tell me. I want to know everything about you." He put his hand on her knee.

She drew a lazy circle on the window.

"Christine?"

She turned to look at him. "My limited experiences with men have not turned out well."

"I'm not going to hurt you, Christine." Matt reached for her hand and caressed her palm.

"It's not that I think you will. But Austin didn't mean to hurt me either. We may not have been romantically involved, but we do have a strong relationship. And it led to so much agony. And there was an incident in high school where I got hurt. It left me badly scarred."

"Oh my God. Were you . . . ? I mean, never mind. It's none of my business."

"I wasn't raped if that was your question. But I was sexually assaulted. And it's taken me over a decade to realize it was a sexual assault. I never came to terms with that. My point is, I just seem to have bad luck when it comes to guys. And I'm scared. I mean, really scared."

"I'm kind of scared, too. I've never been in love. I've had a couple of girlfriends, but I've never felt the way I feel about you. But, Christine, the level of fear you lived with this last year is going to affect every aspect of your life. I get that."

Christine turned his hand over, brought it to her lips, and kissed it.

"I don't know, Matt. I have a lot to sort through and deal with."

"I know you do. Have you ever heard of the Healing Trauma program at Oasis? It's right outside of Nashville?"

"I went to a fundraiser for them once. I've heard they do great work."

"It's an intensive program to help people deal with an experience that overwhelms them. You've had two major traumas in your life. I think you should consider going."

Christine nodded.

"I'll call in some favors and try to get you into the next session if you're interested," Matt said.

Christine's eyes met Matt's. "I love you. You know I do. But I don't know if the time is right. And I can't even believe I'm saying that since I've wanted this for so long."

"You don't have to know now. When you feel like you're ready, I'll be here."

She rested her head on his shoulder. "Thank you."

ALL CHRISTINE WANTED WAS TO collapse in her condo and be alone. But once she was there, she felt lonely.

She texted Julianna. *Just got home. You?*

About an hour away. What an experience the tour bus is. No wonder you stress about it.

It's a moving boy's dormitory. A lot of testosterone and odors.

How are you? Julianna asked.

Christine texted a frowny face.

Call ya when I get in?

How about you just stop by? And bring wine. Lots and lots of wine.

Uh-oh. You got it.

Later, when Christine and Julianna were settled on the couch with a bowl of popcorn on the table and wineglasses in hand, Julianna asked Christine what had happened the night before.

"It was great. I mean, everything I'd wanted happened. My stalker was arrested and no longer a threat, and Matt was with me."

"*With you,* with you?"

"Oh, yeah. In every way."

"And how was it?" Julianna asked, sipping her wine.

"Amazing."

"So that's good, right?"

"Right up until this morning, when it all came crashing down on me. I've spent months living in fear because of my relationship with Austin. And I nearly got raped in high school. The idea of starting a relationship right now causes a panic attack. In some ways, I never expected to have a chance with Matt so I wasn't prepared. A fantasy is one thing. Reality is another. I thought I had dealt with all my crap. But I haven't. I never have. Until you made me acknowledge it, I refused to even call it an assault. But it was. And that memory and fear have never left me."

Julianna leaned back against the couch. "Oh, Christine."

"Matt recommended I go to Oasis for trauma healing. I think it's a good idea."

"I think it's a great idea."

"I need help, Julianna. Until I get myself sorted out, I'm no good to anyone."

"That's fair. Think Matt will wait?"

"He said he would. What do you think?" Christine asked, her eyes rimmed with tears, hoping Julianna would say what she wanted to hear.

"I think Matt's the type that would wait for you forever."

Christine reached over and hugged her friend. "Thank you."

CHAPTER EIGHTEEN

C hristine walked out of the Oasis building to see Julianna leaning against her car. Matt had stayed true to his word and finagled her a place in the trauma healing session that began just ten days after she returned home. She'd spent the week in an intensive program seeing and talking only to the program leaders and fellow attendees. Matt had offered to pick her up, but she didn't know what frame of mind she'd be in so she asked Julianna to do it. Matt said he understood. She hoped he did.

Julianna wrapped her arms around Christine, who returned the hug. "Hello, my friend," Julianna said before letting her go and grabbing Christine's suitcase. She threw it in the trunk and they got in the car.

"Well?" Julianna asked.

"My therapist believes I have PTSD after a year of cyberbullying and being stalked, and then, of course, the incident from high school," she said.

"No surprise there. That's good, right?"

"Yes. That's what I expected. She recommended I find an outpatient therapist. I need to work through some other issues as well."

"Like what?"

"Self-esteem issues that I've had since high school. It's amazing how those years affect us into adulthood. And equating men with danger. It flashes through my mind more often than it should."

"That's a lot to focus on at once."

"Yeah. Who knew I was such a wreck?" Christine said.

"We're all wrecks in our own way. But you have had more to deal with than most. You have a right to be a bit of a wreck."

"But that's what this course helped me with. It addresses emotional pain, compulsive behavior cycles, and disconnection that follows a traumatic experience. Those are all things I've been doing since even before Alicia. But when I pushed Matt away, I came face-to-face with my behavior for the first time."

"And speaking of Matt?" Julianna raised her eyebrows.

"Don't. I'm not ready to go there. It was only a six-day program. I need time," Christine said.

"Let me ask you just one question."

Christine narrowed her eyes. "What?"

"Do you still love him?"

Christine's voice fell to a whisper. "Yes."

CHRISTINE WAS MAKING DINNER when her phone chimed with a text.

It was Austin. *Hey, Chrissy. I hope you're going to be home tonight because I'll be at your place in an hour.*

Christine smiled. She was ready to see him.

I have plans with Julianna at eight.

I'll be there by seven.

Christine changed out of her big, stained T-shirt and put on a blouse. She ran a comb through her hair and put on a little mascara and lipstick. She didn't want Austin to think she was a total mess—especially if he was reporting back to Matt.

She opened the door to see him holding a bouquet of lilies and grinning like a fool. "Get in here," she said.

He wrapped her up in a hug, twirling her around the room. "God, I've missed you," he said. "My therapist told me I needed to see you. She was right."

"Your therapist?" Christine had no idea what he was talking about.

"Do you really think I didn't need some help after this? My God, woman. You've been through hell because of me. That's some pretty heavy shit."

"So, you're saying it's not all about me?" she asked, a big grin on her face.

"Ha. That's what I'm saying."

Christine moved into the kitchen. "Want a beer?"

"Yeah, but only one. I drove here."

"Smart call. 'Cause I'm not driving your drunk ass home."

"Those days are over, Chrissy. I'm growing up. Oh, damn. Sorry. Christine."

"Nah, call me Chrissy. It's been healing to hear it come from someone I know cares about me. Like ripping a Band-Aid off, but very slowly. And are those drunk days really over?"

"Okay, they aren't totally over. But it's time. Hell, I'm thirty-two."

"Your bio says twenty-eight," she said. She handed him the beer and they sat on the couch. "What's this visit about? Personal or professional?"

"Both. I needed to see you. How are you?"

"I'm okay, Austin. I mean it. I'm really okay. Matt was spot-on about sending me to Oasis. It's intense, but you leave with a set of tools that help you through the tough times."

"Matt's always spot-on. With everything."

"Yeah, he is," Christine said.

"Did my Chrissy just make dreamy eyes?"

"Shut up."

"Okay. Moving on. Remember back when I asked you to consider coming to work for me?"

"Yes."

"Hear me out. I'm starting a publishing company. It'll be small at first, probably just two writers and myself. But I need a song plugger, and I want you."

"You've helped raise my clout quite a bit. And thanks to you saving our company, I'm being treated well where I am. I got a promotion and a raise," Christine said.

"I'll double your salary."

Christine froze. "You'll what?"

"I'll double it."

"You can't. You already overpaid for me to live here."

"I can and I will. And it's not pity pay. Starting a business is a twenty-four seven job. You'll earn every penny."

"You can't afford that."

"I'll be able to soon. Residuals are coming in off my hit songs, I'm touring, and I'm selling loads of merch. Next year will be even better," Austin said, his eyes glowing.

"Can we say loads of product? The word 'merch' still causes me to break out in hives."

"Ugh. Sorry. But I can afford it," Austin said.

"And if I say no?"

"I'll have to hire someone else. But I don't want to."

"You're serious, aren't you?"

"I am. What do you say?" He gave her two thumbs-up.

"When do you need an answer?" Christine asked.

"No rush. I hired the writers and want them to focus for a few months on writing every day. I'm paying them a small salary for the first year, so they don't have to worry about a draw. It's not much, but it's what I can afford, and they can at least pay their bills. I know what it's like. I was in their shoes before writing my first hit. Once we have the songs we feel are worth taking around, I'll need you."

"It's intriguing." She sat up straighter, her eyes wide as she considered the possibilities.

"You're not going to turn me down, are you?"

"I don't know, but I promise to consider it."

"Okay. I know you have plans with Julianna, so I'm gonna run. We'll be a powerhouse together. I don't want to do this with anyone else."

They stood and she walked him to the door.

"Did I mention I plan to give you a percentage of the company?"

"Austin."

"I'm just saying, it'll be well worth it to come work with me."

"You're hard to say no to."

"That's the plan. Although you've found it easy enough to say no in the past. Can I ask you a question?" He put his hand on her arm.

"You know you can."

"Did I ever tempt you at all?"

Christine looked at his gorgeous face. He truly was a beautiful person, inside and out. "Of course you did. More than you'll ever know."

"Then why did you always turn me down?"

"Honestly, I don't know. I thought about saying yes many times. But if I must give an answer, it's because I felt like you only kept asking because I kept saying no. And if I ever said yes, you'd have disappeared. I think your interest in me stemmed from the fact you couldn't have me."

"I think it was more than that. But I won't lie. It did keep me interested. That and the fact I think you're one cool chick." He smiled his gorgeous smile and gave her a wink.

"I didn't want to risk what we had with a one-night fling.

And I was pretty sure Matt wouldn't go in after you. So to speak."
Christine blushed, making Austin laugh.

"So to speak. No, that probably would have ended any possibility there."

"Then I'd have slept with you, lost our friendship, and lost any chance with Matt."

"Might not have happened that way."

"But good chance it would have. I could have lost you both."

Austin nodded, accepting the answer. "Love ya, girl." He gave her a kiss on the cheek.

"Love ya back."

He stepped outside just as Julianna opened her door. She peered out at them.

"Jules! What's up, gorgeous?" He gave a salute and walked toward the elevator.

Christine raised her eyebrows at Julianna, who shrugged and headed toward Christine.

"Jules?" Christine asked.

"I told him not to call me that," she said.

Austin stepped into the elevator, whistling on his way. He waved as the doors closed.

"Anything I should know about?" Julianna asked.

"Nope. Not yet . . . *Jules*," Christine said. "Anything *I* should know about?"

"Nope. Not yet."

Christine stared at her. "Watch yourself with that one."

"If and when the time comes, I will."

"Fair enough. Hey, there's a songwriter night at the Bluebird tomorrow. Want to go?" Christine asked.

Julianna looked at Christine with a big smile on her face. "You're going to be okay, aren't you?"

"Yeah. I'm going to be okay."

THE PAIN WAS SEARING. Alicia plunged the knife in repeatedly. Christine tried to fight her off, but nothing made it stop. Right before Alicia lunged one last time, Christine opened her eyes and glanced around to see that nobody was in her bedroom. She always left a light on at night. She wondered if she'd ever sleep without a light on again.

She felt another stabbing pain in her stomach. Cramps. She stumbled to the bathroom and discovered that, once again, she had let her tampon supply run low. "When will I ever learn?"

Christine called in late to work. It was the music industry. Nobody showed up on time anyway.

She threw her hair up in a bun, slapped on some lipstick for good measure, dressed in baggy jeans and a fitted T-shirt, and made her way to Target. She tossed her list of items in the cart. "Lightdays, tampons, Pamprin." She added shampoo and conditioner, a box of facial cloths, and a six-pack of toilet paper. Waiting in line at the checkout counter, she glanced at a rag mag and wondered once again how anyone could believe the stuff they published.

"Christine?"

She shut her eyes. "No," she said. "This could not happen twice in one year. Fate is not that cruel."

"What?" the cashier asked.

"Just talking to myself."

Christine looked over her right shoulder and saw Matt walking toward her. When he got close enough to see the items she was putting on the conveyor, he blushed.

"Is there some sort of menstrual fairy that lets you know when I'm here buying this crap?" she asked.

"Uh, no. I guess we're just this lucky," he said.

"Hi," Christine said.

"Hi."

Matt remained by her side as the clerk scanned her items. Christine felt anxious. She tried to remember her relaxation techniques, but nothing worked. She hadn't been this close to Matt since the morning after they'd made love. Had it already been four weeks? She had come a long way in working through the trauma and was slowly getting her emotions in check, but Matt was in a league of his own when it came to stirring up her feelings.

She paid for her purchases and faced the man she loved.

"Well, it was good to see you."

He pointed to Starbucks.

"I really need to get home and—"

"Please." He dropped his head and let his eyes peer up at her. Then he put his hands in a praying position.

He looked so cute. She couldn't say no. She owed him this. She owed herself this.

"Okay."

She ordered her usual chai and he got a coffee. He paid and they sat down.

"Matt, I—"

"Please let me start."

"Okay."

"These have been the longest weeks of my life, not knowing how you'd feel coming out of Oasis. I know trauma can take a long time to heal from, and I'm a direct connection to Austin and Alicia. There were times when I felt like it was someone on the road, maybe even in our crew, and I watched people so closely. I feel guilty I couldn't do more to help you."

"You caught those two in the beginning and fired them," Christine said.

"I did. But they were just copycats. I should have figured it out earlier. I owed you and Austin better than that. I failed."

"You didn't fail anything. She was good, and smart, and calculating. I never suspected her because she was so nice to me. We suspected Phoebe because she wasn't nice to me. But that should have been the flag that it wasn't her. We don't think like cruel people, Matt. And that's a good thing," Christine said, reaching across the table to put her hand on his arm.

"Thank you for trying to make me feel better. And you're right, we don't think that way. But it has made me double down on doing background checks on the entire crew."

"Would that have caught Alicia?"

"No. It wouldn't. But it might catch someone else. Every time something else happened, I had so much pain for you. Watching it happen was devastating. Especially to someone like you. Someone I cared so much for. Felt so much for," Matt said, putting his hand on top of Christine's.

"Felt?" Christine's chest constricted. Were his feelings for her in the past?

"Felt then and feel now. I love you, Christine. When I assumed I was competing with Austin, I let it go. When I found out I wasn't, I dared to have hope."

"What now?" Christine asked.

"I've been respectful and given you the space you asked for. Hardest thing I've ever had to do was leaving you alone when I felt you needed me the most. I want you in my life, Christine. And I don't want to wait another minute. How about dinner? My place, tonight. I'm cooking."

"Your place? Need I remind you of today's purchases?"

"This isn't about sex. This is about you and me having a date. Sex isn't what I'm looking for."

"What are you looking for?" Christine asked.

"Nothing. Everything," he said, and Christine melted. His eyes met hers and he looked at her in a way no other man ever had. She saw a mix of love, admiration, and respect.

Christine's eyes threatened to fill with tears. She was tired of crying and wanted to regain her composure. She needed to move, keep busy. She stood, gathering her stuff.

Matt stood, too, and threw away their empty cups. He reached for her bags and walked her to her car.

She opened the door, and he put her purchases inside on the seat. Then he closed the door, gently pushed her back against it, and put his hands on either side of her.

She wrapped her arms around his neck and he leaned in. He hovered above her lips, giving her a chance to say no.

She didn't.

She felt his entire body meld with hers as he kissed her, fully and completely.

He pulled away and nuzzled her ear. "Christine?"

"Yes?"

"I'm calling in my rain check."

CHRISTINE HUMMED TO HERSELF as she cleaned her condo. After seeing Matt at Target, she'd decided to take the day off. Her cramps were gone, and she felt great. She thought of the Claritin commercial when the film is stripped away; the sky becomes blue again and the grass looks greener.

She texted Julianna: *Matt and I have a dinner date tonight at his place. He's cooking.*

Woo-hoo! Should I wait up to hear about it or is it a sleepover? I was at Target buying tampons.

So, he loves you even when you're not a sure thing.

Apparently so. Who would have thought? Christine texted.

I would. Have fun. I'll have a cup of hot tea or wine waiting when you get home.

CHRISTINE TOOK HER TIME getting ready. A long, hot shower felt good. She let her hair air dry and chose comfortable jeans and a casual yet fitted T-shirt. She could be herself with

Matt. That felt nice. She started to walk out of her bedroom, paused at the door, and walked back to her closet. She took out her high school yearbook and opened it to the senior pictures. She turned the pages, finding each of the guys who had circled her that night. She paused longer on Bryan's photo.

"You guys suck," she said. "You're abusive assholes who will never understand what you did to me. But you will no longer rule my relationships with men. It's over. This fear that has followed me around since that night is gone. I win. Christine Matthews survived. Chrissy is not a damn sissy. She's one strong hell of a woman."

She slammed the book shut, put it back on the shelf, and walked away. Then she went back, took the yearbook out, and looked at Bryan's photo again. He looked like a kid now, although still big and burly. *What was wrong with you that you did that to me?*

She thought about all she'd learned in Bible study. Then she remembered the Kane Brown song "Learning" and its message of forgiveness. There was only one thing that would make her truly move on. "Bryan, I forgive you," she said.

She stuffed the yearbook back in its place. As she left her apartment, she felt lighter. The sky looked clearer than ever before. The stars shined brighter. It was a good day to start the rest of her life.

CHRISTINE STOOD ON MATT'S DOORSTEP. At that moment, she decided to take the job with Austin. Not only because he offered more money than she was paid at Hit Songs Publishing, but also because she'd be part of something that would be hers as well as his. She'd be able to stay in her condo and pay for it herself. It had taken thirty years for Christine Matthews to figure out who she was and what she was worth. She had a lot of catching up to do. But she was ready to start.

She rang the bell.

ACKNOWLEDGMENTS

've long dreamed of the opportunity to have an acknowledgment page to thank the people who have stood by me, encouraged me, read what I've written, and been my cheerleaders. They are more than I can mention.

Country singers are often praised for thanking God for their talent and opportunity, and I'd be remiss not doing the same. To my loving husband, Randy, whose mantra was "Don't give up. No matter what it costs, keep chasing your dream." I also thank God for my supportive and loving parents, who taught me the wonderful world of reading at an early age. My mom who passed on her love of writing, and dad who would call and say, "You have to read this book. It's our kind of book." My sister and soulmate, Kelly, who I grew up reading with and who followed her love of books into a career in education. My besties, Sandi and Jodi, for reading everything I write; and the kids in my life who constantly inspire me: Will, Kayla, and Cleeford. And to the man who has my donated kidney, David, for inspiring the first book I ever wrote.

I must thank my Broken Bow Records bosses and coworkers who never once asked, "Is this little writing thing getting in the

298 ★ LOVE ON TOUR

way of your record promoting?" Because they trusted me not to let it, and instead they encouraged me to pursue it . . . Jon, JoJamie, Layna, and Dawn.

Gratitude goes to my agent, Liz Kracht, at Kimberley Cameron & Associates, for being the first agent to believe in me and staying with me through ups and downs in both our lives; and Tricia LaRochelle for the many, many edits and formatting.

For Brooke Warner and Addison Gallegos for taking on this project and walking me through my many questions and blank stares. And the rest of the She Writes author community for offering their support. Thanks to Crystal Patriarche, Hanna Lindsley, Grace Fell and Mark Logsdon for their invaluable advice on publicity. And Will Hornby for enhancing my social media presence.

To the amazing artists I've worked with in my music career, who taught me the joys of the country music industry, and for allowing me to bask in their achievements . . . especially the BBR artists I currently work with: Jason Aldean, Lainey Wilson, Dustin Lynch, Craig Morgan, and John Morgan; and BBRMG artist Alexander Ludwig. And to Willie Nelson, whose music won my thirteen-year-old heart causing me to pursue my career.

To one of my favorite authors, Tracey Garvis Graves, who allowed a struggling writer to reach out after reading *On the Island*, and for being a success story and motivator for every author who starts out on a non-traditional publishing path. And to author Jeff Zentner for becoming a mentor.

To everyone who reads Love On Tour, thank you for making my dreams come true and for giving my characters an audience. The idea that you are taking the time to purchase my book and read it means everything.

Most of all, the inspiration for this story, the "behind-the- scenes" people in the music industry, especially the tour managers. For every time you found me extra concert tickets for that last-minute radio request or a bunk on the bus when transportation proved tricky, provided secure parking so I didn't have to wander in the dark looking for my car, and covered me when my flight was canceled, delayed, or I had a family emergency. Thank you for treating me as a part of the tour, the road family, and respecting the job I needed to do and helping me do it on your turf. My gratitude runs deep . . . especially to the TMs I currently work with: Jake, Meg, DMC, Jerry and Dave.

ABOUT THE AUTHOR

LEE ADAMS was born and raised on the outskirts of Baltimore, MD. She has been active in the country music industry since the 1980s, working at a radio station before joining Decca/MCA Records and then Broken Bow Records, where she has been VP of Promotion since 2007. She has worked more than fifty #1 songs and is a current member of the Academy of Country Music and the Country Music Association. Lee and her husband of thirty-five years, Randy, adopted a teenager from Haiti in 2017. They live on the Potomac River in Falling Waters, WV.

Author photo © Kevin Grace

Looking for your next great read?

We can help!

Visit www.shewritespress.com/next-read
or scan the QR code below for a list
of our recommended titles.

She Writes Press is an award-winning
independent publishing company founded to
serve women writers everywhere.